BRENDA JACKSON

The House on Blueberry Lane

THIS MATERIAL ON LOAN FROM

TTLE PUBLIC

RARY

NISHED

"Brenda Jackson writes romance tha[t]
and characters you fall in love wit[h]
—**LORI FOSTER**, *New York Times* bestsel[ler]

A CATALINA COVE NOVEL

ISBN-13: 978-1-335-62097-2

9 781335 620972

50899

EAN

Praise for the novels of Brenda Jackson

"The only flaw of this first-rate, satisfyingly sexy tale is that it ends."
—*Publishers Weekly*, starred review, on *Forged in Desire*

"Jackson was the first African-American author to make both the *New York Times* and *USA TODAY* romance bestsellers lists. And after twenty years in the business, books like *Love in Catalina Cove* prove that she's still a prevailing force in romance."
—*BookPage*

"For true romance lovers, *Forget Me Not* will make your heart sing."
—*Frolic*

"[A] heartwarming romance."
—*Library Journal* on *Love in Catalina Cove*

"Jackson's winning formula of heat and heart will draw readers in."
—*Publishers Weekly* on *The Wife He Needs*

"[Jackson's] signature is to create full-sensory romances that deliver on the heat, and she duly delivers.... Sure to make any reader swoon."
—*RT Book Reviews* on *Forged in Desire*

"Brenda Jackson is the queen of newly discovered love... If there's one thing Jackson knows how to do, it's how to pluck those heartstrings."
—*BookPage* on *Inseparable*

"Jackson is a master at writing."
—*Publishers Weekly* on *Sensual Confessions*

**Also available from
Brenda Jackson
and HQN**

Catalina Cove

LOVE IN CATALINA COVE
FORGET ME NOT
FINDING HOME AGAIN
FOLLOW YOUR HEART
ONE CHRISTMAS WISH

The Protectors

FORGED IN DESIRE
SEIZED BY SEDUCTION
LOCKED IN TEMPTATION

The Grangers

A BROTHER'S HONOR
A MAN'S PROMISE
A LOVER'S VOW

For additional books by
New York Times bestselling author Brenda Jackson,
visit her website, www.brendajackson.net.

BRENDA JACKSON

The House on Blueberry Lane

HQN

ISBN-13: 978-1-335-62097-2

Recycling programs for this product may not exist in your area.

The House on Blueberry Lane

For questions and comments about the quality of this book, please contact us at CustomerService@Harlequin.com.

HQN
22 Adelaide St. West, 41st Floor
Toronto, Ontario M5H 4E3, Canada
www.Harlequin.com

Printed in U.S.A.

To the man who will always and forever be
the love of my life, Gerald Jackson Sr. My hero.
The wind beneath my wings. My everything.

To those attending the
Brenda Jackson Readers Reunion Cruise 2023,
this one is for you.

Leave there thy gift before the altar,
and go thy way; first be reconciled to thy brother,
and then come and offer thy gift.
—*Matthew* 5:24

The House on
Blueberry Lane

CHAPTER ONE

VELVET SPENCER SAT in front of her TV with a glass of wine in one hand and the remote in the other. There had to be something worth watching other than romance movies, cop shows and sci-fi films. She was in the mood for none of those. In her present frame of mind, she should just finish her wine and go on to bed. She loved her job as a teacher but was glad she didn't have to dwell on lesson plans for a while. School had ended for the holidays and with nothing planned this week, she thought she might drive into New Orleans to start early Christmas shopping. Shopping was always a girl's best friend.

Anything was better than sitting around and letting her thoughts dwell on that town hall meeting she'd attended last Thursday, when she'd seen Jaye Colfax for the first time in two years. That's when she had ended their relationship and left Phoenix without telling him she was leaving or where she was headed. For two years she had tried building another life for herself without him in Catalina Cove, and had done a fairly good job.

And now he was here.

His presence was already the talk of the town. Everyone at that meeting had been introduced to the wealthy entrepreneur who had purchased the only bank in Catalina Cove. Women were whispering about how drop-dead gorgeous he was and speculating about what it would take to capture such a man's eye. She had been tempted to tell them unless they were in for an affair that led nowhere, not to waste their time.

Afterward, she couldn't get home quick enough to call her best friend, Ruthie, to tell her that Jaye was not only in town but would be here for a while to get his newly purchased asset, Barrows Bank, up and running.

Her best friend was just as shocked as she was. Ruthie even brought up the possibility that Jaye had somehow found out her whereabouts and that was why he was in Catalina Cove. Velvet knew that theory wasn't true. Jaye didn't run after women. Besides, why now, after she'd been gone two years?

Velvet put the remote on the table and went into the kitchen. She was about to pour some more wine when her doorbell sounded. Who in the world could that be? Maybe it was her neighbor, Delisa Mills, letting her know she was back in town.

Delisa wasn't just her neighbor but also her landlord. The woman had inherited the huge Victorian-style two-story home that could house a family of fifteen easily. Not needing all that space, Delisa had transformed the house into a duplex with separate entrances—one from the side and one from the front—all without altering the style and elegance of the beautiful and spacious house. Velvet lived in the lower section. Her three bedrooms, two bathrooms, kitchen and dining area fit her needs and suited her just fine.

Delisa lived above in the second story. A divorcée in her late fifties, Delisa loved to travel and spent most of her time out of the country. She thought the older woman was friendly, and as far as Velvet was concerned, their arrangement worked out great.

When she reached the door, she asked, "Who is it?"

"Jaye Colfax."

Velvet's heart nearly jumped out of her chest. What was Jaye doing here? How had he found out where she lived? Drawing in a deep breath, she tried to calm her erratic heartbeat. Glancing down at herself, she was glad she was decent since she hadn't changed out of the slacks and blouse she'd worn to her dentist appointment that day. With slightly trembling hands, she opened the door.

The porch light illuminated his features, and she went still, taking in just how handsome he was. Jack Colfax, Jr., known to his friends as Jaye, stood there looking simply gorgeous, from his head to his toes and every part in between.

"Jaye. What are you doing here?"

"May I come in, Vel, so we can talk?" he asked with an unreadable expression.

Hearing him say her nickname, which nobody in Catalina Cove used, gave her pause. Ruthie called her that all the time but hearing Jaye say it brought a lot of memories rushing through her mind...and her body.

"Vel?"

He'd said it again. She could easily say no, he couldn't come in, and they had nothing to talk about. She had put distance between them for a reason. She had given up talking to him then, why should they talk now?

She could tell him just what she thought of him but knew that wouldn't be a smart move. He was the new banker in town and agitation between them could call for awkward moments she'd rather not deal with.

If nothing else, they needed to talk about the best way to handle things since nobody in Catalina Cove, except for Sierra Crane, knew about her and Jaye's past. Upon moving to the cove, she and Sierra—who owned the local soup café—had struck up a close friendship.

"Yes, please come in," she said, stepping back.

When Jaye crossed the threshold, her gaze roamed over him. He was six foot two, but he appeared taller than she remembered. He was dressed in a tailor-made suit, one that fit his toned body to perfection.

Regaining control of her senses, she closed the door behind him and repeated her question. "What are you doing here, Jaye?"

"I think we need to talk."

Yes, he'd said that, and they had, back when it mattered, and it had gotten them nowhere. "I was about to have another glass of wine, would you like one?"

"Yes, thanks." There was no need to make sure what she was drinking was what he'd want because she and Jaye always liked the same wine. In fact, they liked most of the same of everything—food, places to visit, music, movies, political party. They'd been perfect together. Perfect for each other. Too bad he hadn't seen or accepted that.

"Please have a seat. I'll be right back." She hurried to the kitchen, holding her breath. It was only when she leaned against the counter that she exhaled. When she'd rented this house, she'd never imagined that Jaye would ever walk through the door, sit on her sofa or

share a glass of wine with her. She'd figured when she'd
left Phoenix she'd made a clean break. Obviously not.

But then, she couldn't place the blame solely at Jaye's
feet. He had been upfront with her from the beginning.
He wasn't the marrying kind, he'd said. All there would
be between them was companionship and sex, sex and
more sex. He'd also made it clear when she'd pushed
for exclusivity that although they wouldn't date others, it was still just an affair. She would be a bedmate
and never a wife.

He didn't love her and could never love her. She
thought that she could be content with their arrangement, had convinced herself she could settle. It took her
three years to accept that she couldn't change his mind
about loving her, and she knew she deserved more. She'd
also known she would never get that *more* from Jaye. His
mother had broken his father's heart, and Jaye had vowed
from an early age never to let someone hurt him that way.

Calming her shaking hands, she reached into the
cabinet to retrieve another wineglass and filled it halfway. That's usually all he ever wanted. They used to
joke about whether the glass was half-full or half-empty
all the time.

After topping off hers, she left the kitchen carrying
both glasses to find him standing in the middle of her
living room, glancing around.

He looked up when she entered. "This is a nice place,
Vel."

"Thanks." As she handed him the wineglass, their
hands touched and she felt a zing of energy and knew he
had as well. Okay, so they'd just proved that sexual chemistry was still alive and well between them. Big deal.

They both sat. As she watched him sip his wine, she thought what she always thought—he looked sexy doing it. The way his lips caressed the rim of the glass and how he would take slow seductive sips...

She cleared her throat. "So why are you here?" she asked for the third time.

Jaye lowered his glass. "It was a rather startling moment seeing you the other night at that town hall meeting."

She shrugged. "You mean you didn't deliberately buy Barrows Bank when you discovered this is where I was living?" she asked coolly.

He took another sip of wine before saying, "Is that what you believe?"

She chuckled and shook her head. "No," she said honestly. "It's not in your makeup to care enough for any woman to go to that much effort. I know you being here was just a coincidence neither of us counted on. I'm sure you were hoping never to see me again."

His brows pinched with irritation. "Have you forgotten that you left me and not the other way around? And without letting me know you were leaving and where you were going."

"You sound pissed. Why? I gave you your freedom."

"I don't recall asking for it."

No, he hadn't. He would have been perfectly fine letting things continue as they were. An affair that led nowhere but to the bedroom. It never dawned on him that perhaps she wanted more. Maybe it *had* dawned on him, but he'd made it clear a number of times he would never fall in love with any woman.

"I did what I felt I had to do, Jaye."

He didn't say anything, didn't even bother to ask her what she meant. But she knew that he knew.

He finished another sip of wine and said, "How do you think we should handle things, Vel? To get the bank up and running the way I want, I'll be living in town for about six to eight months. Maybe less once I hire a bank manager. I don't want any awkward moments between us. Any suggestions?"

"Yes, you could stop calling me Vel. Everybody in town calls me Velvet. If they hear you call me that, they'll know we had a past."

"And you'd rather they didn't know that?"

She nodded. "There's no reason they should. What was between us is in the past and it should stay there."

"Alright. Anything else?"

She drew in a deep breath. "Yes. Nobody in town knows who I am."

She saw the bemused look on his face, and then when he realized what she meant, he smiled. "In other words, nobody in Catalina Cove knows you're the Spencer's restaurant heir."

"No, they don't."

"Even though there's a Spencer's in town? One of the few fast-food places I heard they've allowed to open here?"

Spencer's was a popular restaurant that was known for their hamburgers, French fries and milkshakes. A few years ago, several other items were added to the menu, including pizza. From what Velvet had heard, Reid Lacroix, the wealthiest man in town, had been against any fast-food chains opening in the cove. However, once his granddaughters made it known that Spencer's was their favorite restaurant and the closest one was in New Orleans, he had made sure that one opened up in the cove. The town had gotten a McDonald's for that same reason.

"Actually, there are two people who know. Reid Lacroix and my friend Sierra Crane. Both are sworn to secrecy. No one else has made the connection and there's no reason they should since I'm not involved in the business side of the company. As you know, I have very capable people running things back in Seattle on my behalf."

"Yes, you do," he said. "I hear you're about to expand into Canada and the UK."

"Yes, that's true."

Her parents had always known she didn't want to be involved in the family business and that being a teacher was her dream. They hadn't been overjoyed but had let her be. Their deaths eight years ago had changed things. While coming home one night from a party, their vehicle was carjacked and both were murdered in the process. It was a senseless killing and took away the two people she cared about most.

"I understand you're still teaching."

"Yes. I like teaching."

"And you're good at it."

"Thanks. Well, that about covers everything."

"Not quite. There's something you need to know."

Velvet lifted a brow. "What?"

"Where I'll be staying."

She tilted her head. "Why would it concern me where you're staying?"

"Because I'm renting the house right next door. I

understand your neighbor, Delisa Mills, leaves town for extended trips. The realtor that I hired was able to find me a place with only a six-month lease. Imagine my surprise when I discovered it was right above you. I could try to find another place if my being so close is going to bother you."

Velvet tried to keep her expression neutral but deep down she was fuming. For two years, she had moved on with her life, trying to get herself free of Jaye Colfax and now, out of the clear blue sky, he not only popped up in Catalina Cove, but he was moving *next door*, living right above her? In the house on Blueberry Lane? What on earth had she done to deserve this?

"Vel?"

She glared at him. "No, Jaye, your living upstairs will mean nothing to me."

He smiled...actually smiled. Did that mean it meant nothing to him, too? He thought it would be okay if he moved in and began parading women in and out of his part of the house when she was so close by? There was no doubt in her mind that since their breakup he had continued his sex-only arrangement with women. He'd certainly captured a lot of interest at the town hall meeting the other night.

"I think we've covered everything, Jaye," she said, taking his wineglass from him—although there was still wine in it—and then turning to head for the door to let him out.

"Yes, I guess we have." When they reached the door, he said, "I'll be staying at that bed-and-breakfast in town, Shelby by the Sea, until the first of the year, before moving in."

"Okay. Good night, Jaye."

"Good night, Vel."

"And please remember, Jaye, from now on, I'm Velvet."

"I'll remember."

She closed the door and leaned against it, feeling totally frustrated. Just like that, Jaye Colfax was back in her life, living directly above her whether she liked it or not.

JAYE COLFAX ENTERED his room at Shelby by the Sea, noticing that it was a very nice place with all the comforts of home. Jerking off his tie and removing his suit jacket, he tossed both on the bed before heading to the window. He had requested an ocean view, and that's just what he'd gotten. Even at night, he could see the lights of several boats, which meant some people were night fishing.

He drew in a deep breath as he recalled his conversation with Velvet. He had been prepared to be totally honest with her and tell her the reason he was here—to claim her love.

However, something she'd said had stopped him from being forthright. She had joked about him deliberately buying the bank when he'd discovered this was where she was living. Then she'd admitted she knew he hadn't done that because it wasn't in his makeup to care that much for any woman. He'd decided at that moment to prove how wrong she was, and that it *was* in his makeup to care that much.

When he felt the time was right, he would let her know how miserable he'd been the last two years and how it had taken her leaving for him to realize how much he cared for her. He loved her. Letting her leave had been the biggest mistake of his life, one he intended to rectify. Only then would he tell her how he'd hired a private investigator to find her...and also admit that Larson Barrows hadn't really been ready to retire. It had taken Jaye making an offer for the purchase of his bank that was so sweet the man couldn't have refused—or he would have been a fool to do so. The same thing with becoming her neighbor. He had made it worth Delisa Mills's while, financially, to stay out of the country at least six to eight more months.

Bottom line, Jaye had done what he'd felt was necessary to claim the woman he loved. The woman he had lost by his own stupidity. Hopefully, in the end, she would see that he intended to do what he should have done years ago—accept her place in his life.

Instead, he had hurt her deeply and, more than anything, regretted what he'd done. Now he would work like hell to un-break her heart and show her they were perfectly matched. There was no other woman for him.

He loved her and he intended to prove it to her, but on her time, not his. If it took longer than six months, he was fine with that, because he was in it for the long haul. He'd discovered that Catalina Cove wasn't so bad. In fact, it was a nice coastal town on the gulf, just an hour's drive from New Orleans.

Jaye was determined that when he left the cove, he would be leaving with Velvet—as his wife.

CHAPTER TWO

One month later

"Is EVERYTHING COMING together for your wedding?" Velvet asked her good friend Sierra Crane as they shared breakfast at the Witherspoon Café. It was a restaurant in Catalina Cove, known for serving a wonderful breakfast that included their signature blueberry muffins and also a delicious lunch and mouthwatering dinner.

Velvet thought Sierra was glowing and had been since she and Vaughn Miller announced their engagement last month on Christmas Day. Velvet hadn't been surprised. It had been obvious to anyone who'd observed the couple that they were in love. The wedding would be held in March on the grounds of Vaughn's family estate, Zara's Haven.

She and Sierra had moved to Catalina Cove around the same time. For Sierra, it had been returning home after her divorce, to the place where she'd been born, to raise her six-year-old goddaughter, Teryn. And for Velvet, it had been relocating to a place far away from Jaye Colfax to heal her broken heart.

"Yes, everything is set," Sierra said, smiling from ear to ear. "I think Teryn is even happier than I am. She adores Vaughn."

"Well, I don't know three individuals more deserving of happiness," Velvet said, after taking a sip of her coffee. Like Sierra, Vaughn Miller had been born in Catalina Cove and moved away after high school. He returned to the cove several years ago and would soon become the CEO of the cove's largest employer when the present CEO and the richest man in the cove, Reid Lacroix, retired later this year.

"What about you, Velvet? Don't you think you deserve happiness as well?"

Velvet tilted her head and looked at Sierra. There were only two people in the cove who knew her history. People she trusted. The first had been Reid Lacroix. He had known her parents since they'd attended college at Yale together, and her dad and Reid had been on the university's rowing team.

It was at her parents' memorial service when Reid had approached her and said if she ever needed to get away, she should visit Catalina Cove. It was just the place to heal from the pain caused by grief. Velvet hadn't taken him up on his offer then, but she had a few years later when she'd visited the cove to heal from another type of pain—a broken heart. While staying for the weekend at the bed-and-breakfast, Shelby by the Sea, she had fallen in love with Catalina Cove and decided to move from Phoenix and make it her permanent home.

Knowing Sierra was waiting for her response, Velvet said, "Yes, everyone deserves happiness."

"Even you?" Sierra prodded.

She knew why her friend was asking and gave her

the only answer she could. "Yes, even me. However, for some, happiness can be an elusive thing. Just like love."

"Only if you decide not to go after it."

"But I did go after both happiness and love, Sierra. And that didn't get me anywhere."

"Promise me you won't give up on them. Take it from someone who had to learn the hard way. I almost lost the love Vaughn had offered to me because I didn't want to take a chance on my heart getting broken again. Now I'm glad I took that chance."

Sierra paused, then asked, "How is that neighbor situation working out with you and Jaye Colfax?"

Velvet took a sip of her coffee. "Not so bad, considering we're technically living under the same roof. He officially moved in a few weeks ago. Although I've caught glimpses of him through my window, our paths haven't crossed."

"I guess that's good for you, then."

"Yes, considering the man I left Phoenix to avoid ends up moving to the same town where I am and becomes my neighbor."

"Umm, maybe that was divine intervention," Sierra said, smiling over the top of her cup.

"Or it could be somebody up there doesn't like me very much."

"*Or*...it could be that somebody up there likes you a lot."

"Meaning?"

"What if he's changed?"

Velvet rolled her eyes. "Jaye Colfax? Not a chance. Honestly, it doesn't matter if he has. I no longer love Jaye. I admit my heart went pitter-patter when I saw him at that town meeting, and for a moment I thought I still loved him, but now I know that I've gotten over him and have moved on."

Sierra leaned over the table and whispered, "Well. I got it from a very reliable source that Jaye Colfax put a stop to any gossip about him being on anyone's *must-do* list. He even made sure Laura Crawford knew he wasn't available."

That made Velvet smiled since Laura wasn't one of her favorite people. The woman, whose family was one of the wealthiest in town, looked down her nose at the less fortunate. In other words, she was a snob. So was her brother, Webb.

Velvet had noticed the first week Jaye moved in that a few different women tried to visit. It was obvious they hadn't made it over his threshold. No real surprise there. The one thing she knew about Jaye was that he preferred doing the choosing and the chasing. In other words, women who sought him out were a turnoff and he didn't have a problem letting them know it.

Velvet looked at her watch. "I need to leave to get to school on time."

"Okay, and remember what I said. You deserve to be happy just as much as anyone else."

VELVET WASN'T SURE why Sierra's words lingered in her mind for the rest of the day, even when her full concentration should have been on her students. She taught high school and volunteered as a gymnastics coach two days a week. Since moving to the cove, both had kept her pretty busy—too busy to think about the reason why she'd moved here. And now that very reason, Jaye Colfax, had moved right next door.

"Is there a reason you wanted to see me, Miss Spencer?"

Velvet blinked, immediately recalling she had asked Lenny Bordeaux to meet with her after school. "Yes, Lenny," she said, standing and smiling up at the lanky fifteen-year-old who was taller than she was. "Please have a seat." When Lenny had settled into one of the student desks, Velvet leaned back against her desk and asked, "How have you been, Lenny?"

He shrugged his shoulders and said, "Fine."

She nodded. "Remember back in November I met with you about your grades? Specifically, the issue of you not turning in your homework assignments, as well as not passing the weekly quizzes. I was hoping things would change but your grades still haven't improved."

Lenny shrugged again. "I've been busy."

She lifted a brow. "Busy? Doing what may I ask?"

He hesitated and then said, "Fun stuff."

"Fun stuff?" she asked to make sure she'd heard him correctly.

"Yes, fun stuff," he said. "I got a car for Christmas, and I've been enjoying it. Then there's the video games I got for Christmas to improve my baseball skills."

Velvet didn't say anything for a moment, disappointed that he saw doing all that *fun stuff* as more important than doing his schoolwork. And did he say he'd gotten a car for Christmas? Was he even old enough to drive? Granted he was tall for his age, but still...

"I thought you had to be sixteen to get your driver's license. You're only fifteen."

"That's the rule, but my dad got around it by applying for me to get a hardship license since I'll be sixteen this summer. That way I have full driving privileges now."

A hardship license? She thought those were only issued when driving was really necessary to get to school. Velvet saw no reason he couldn't walk to school like all the other ninth graders. Unlike high schools in other places, Catalina Cove's junior high school consisted of grades seven through nine, and senior high were ten through twelve.

"Don't you think making sure you do your homework assignments and preparing for the weekly quizzes are important?"

"Yes, and I'll get around to studying eventually."

Get around to studying *eventually*? Did he think he had a lot of time left to turn his grades around? She knew he loved to play baseball and his dream was to make the varsity team. "You like playing baseball?"

"Yes. I hope to get drafted to play in the majors right out of high school."

She nodded. Although that was a few years away, it was good that he had goals. However, she thought he had his current priorities mixed up. She hated to be the one to burst his bubble, but she needed him to be aware of a few things. "Wanting to one day become a professional baseball player is great, but you need to complete high school first. In order to move on to the next grade, Lenny, you'll need to pass all your core classes. Algebra is one of them. If you fail, you'll have to repeat the class or take it over the summer before going on to senior high school."

He shook his head. "I'll be in baseball practice over

the summer. I plan to play on the varsity team in the fall."

"Not if your grades don't improve. I'd be willing to tutor you after school."

"My dad says I don't need to pass algebra."

She lifted a brow. "Excuse me?"

"My dad said I don't need algebra to play for the varsity team."

Now Velvet was really confused. Why would his father tell him something like that? She had sent a letter to his parents when she'd met with Lenny in November, letting them know how serious things could get without improvement. Did they not receive the letter?

"I'll be glad to talk to your father and when I do, I'll tell him the same thing I'm telling you now, Lenny. If your grades don't improve, you will fail my class." She wasn't going to back down on her position regardless of what his father might have told him.

"May I go now?"

"Yes, you may go."

She watched Lenny walk out of the room. She had offered to tutor him, but he honestly believed he didn't need to pass algebra because of what his father had told him.

Well, she'd had her talk with him and would follow up and send another letter to his parents. But for now, she would go home and enjoy her weekend.

GOOD TIMING, JAYE THOUGHT, bringing his car to a stop at the same time Velvet pulled into their shared yard.

All six houses on Blueberry Lane backed up against massive yet scenic blueberry fields. What he liked about this house was that it was the only one in a quiet cul-de-sac and had the most land and trees. People rarely drove into the cul-de-sac and he liked the privacy and planned to use it to his advantage.

As he got out of his car, he felt deep flutters in the pit of his stomach. Although he'd kept his distance from Velvet, there wasn't a morning he hadn't stood in his kitchen, after returning from his morning jog, and through the window watched her get into her car to leave for school.

"Hello, Mr. Colfax," Velvet said to him as she exited her car.

If she was intent on keeping things formal between them, he would let her. *For now.* "Miss Spencer. And how was your day?" he asked as his gaze raked over her, taking in everything about her, especially her gorgeous smooth, creamy and flawless cocoa-colored complexion, shoulder-length dark brown hair that fell in waves to her shoulders, her black eyes and high cheekbones.

"My day was challenging, and yours?"

He smiled. "Challenging as well, but I'm finding this is a good town with a lot of nice, hardworking people."

"Yes, I love it here. It's peaceful."

Had she said that as a hint that her life was here now and not in Phoenix?

She then said, "Well, have a nice evening."

"You do the same." There was no need to tell her that as long as he slept alone and didn't wake up with her in his arms, it wouldn't be a nice evening, night or morning. He watched her hurry up the steps to her door, open it and then close it behind her.

He grabbed the bags from the passenger seat; he'd

picked up dinner from the Witherspoon Café. He headed up his walkway to the side of the house where his entry door was located, but not before glancing back at the door through which Velvet had disappeared.

VELVET CLOSED THE door behind her, then leaned against it, drawing in a deep breath. The moment she'd gotten out of her car and seen Jaye, she had been transported back to the time when seeing him would have been the highlight of her day…and then her night. Those days were long gone. Now she left her house and returned home, hoping she wouldn't see him at all.

Typically, there was no reason for their paths to cross since she had teachers' hours and he had bankers' hours. That meant she was in her classroom getting her day started before he even left for work. However, because he was an ardent morning jogger, she would get a glimpse of him out her kitchen window while enjoying her morning coffee. There was nothing like starting her day seeing all those rippling muscles, firm abs and bulging biceps. It was a good thing he jogged through the blueberry fields behind the houses and not out on the open road. She could just imagine being a female driver and seeing all those toned muscles sprinting about. It would probably cause car accidents.

She pushed away from the door, recalling how when they'd been a couple, Jaye never invited her to go jogging with him, even those days when she would spend the night over at his place. He said jogging in the morning was his personal time alone to clear his head. It was when he could really think, strategize and plan his day.

Sighing deeply, she placed her briefcase on the din-

ing room table and wondered if Jaye had recognized it
as the same one he'd given her as a birthday gift. Unfortunately, it hadn't it been the engagement ring she'd
been hoping for.

What had been the turning point in their relationship was overhearing Jaye tell his best friend, Mercury
Steele, that he loved her, but had quickly explained that
meant he loved *to bed* her. That's when she had finally
seen the handwriting on the wall. After engaging in an
exclusive relationship with Jaye for three years, he still
had no intention of ever settling down and marrying her.

Needing a drink, she went into the kitchen for a glass
of wine. Every time she saw Jaye, it would remind her
of just what she hadn't done in two years—namely,
made love with a man. When they'd been a couple, she
and Jaye had maintained a very active sex life. It didn't
take long to realize her battery-operated toy couldn't
replace the real thing and she'd gotten rid of it, deciding to do without. She'd been fine since then but now
her body's radar seemed to hone in on the very person
who had taken care of its needs for three solid years.

Not wanting to think about that, she took a sip of
wine and then went back to the dining room to pull the
papers from her briefcase. She always gave an algebra
quiz on Fridays. Sitting at the table, she began grading
papers, deciding to do it now rather than wait until Sunday evening. Less than an hour later, she was finished.
All the students had aced the quiz, except for Lenny.

When Velvet heard her cell phone ringing, she
smiled, recognizing the ringtone. It was her best friend,
Ruthie, who'd been her college roommate and the rea-

son Velvet, after her parents' death, had relocated from Seattle to Phoenix.

"Hey, Ruthie. How are the wedding plans coming along?" Ruthie was getting married in June.

"Great! I'm working with a wonderful wedding planner, and she has a lot of great ideas."

"That's wonderful."

"I just wanted to check in to see how you're doing and ask if you've seen your sexy neighbor lately."

Velvet rolled her eyes, knowing Ruthie thought the entire situation with her and Jaye was rather amusing. She had spent two years putting as much distance between them as she could and then fate delivered him practically to her door.

There was no need to tell Ruthie that she saw Jaye most days; especially when she made sure she was standing at a particular spot in her kitchen to catch a glimpse of him leaving to go jogging. "Funny you should ask. I saw Jaye today when I came home. He was coming home as well."

"And?"

"And we spoke and then I went inside my side of the house, and I assume he went inside his."

"Umm, did you get all hot and bothered when you saw him?"

"Why would I? I don't love Jaye anymore."

"Who said anything about love? I'm thinking of hot sex. The two of you used to mate like rabbits, and if I recall, just a couple of months ago you mentioned the idea of engaging in a steamy affair just to take the sexual edge off."

Did Ruthie have to remember every single thing she said? "That was all talk."

"Was it?"

"Yes, but if I did decide to hook up with a guy to take the edge off, it definitely wouldn't be with Jaye."

"Why not? I think the situation would be ideal since the two of you share space."

"We don't share space. He has his own place and I have mine. They're just connected."

"Well, regardless, he lives right above you, Vel."

"Your point?"

"My point, as I was saying, is that if you were to have an affair with him, at least you'd know you wouldn't be disappointed. Besides, you claim that you don't have feelings for him anymore. If that's true, then I'd think you'd prefer jumping into the sack with someone you know rather than someone you didn't. Especially if it's someone who has the ability to make multiple orgasms an art form. Need I remind you those were your words and not mine?"

Velvet figured it was time to end their call. The last thing she wanted to remember was how well Jaye could make her scream and about all those orgasms. "I just finished grading papers and now I need to record grades, Ruthie. I got to go."

"Okay, but when horniness gets the best of you, I think it's wonderful that Jaye is living so close."

"Goodbye, Ruthie."

"Goodbye."

Velvet clicked off the phone, wishing Ruthie hadn't reminded her of how good she and Jaye were in bed, not to mention that suggestion about taking him on as a lover. There was no way she would consider something like that, no matter how horny she got.

She took another sip of wine and leaned back in her chair. She had been living in Phoenix less than a year when she'd met Jaye. His banking corporation had been one of the sponsors of a job fair put on by her school at the civic center.

As Velvet sat there, she couldn't help but remember when she and Jaye met.

CHAPTER THREE

Five years ago

"EXCUSE ME. ARE YOU the person in charge?"

Velvet looked up to the handsome face of the man standing at her table. Immediately, she was caught speechless by the dark eyes staring down at her. They had to be the most captivating pair of eyes she'd ever seen. The absolutely gorgeous man wore a dark suit, looking like he'd stepped from the pages of *GQ* magazine, and would definitely clinch it for any hot-blooded person.

While his gaze held hers as intensely as hers held his, she suddenly realized it was for a different reason. He had asked her a question, but her brain had temporarily shut down. "I'm sorry. What did you ask?"

A sexy smile curved the corners of his lips as he repeated the question. "I asked if you're the person in charge?"

Since the other teacher, Charlotte Madison, who had been working the booth with her at the job fair left early, that meant Velvet was it. "Yes, for now. May I help you?"

"Yes, I believe you can," he said, extending his hand

to her. "I'm Jaye Colfax and my bank is one of the sponsors of this event."

She nodded, trying to ignore the heated sizzle that passed through her when she took his hand. What on earth was happening to her? She had never experienced an instant attraction to a man in all her twenty-five years. "Yes, Mr. Colfax." She recalled seeing his name on the sponsor list. In fact, categorized by the amount of donations received, his company headed the list. "I'm Velvet Spencer, one of the teachers at Dunbar High School. We definitely appreciate your sponsorship. How can I help you?"

"Due to a meeting, I didn't get to come as early as I'd planned and was wondering how things went today?"

A smile touched her lips. "Things went very well. As you can see, a lot of businesses participated. Most of the students who came through got a good idea of all the opportunities available after graduation. For those who don't have the funds to go to college, I believe they were surprised to learn about the scholarships available to them."

"That's good, and please call me Jaye."

"Okay, and I'm Velvet." She shared some of the survey results they'd gotten from the students so far, and he was impressed so many had taken the time to provide feedback. "We were just as surprised, but then a lot of them are anxious as well as excited about finishing high school and becoming independent."

He chuckled, glanced at his watch and then looked back at her. "It's nearing dinnertime. Do you have plans?"

She blinked. "Plans?"

"Yes, for dinner."

She held his gaze. "No, I don't have plans."

"Neither do I. Would you join me?"

Velvet hated seeming dense, but she was having a hard time keeping up with him. One minute they were discussing the job fair and another minute he was asking about her dinner plans. "You want to take me to dinner?"

"Yes."

Velvet looked straight into Jaye's eyes, figuring there had to be a catch somewhere. "Why?"

"Why not, Velvet Spencer? You did just say you didn't have plans. Do you not plan to eat later?"

"Yes, I plan to eat."

"Is there any reason you can't do so with me?"

As far as she was concerned, there were a number of reasons, but she decided to state the main one. "I don't know you."

"I don't know you, either, but I would love getting to know you. I'm especially curious about your name."

"Most people are."

"So what about it, Velvet? Dinner?"

Velvet hesitated briefly before glancing at her watch. Then she looked around. The job fair was officially over. All the students had left and the businesses were packing up to leave. He was the top donor to the high school as a job fair sponsor, and she had a feeling her principal wouldn't like it if she rubbed the man the wrong way. "Okay, I'll join you for dinner. It will take me a few minutes to break things down, though. Charlotte, my job fair team partner, had to leave early."

"I'll help."

"You sure?"

"I'm positive."

"Okay." She thought that was considerate of him.

Silently, he helped her take down the banners and she was glad he was there. Otherwise, she would have had to stand on a chair. But he was tall, probably at least six two, and easily took down the hanging signs. He also helped pack up the streamers and stack of left-over handouts.

She tried not to look at him but found she couldn't help herself. He had removed his jacket and tie and she thought his white dress shirt and dark gray slacks looked good on him. Some men wore the clothes and there were clothes that wore the man. Jaye Colfax definitely wore the clothes. He had looked darn good in his suit and now she couldn't help noticing how well he looked in shirt and slacks.

He glanced up at her, and her heart started pounding. She wasn't used to so much masculinity on display.

"What do you intend to do with this?" he asked, picking up the box like it weighed nothing, when it had taken both her and Charlotte to carry it in.

"It needs to go to my car. I can get a cart for you to roll it out."

"No, I got this."

She nodded, thinking he most certainly did. He lifted the box to his shoulder, and she could clearly see muscles flex beneath his shirt.

"Alright then, please follow me," she said, grabbing her purse. She also gathered up his jacket and tie. Maybe she was imagining things, but she thought she could feel his body heat in them. She certainly picked up his masculine scent in the clothing.

Velvet led him out the building to where her SUV was parked. After unlocking the trunk, she stepped aside for him. He placed the box inside with the same ease as when he had lifted it to carry it outside. The man didn't break a sweat.

He closed the trunk and turned to her. "So, what type of foods do you like to eat, Velvet?" he asked her.

She handed his jacket and tie to him and watched him slide into his jacket, then tuck his tie into the pocket.

"I enjoy seafood," she answered.

He nodded. "Then Captain Scampi is the best place. Fresh seafood is flown in daily. Have you been there before?"

"Yes, once."

He lifted a brow. "Only once?"

"Yes. I moved here from Seattle less than a year ago and went to Captain Scampi a few months back for my girlfriend's birthday. The food was delicious."

"It always is." He smiled before looking at his watch. "Depending on traffic it's twenty minutes from here. We can go in my car, and I'll bring you back to get your car later."

"There's no need. I can just meet you there."

He nodded. "I will be there waiting."

I will be there waiting… Why did his words stir something deep within her? Something elemental. Shrugging away those thoughts, she moved to the driver's side of her vehicle. "You think you'll beat me there?" she asked, grinning.

He grinned as well, and she felt another stirring in

the pit of her stomach. Jaye Colfax was way too handsome for his own good.

"Yes," he said, and she knew pretending she wasn't attracted to him would not be easy.

As she buckled her seat belt, she watched him walk to a sports car, a red Tesla Roadster. She threw her head back and laughed. Yes, he would definitely get there before her.

JAYE HAD ALREADY snagged a table that had a beautiful view of the mountains when he looked out the window and saw Velvet Spencer pulling into the parking lot. The woman was hot and that's all it had taken to kick his libido in gear.

He felt the phone in his pant pocket vibrate and figured it was his best friend, Mercury Steele, wondering where the hell he was. They were to meet up for their usual happy-hour drinks at Notorious, a popular nightclub in town. Included in their plans were their pick of women who were always eager for a quickie. But not today for him. Mercury would just have to do it alone. He would explain things to him later and there was no doubt in his mind his best friend from grade school would understand.

He watched Velvet walk from her car to the restaurant and noted several other men in the restaurant were watching her, too. The moment he'd walked into the civic center, he had noticed her. There had not been anything particularly revealing about the outfit she was wearing, a pretty print dress that hit her knees and a short-waisted jacket. But the outfit complemented a small waist and a pair of gorgeous legs. Did he mention gorgeous legs? Everybody knew he was a leg man. He liked all the other parts, too, but a pair of gorgeous legs had always been his downfall and could get his libido riled up real fast. And when his gaze had shifted from her legs to her face, it was a wonder his tongue hadn't fallen out of his mouth. He thought the woman was stunning and sexy all rolled into one. It had taken him a minute or two to suck in a deep breath before heading in her direction with one purpose in mind. He wasn't a man who dwelled on the there and after; he mainly concentrated on the here and now.

He would have made it over to her booth sooner had he not been stopped by several people who he knew him, either from his high school days or business dealings. That's one of the pitfalls of living in your hometown. People not only knew you by name, but they also knew you when…

Jaye could add a lot of words after the word *when*. That's how things were when you were a close friend to those Steele brothers. All of them had notorious reputations around town regarding their sexual exploits. Reputations that they'd rightly earned. What could he say? He had earned his as well.

He stood when he saw Velvet enter the restaurant and look around. The place was packed, yet it seemed to him that all eyes were on her…and then on him when he stood. He saw the knowing looks in a few pairs of eyes, especially those who knew of his womanizing reputation. For some reason, it annoyed him that they'd immediately assume she was his next conquest. But why should it bother him when she was?

Still, there was something about Velvet Spencer's

smile that got him below the belt. She'd said she'd been in town less than a year so she might not have heard about him—mainly that he liked women. He enjoyed bedding them and the one thing he wouldn't do was get serious about one. Ever.

He figured she probably didn't know of his reputation. Otherwise, chances were she would not have agreed to go out to dinner with him. From the moment they'd engaged in conversation, he'd known something about her was different than his usual conquests. He just wasn't sure what that difference was. One thing he did know was that everything he saw about Velvet spelled class. Not that I-want-to-be-classy or I-am-trying-to-be-classy. She seemed to wear an invisible banner that stated I am classy.

It was there in her smile, in the way she walked and even when she talked. He could sit and listen to the sound of her voice for hours. That's why more than anything he wanted to get to know her…before he took her to bed. That meant he didn't have much time because he intended to achieve the latter tonight. Plus, he had that meeting in the morning with the Empire Group that he needed to prepare for. Hmm, he found it odd that for the first time he wanted to get to know a woman before bedding her.

Most people credited him with being a good judge of character and could pretty much sum up a person and their worth within the first ten minutes of meeting them. That skill definitely helped him as a banker who didn't have time for bullshitters, scammers and fraudulent asses who thought they could pull something over on a Colfax. It wasn't happening. That was the main reason he had a feeling there was more to Velvet Spencer than her unusual first name.

"You did beat me here, but I'm not surprised," she said, finally reaching their table and taking the chair he pulled out for her. "I like your car, by the way."

"Thanks. Maybe one day I'll take you for a spin," he said, returning to his chair.

Jaye knew the words weren't true because tonight was one and done. At least that's the way the ball usually bounced. He wasn't a man who hung around a female if, for whatever reason, she thought she could get her claws into him. Nor did he particularly like an aggressive woman who targeted the man. He liked being in control and went after the woman he wanted and not the other way around.

"Thanks for the offer, but no thanks."

No thanks? Had she just turned down a chance to ride in his car...for the second time that day? Didn't she know there weren't many women around town—he honestly couldn't think of a single one—who wouldn't want to take a spin in his car with him? If nothing else, other than to be seen.

At that moment, the waitress walked up and smiled. "Hey, Jaye." She looked over at Velvet and didn't smile as much. In fact, she seemed annoyed. He honestly didn't know why. Monica had been one of his many one-and-dones from their high school days. She had gotten a divorce last year and since then had come on to him a few times. However, he'd made it pretty clear that he wasn't interested. And just like in high school, it appeared she didn't know how to take *no* for an answer.

Monica looked back at him without even acknowledging Velvet. "You want your regular, Jaye?" Then he recalled that common decency wasn't one of her strong suits. Regardless, he would not let her disrespect any woman who was with him.

He held her gaze. "What I really want is for you to give my dinner date the same courtesy and respect you're giving me."

The smile vanished from her face and an innocent look appeared. "I have no idea what you're talking about."

"I think you do, but since you claim you don't, I want another server for our table and stay away from the kitchen if you want to keep your job."

Instead of saying anything, Monica stormed off. He watched her talk to another waitress who turned and came to their table. It was Cissy. He knew and liked her. She and another classmate, Randy Corrington, had married out of high school and now had a couple of kids.

She smiled both at him and then Velvet...like Jaye thought any good waitstaff should. "How are you guys doing today?"

"I'm fine," Velvet said, smiling back.

"So am I, Cissy," Jaye said. "How's Randy?"

"He's doing fine. His electrical company is pretty busy these days. We appreciate your brother Franklin putting in a good word for him."

Jaye shrugged. "Randy's work speaks for itself and Franklin knows it."

Moments later Cissy had taken their order and gotten their drinks. Jaye was glad he was sitting facing the kitchen. He had warned Monica not to go near it, and she better take heed to his warning since the owner was a good friend of the Colfax family. It didn't take much for him to recall one other time a waitress had gotten pissed at his one-and-done policy. Although he had spelled it out for her from the beginning, she had wanted more. When he'd refused, she deliberately put maximum strength hot sauce in his chili. His tongue had burned for a week.

When he and Velvet were alone again, she looked at him and said, "You didn't have to dismiss that first waitress. I was fine."

He frowned. "Well, I wasn't. Nobody disrespects my date." And he meant it. A smile replaced his frown when he said, "Now you want to tell me the story behind the name Velvet?"

She chuckled and his breath got lodged in his throat. When did the sound of a woman's chuckle ever do that to him? Okay, he would be the first to admit he was physically attracted to her, and it was a strong attraction. Stronger than most. But still, he wasn't one to let a woman—no matter how beautiful, curvy or leggy—go to his head. At least not the one connected to his neck. The other one he had no problem stimulating.

She took a sip of her iced tea through her straw and, suddenly, he got hard. Damn. He shifted in his chair, grateful he was sitting or else he would have embarrassed himself. For a man, an arousal was something you couldn't hide.

When she smiled over at him, he felt a tinge of something so foreign he grabbed his own glass of iced tea and, not bothering with the straw, took a huge gulp. It was either that or the heat consuming his midsection would get the best of him.

"My paternal grandmother named me," she said. "She was a huge Elizabeth Taylor fan and *National Velvet* was her favorite movie. She gave birth to one son, my father. So she missed the opportunity of naming a daughter Velvet. My parents let her do the honor with her first and only granddaughter."

Jaye nodded. "Do you have any brothers?"

"No. I was my parents' only child. What about you? Any siblings?"

"Yes. My father has three sons. I'm the oldest."

She nodded. "You mean your parents have three sons, right?"

He frowned. "No, I meant what I said."

A moment of silence stretched between them, and he felt the need to apologize. "I'm sorry. I didn't mean to sound so abrupt. It's just the subject of my mother is a touchy one with me."

"Oh."

Jaye felt he'd told Velvet all she needed to know. In fact, he'd told her more than he told most people. It wasn't any of their business. Besides, he had only just met her that day. But still, for a reason he didn't understand, he felt he needed to explain since he knew, unlike some women, she was too kind and considerate to ask why.

After taking another sip of tea, he said, "My mother left my father for another man when I was twelve. And she never looked back."

"I'm sorry, Jaye," she said softly. "I am truly sorry."

He held her gaze, seeing sadness and not pity in her eyes. Some people didn't know there was a difference, but there was. He could handle the sadness, but he didn't want anyone's pity. Jack Colfax, Sr., and his sons had survived just fine without Eartha Colfax in their lives. The woman hadn't been mother material, anyway. She'd been the great pretender.

Although his brothers might have been too young to understand, he hadn't. He'd known the nights when his father had been working two jobs, first as general manager at a bank during the day, and then as a professor of finance at a university two nights a week, so his wife could be a stay-at-home mom.

But she hadn't been a stay-at-home mom. She hadn't come close. While her husband had been working himself hard, she'd been having affairs right under his nose. He'd been too trusting and too loving. He hadn't known anything until she'd asked him for a divorce so she could marry her lover. Jaye had seen firsthand the hurt and pain his father had suffered because of loving a woman.

"It wasn't your fault," he finally said. "My father, brothers and I did just fine without her."

She still had that sad look in her eyes and he felt a tightness in his chest. He was tempted to reach out and smooth her sadness away, knowing it was there because of him. He had told her too much. More than he'd told any woman. Why? And why was he allowing Velvet Spencer to get under his skin?

Jaye was glad when Cissy returned and placed a huge delicious-looking seafood platter for two in the middle of their table.

CHAPTER FOUR

AN HOUR OR SO later, any apprehensions Velvet may have had about joining Jaye for dinner were gone. She was totally enjoying herself and thought he was a likable guy. Her heart had ached for him when he'd told her about his mother. Regardless of what he'd said, she figured his mother's actions had affected him. She had a feeling he regretted sharing that much of himself and usually didn't do so. Probably because it was too painful to recall.

He had quickly switched the subject to his father, and she could tell the older Jack Colfax was someone Jaye admired tremendously. He had told her how his father had opened his first bank ten years ago and now there were several of them on a national scale and they were looking to spread to other areas.

He wasn't boastful or arrogant, but she could tell he was proud of his family's success and accomplishments, and how important it was for his father to pass some sort of legacy to his three sons. She understood because she had felt the same way about her parents. Both had worked hard to turn their first Spencer's restaurant into a smashing success. By the time they had celebrated the restaurant's fifteenth anniversary, there were over a hundred Spencer's across the United States.

Although she had worked alongside her parents in growing the family business, her parents had known that her true love was teaching. Not once had they tried to shift her focus from that and she appreciated them for it. From listening to Jaye talk about his father, she could tell they had a close relationship, like the one she'd had with hers. It was sad that his mother hadn't stayed in contact with her sons after his parents had divorced.

More than once tonight during their conversation, their gazes met and held. Each time it happened, she became even more fully aware of him as a man. A man who got her blood stirring. And she had a feeling it wasn't one-sided. There was no way it could be when the intensity of his gaze was radiating a degree of desire she could actually feel.

"I've told you a lot about myself, Velvet. Now tell me about you. What made you leave Seattle to settle here in Phoenix?"

She didn't say anything for a minute and then said, "A year after I graduated from college, I lost my parents in a carjacking."

The look in his eyes flashed from shock to outrage and then to sadness. "I'm sorry, Velvet. I am truly sorry."

"Thanks. The authorities got the guy, but all I could think about was how senseless their deaths were. He could have taken their car and left them by the side of the road, but instead he killed them."

There must have been something in her voice that touched him and beckoned him to touch her. He reached out and gently caressed the side of her face as if he were trying to smooth away the pain and sadness he saw there.

Velvet liked his touch. It calmed something within her. Namely, the torment she felt whenever she thought about her parents' deaths. As his fingers continued to caress her skin, his gaze traced a slow path over her face, as if cementing each of her features to his memory.

"That had to have been hard on you."

She nodded, fighting back her tears from pain that was still raw. "It was. They were all I had, and we were close. I remained in Seattle long enough for the guy to go on trial and be sentenced. Then I felt I had to get away and move someplace else."

"What made you decide on Phoenix?" he asked in a comforting voice.

"My best friend from college, Ruth Bethea. This is her hometown, and she would always tell me what a great city it was. We're both teachers and when there were vacancies at her school, she convinced me to come here and so I did."

A smile curved his lips. "And I'm glad you did."

Velvet tried not to be taken with Jaye but discovered she was. Although she was twenty-five, she hadn't done a lot of dating. After high school, most of her time had been spent at the universities, obtaining her bachelor's and master's degrees, both within four years. Most of her free time had been spent traveling around the country with her parents as they checked on their restaurants. Once a year, the three of them also traveled abroad to different countries.

Because of their wealth, her parents had cautioned her early that there were just as many gold-digging men as there were women. She had found that to be true when she had met Lamont Owens in her senior year of college. They'd dated three months, and she had liked him. But then one night he had bragged to one of his friends about his plans to marry her and make sure he ran the Spencer's Corporation when her old man retired. He only saw her as an investment for his future. Ruthie had overheard him and told Velvet. That's when she had dropped him like a hot potato and had been glad they hadn't shared a bed. After Lamont, no guy had interested her enough to move to anything serious.

Until now.

Jaye interested her. Never had she felt such strong vibes off a man. Whenever he looked at her, leveling those dark eyes on her, she had to fight to keep from moaning. Even the sound of his voice was a turn-on. He was extremely handsome. Tall, dark and sexy certainly described him to a tee. Whenever he smiled, it seemed the entire world should smile right along with him.

His chestnut-colored skin looked smooth as silk and the neatly trimmed beard around his mouth offset a gorgeous pair of lips. When had she been taken with a man's lips before? Then there was that little dip in the center of his upper lip that did something to her. Made her want to take her tongue and—

"How do you like living in Phoenix so far?" he asked her.

She shifted her gaze from his mouth to his eyes. Had he noticed the attention she'd been giving to his lips? "I like it here. I admit that I had to get used to how dry it is since I came from a place that rained a lot."

"I'm sure that did take an adjustment."

Her gaze had shifted back to his lips. She met his eyes once more when she caught the tail end of what he'd said. "An adjustment to what?"

He smiled. "The difference in the weather between Seattle and Phoenix."

"Oh." Velvet knew she should be keeping up with the conversation, but she was fighting to focus on what he was saying rather than the lips his words were flowing through.

"I could stay here and talk to you for hours, Velvet."

She was glad to hear him say that because she felt the same way. Besides being handsome, the man was suave, intelligent and a great conversationalist. He was well versed on a number of topics. But then so was she, and they had covered a lot of them. "I like talking to you, too, Jaye."

Not only had they talked but they'd laughed about a couple of television shows they had seen. They were both into reality shows, which were so far from being genuine that they couldn't help but find them amusing.

He glanced at his watch. "This place will be closing in an hour. I guess it's time for us to leave."

She looked at her own watch. Surprised, she saw it was close to ten o'clock. She couldn't recall ever staying out this late on a school night. Jaye must have seen the surprised look on her face and said, "I should apologize for keeping you out late. It's a school day tomorrow. I bet you're usually in bed by now."

He was right. Normally, she was. However, she'd been enjoying his company so much she hadn't noticed the time. Although she hadn't asked his age, she figured he was in his early thirties. Usually, she dated guys closer to her age. But then, could she really consider this a date? Granted, he'd asked her out, but it wasn't as if it had been preplanned or anything. For heaven's sake, she was wearing the same outfit she'd left in this morning for school. It was definitely nothing to impress a man.

After he got their waitress's attention, she arrived with their check. Moments later, he stood and said, "I'll walk you to your car."

Velvet took the hand he offered and stood. Already, she wondered if she would see him again after tonight. The parking lot, which had been filled to capacity when she'd arrived, was practically deserted now.

When they reached her SUV, he said, "I enjoyed spending time with you, Velvet." He paused a moment and said, "I'd love to see you again."

A flutter of excitement raced through her. "That can be arranged, Jaye, because I'd love to see you again as well."

The dimpled smile that spread across his face triggered the throb she felt in her heart. "How is your schedule for this weekend? I'd like to take you out to dinner again."

Not to appear over eager, she took her time before saying, "I'm free this weekend."

His smile widened and it carried a sensuous heat that she felt in the pit of her stomach. "Good. What's your phone number?" he asked, while pulling his cell phone out of his jacket.

He punched in her number as she rattled it off to him. When her phone rang in her purse, he said, "Now we have each other's numbers. I look forward to seeing you Saturday. I'll call you later this week to let you know where we'll dine."

"Alright." She wanted that information so she could dress appropriately.

He held her gaze while placing his phone back in his jacket. He took a step closer and said in a deep husky voice, "I guess this is where I say good-night and we part ways."

She nervously licked her lips as her gaze moved from his eyes to his mouth to stare at his lips again for the umpteenth time tonight. Would he kiss her goodbye? The thought of those luscious lips on hers was too much to think about.

"Four times," he said, moving closer to her. The lampposts in the parking lot weren't shining directly on them, however, they provided enough light for her to see his features.

"Four times?" she asked, not sure what he meant.

"Yes. Four times tonight you've licked your lips with your tongue. Do you know what happens to me whenever you do that?"

Velvet had no idea. She hadn't even known he'd been counting. "No."

"Each time made me want to lean in close to you and do this."

The next thing she knew, his hand had moved to her waist at the same moment his mouth slanted over hers. Jaye Colfax was kissing her in a way that she had never been kissed before. Granted, she hadn't been kissed a lot in the past; she was comparing this with the few times she had. Jaye's kiss was heating her insides to a degree she hadn't known was possible. This was a new phenomenon, introducing her to the kind of passion she'd only read about, heard whispered about and dreamed about.

Nothing could have prepared her for this. Definitely not those sloppy kisses she'd shared with Lamont—and he'd thought he was an expert. There was no doubt in her mind that Jaye Colfax was the real expert, firing up her desire. If they kept going, it would be blazing out of control.

It was as if he was claiming her mouth, his tongue traced every inch of hers in a meticulous manner, making sure he left no spot untouched. He went about it painstakingly slow, with a thoroughness that made her moan.

The hands at her waist tightened and drew her even closer to him. That's when she felt it, his hard erection against her middle. The thought that he wanted her as much as she wanted him overwhelmed her, and the heat that suddenly flared between her legs made her moan again.

Suddenly, he ended the kiss. She thought she saw a strange look on his face, as if he hadn't expected to be taken with the kiss as much as she had. "I think I better let you go now," he said, licking his own lips.

"Alright."

When he opened the door to her SUV, she slid in. He surprised her when he leaned down and said, "I'm following you home to make sure you get there okay."

"You don't have to do that. I live in a gated community so I should be fine."

He shrugged. "Doesn't matter. I'll follow you to the gate."

Since he seemed determined to see her home, she simply nodded. He had parked on the other side of the lot, so she gave him time to reach his car before pulling away from the restaurant. On the drive home, all she could think about was that kiss. A kiss she would always remember. A kiss in a parking lot where anyone could have seen them. It was so unlike her to carry on with a man in that manner in a public place, but she had no regrets.

Every so often she would look in her rearview mirror to see that he was directly behind her. She couldn't help but appreciate his thoughtfulness in wanting to make sure she arrived home safely. Fifteen minutes later, she had reached the entrance to her gate and when she pulled into the security station, he beeped his horn before driving off.

Moments later after she entered her condo, all she could do was smile at the thought that she had finally been kissed the way she'd always dreamed of a man kissing her. And she'd enjoyed it tremendously.

WHAT THE HELL HAPPENED?

That question was rolling furiously through Jaye's mind as he entered his condo and tossed his keys on the table in the foyer. He rubbed a hand down his face in frustration. Velvet Spencer was supposed to be a one-and-done. By this time, they should have experienced at least two orgasms and working on the third. In her bed or his. Instead, he was at his place without her and wondering how in the hell that had happened.

The sexual chemistry that had flowed between them all through dinner had been so intense it had kept him aroused the entire time. What was it about her that had made him forget to breathe a few times? He'd gotten even more turned on whenever she talked, licked her lips, moved her hands or ate her food. Hell, he'd felt his erection twitch every time she blinked her eye.

He'd felt sexual chemistry before, but never of this magnitude. The one he'd shared with Velvet tonight had been a potent mix of raw sexuality and sensuality he hadn't known could exist. The woman was pure temptation personified. Yet, when they'd kissed, he sensed an innocence about her. One thing he usually didn't waste his time with were innocent women. But there was something about Velvet that made him want to see her again. She generated an unprecedented degree of desire and lust within him. Now more than anything, he wanted to know how she'd managed to do something that no other woman had done for him.

He had made it to the bedroom and was about to strip for his shower when his cell phone rang. It was his best friend, Mercury Steele. "Yes, Mercury?"

"You better have a good reason for not showing up, Jaye. Candie was there and she'd brought a friend along. A real looker. I ended up having to entertain them both myself."

Jaye rubbed his hand down his face and decided to give Mercury the short reason he hadn't shown up. "I met this woman."

Mercury laughed. "Say no more. I understand."

He figured Mercury would. Mercury knew him just like he knew Mercury. They had been best friends since first grade and basically thought alike. When it came to women, they enjoyed them for sex. Love had nothing to do with it. At least for Mercury, it no longer did. There was that time in college when Mercury had fallen for a woman. She had taught Mercury a hard lesson. The same one Jaye's mother had taught him. Women are to be enjoyed but never consider making one a permanent part of your life.

"Look, Mercury, I'm tired and after my shower I'm going to bed."

"Tired? Going to bed? It's not even eleven o'clock. Damn man, she must have worn you out."

Normally, Jaye was a night owl and wouldn't be in bed before midnight. His friend would be surprised to learn that tonight he hadn't indulged in a one-and-done like Mercury assumed. He hadn't gotten beyond that first kiss. But even now that kiss was messing with him big-time. When had a woman's lips ever tasted so good?

"Good night, Mercury." He clicked off the phone.

A short while later, Jaye had showered and was in his pajama bottoms. He went to the wet bar in his dining room, needing a shot of something strong. He reached to pour a shot and then stopped. No woman had ever driven him to drink, and he wouldn't let one do so now. His intense attraction to her had to have been a fluke. He got to women; he never let one get to him. That wasn't the way he operated, and he'd been told by women that he was a smooth operator. One of the best.

Now that he was back on familiar ground, his common sense had returned, and maybe the best thing to do was to come up with an excuse and cancel his date with Velvet this weekend. He rubbed a frustrated hand down his face. No woman alive could make him run in the opposite direction. So why was he giving Velvet that much power over him? He was determined to find out what it was about her that revved up all that was male within him. What was it about her that made him want to call her even now just to hear her voice again?

What the hell was wrong with him?

The one good thing was that the attraction hadn't been one-sided. He was a man who knew women. He could read one like he could his favorite book. Being coy was something he could detect a mile away. But there was nothing coy about Velvet and that's what confused the hell out of him. She'd wanted him as much as he'd wanted her. Yet for some reason, she hadn't seemed to recognize the intense attraction for what it was. He had.

He'd known each and every time she'd stared at his lips, because she would lick her own lips, as if wondering how he would taste. That was one of the reasons he had kissed her the way he had. He'd held nothing back. Hell, he'd even wanted her to feel his erection. There shouldn't be any doubt in her mind he had wanted her as much as she'd wanted him.

And he would have her.

Then he would move on just like normal. He smiled, satisfied that he was back to himself. There was something else, however, that piqued his interest. Ortega Yacht Condos were some of the most expensive in the city. He would know since he had thought of moving there himself, but he'd preferred the luxury condos closer to town. How could Velvet afford to live there on a teacher's salary?

And why did he get the feeling she was a well-polished, sophisticated and classy woman? She might be a teacher but he could sense there was more. It was there in the way she arranged things on their table so they could enjoy the meal they were sharing. And then the way she held her eating utensils with an etiquette that suggested a polished upbringing.

And then there was her vast knowledge of various topics. Granted, she was a teacher, which could be the reason. However, in just that short of time they'd spent together, he'd sensed an intelligence that surpassed any woman he'd dated before. Hell, when they'd been talking about stocks, bonds and investments, she had known just about as much as he did, and he was considered a financial whiz.

Jaye frowned. He definitely would go out with Velvet again. His hot-as-the-dickens schoolteacher was a mystery that he intended to solve.

"How did the job fair go yesterday, Velvet?"

Velvet glanced up at Ruthie. She was fortunate that she and her best friend taught at the same school, just different grades and subjects. Ruthie loved English and was great at teaching it. Students signed up early to get into her classes. She had a way of taking a sentence and dissecting it to no end. They'd hit it off as roommates in college and remained close friends since.

"It went well. I had fun," she answered. Then she leaned over the table where they were having lunch in the school cafeteria and whispered, "I even had a date afterward. Well, it wasn't a normal date, but he asked me out to dinner, and I went and totally enjoyed myself."

Ruthie raised her eyebrows. "Whoa, back up a minute. Who is he?"

Velvet lowered her voice. "The guy who showed up at the end of the job fair and asked me to dinner. Please keep up, Ruthie."

Ruthie shook her head. "I'm trying to, Vel. Now, who's the guy that showed up at the end of the fair and asked you to dinner?"

"One of the sponsors. Jaye Colfax."

Ruthie, who'd been sipping her drink through a straw, began coughing when some of the liquid went down the wrong way. Velvet was out of her chair in a flash and beating on her back. "Okay, Vel, I'm going to live and we're drawing attention."

Velvet returned to her seat. "I just wanted to make sure you were okay."

"I am," Ruthie said, taking a slow sip of her drink before adding, "However, I'm not sure you are. Did you say you went out with Jaye Colfax?"

Velvet smiled. "Yes, you know him?"

Ruthie rolled her eyes. "What single woman living in Phoenix doesn't? Remember, I told you about those Steele brothers? All six of them."

Velvet nodded. "You *warned* me about them when I first moved to town."

"And with good reason. They aren't considered the Bad News Steeles for nothing. Well, Jaye is friends with them. In fact, he and Mercury Steele are best friends, and he's no different than they are when it comes to women."

Velvet stared at Ruthie. "Are you sure? He was a perfect gentleman last night."

Ruthie cocked a brow. "And he didn't try anything with you? Like kiss you or ask to share his bed? He likes one-night stands. And before you ask, the answer is no, I've never dated Jaye or any of the Steeles. I went to school with the youngest Steele, Gannon, although he was a grade or two ahead of me. He was nice but no different from the rest when it comes to being womanizers."

When Velvet didn't say anything, Ruthie stared at her and then asked, "Well, did he come on to you?"

Releasing a sigh, Velvet said, "Jaye asked me to dinner, we shared a delicious meal and wonderful conversation. Afterward, he walked me to my car."

"And?"

"And we kissed, but not one time did he bring any mention of sex into the conversation."

Ruthie rolled her eyes. "He didn't have to. The man is sex on legs. I'm surprised he didn't suggest that you go to his place or yours."

"Well, he didn't."

"But the two of you did kiss?"

"Yes, and it was the best kiss I've ever experienced. It made any I've shared in the past obsolete."

"And you want me to believe he did not come on to you sexually?"

"That's right. He didn't. However, I will admit that there were a lot of vibes between us. Even a novice like me could tell we were attracted to each other. And I felt it in the kiss, but at no time did he suggest I go home with him, and I certainly didn't invite him to my place. Although, I was tempted."

"Velvet!"

"Well, I was, so don't be shocked. Like you said, he is sex on legs. I like him. He didn't try anything and even followed me to the security gate of my condo to make sure I got in okay."

Ruthie waved off her words. "It's a setup."

"A setup?"

"Yes. For some reason, he's slowly reeling you in, Velvet. I bet he's asked to see you again."

Velvet nodded. "Yes, we have another date this weekend."

"Be careful, Velvet. Jaye Colfax means you no good. Although I hear he warns women off about getting into him because he's not into serious relationships. They fall for him, anyway. There's a slogan around town that says *if you don't want your heart broken, then stay away from Jaye.*"

Velvet frowned. It was hard to believe they were talking about the same person. The Jaye Colfax she'd met pushed her buttons true enough, but at no time did he try encouraging her to sleep with him or coming across as if he was only interested in sex. "I will be careful, Ruthie."

"I hope so. Men like Jaye only want one thing and when he gets it, he'll walk away. I don't want to see you get hurt." Ruthie paused and then asked, "Did you tell him who you are? That you are an heiress?"

"No, it never came up, although I did tell him about my parents. I have no reason not to share who I am with him, though. From what I understand, he and his family have plenty of money and he didn't come off as someone who would need mine."

"At least that much I can vouch for. He's a nice guy, well-mannered, successful and professional. His only downfall is that he is bad news just like those Steeles."

Velvet shrugged. "He's not looking for a serious re-lationship with a woman and I get that."

"But you want a serious relationship with a man, Vel. I know you. Casual sex isn't your thing."

Ruthie was right. Casual sex wasn't her thing. She always dreamed of having the same solid and loving re-lationship that her parents shared. And she wouldn't set-tle for anything less. "I might be just the one to change his mind, Ruthie."

Ruthie shook her head. "Don't hold your breath for that to happen. Jaye Colfax is a total player. Don't let him break your heart. Promise me that you won't let him do that."

Velvet saw the deep concern in Ruthie's eyes. "I promise, Ruthie. I won't."

CHAPTER FIVE

Present day

VELVET WOKE UP bright and early the next morning, immediately remembering what year it was and the fact that she was not in Phoenix but in Catalina Cove. Taking her thoughts down memory lane had been difficult, and she ended up drinking more wine than she'd intended. It was a good thing there was no school today. She enjoyed her weekends, especially those where she had nothing planned.

Then she quickly remembered she did have something planned today. A bridal meeting hosted by Sierra. She had asked Velvet to be one of her bridesmaids. Velvet felt honored to have been chosen and looked forward to the get-together at noon. She quickly pushed the thought to the back of her mind that she was always a bridesmaid and never a bride. In June, she would be a bridesmaid in Ruthie's wedding, too.

"Oh, well," she muttered, getting out of bed. If anybody would have told her that she would be looking thirty really close in the face and still be single, she would not have believed them.

She'd been so convinced Jaye truly loved her and would realize it and make her his wife. She'd been crushed to discover he hadn't loved her at all—just the sex. Heck, she'd loved the sex, too, but that was only a part of what their relationship had been about. Too bad he hadn't known that.

Unfortunately, she had broken the promise she'd made to Ruthie. Her friend had asked her more than once not to let Jaye break her heart. She had promised Ruthie that she wouldn't, but in the end she'd allowed him to do that very thing.

She heard a noise and knew it was coming from outside. Moving to the bedroom window, she nudged the curtain slightly aside and saw him. Jaye was whistling while busy painting the storage shed in the backyard. Although it was something Delisa had planned to have done at some point in the future, why was Jaye spending his Saturday morning doing it? It wasn't like he owned the place. He was just a tenant like her. But then she knew that Jaye was a man who liked using his hands. Whether it was cooking, building or repairing things, or…using those hands on her.

She pushed the thought from her mind and recalled that Jaye's paternal grandfather had owned a huge construction company in Phoenix, and while growing up, Jaye and his brothers had worked alongside their grandfather. That was the reason Jaye could build almost anything. She recalled one weekend he had installed new kitchen counters and he'd enlarged her patio deck one summer. The one thing she'd liked about Jaye was that he never let his wealth dictate any limitations. He always said that no job was beneath him if the work needed to be done or if he wanted to do it.

Velvet had felt the same way. She knew there would

be some who would not understand why the Spencer's restaurant heiress would want to teach instead of functioning as CEO of her mega corporation. She was asked that all the time while living in Seattle and she began her teaching career. She got tired of explaining herself to people, although she'd been tempted to tell them many times it really wasn't any of their business.

That was one of the reasons she'd made the decision not to broadcast her connection to the restaurant chain when she relocated to Phoenix. She'd kept that same mindset when she'd moved to Catalina Cove. Those she wanted to know knew. She was never one to flaunt her wealth.

Velvet continued to watch Jaye work and was ready to drop the curtain back in place if he glanced toward the house. The last thing she wanted was for him to see her staring out the window at him. But dang, she was definitely enjoying the view as her eyes followed his every movement. His hands certainly knew how to handle a paintbrush.

If she recalled, his hands knew how to handle just about anything…

Sharp, intense, sensations flowed through her when she remembered how those same hands knew how to handle her. She would come apart under the ministrations of those very skillful and gifted hands. Just watching how they were stroking paint on that building reminded her of the feel of them stroking her the same way. The memories caused heat to flare within her. Two years had been a long time to go without being made love to when Jaye had made love to her every single night.

She was about to drop the curtain in place when he

shifted positions. But instead of looking toward her window, he turned and she could now only see his back. When he stretched his tall frame to paint an area higher up, her eyes stretched with him. She always thought he had a nice physique and that hadn't changed. January weather in the cove was comfortably cool, but forecasters said today would be in the seventies, so Jaye wasn't wearing a jacket. She thought the way his T-shirt and jeans were fitting his body should be outlawed. Jeans that hugged his firm hips and strong thighs. She couldn't help remembering the tight hold those same thighs would have on her while thrusting hard into her over and over again.

The memory set the area between her legs throbbing. That was the last thing she needed now. Just recalling their time together was filling her with an intense need that was nearly unbearable.

She would take a shower to cool off. Then she would get dressed and meet Sierra and the other bridesmaids for lunch at the Green Fig. Jaye had another side of the building to paint and, hopefully, by the time she returned, he would be finished and back inside. If past weekends were anything to go by, she wouldn't be seeing him again today, which made her wonder how he spent his weekends. Then she recalled what Sierra had said about Jaye refusing to date any of the single women in town. But those had been the ones who'd thrown themselves at him. Would he eventually meet someone of his own choosing?

Velvet took another look at Jaye and that fine body of his before dropping the curtain in place and moving away from the window.

Jaye had known the exact moment Velvet began looking at him. Out of the corner of his eye, he'd seen the curtain move and had known she was there. The primitive evidence being the way his body had reacted…the way it always reacted whenever she looked at him in a certain way. He had been tempted to turn around so she would know he was fully aware of her presence but then decided against it. She'd once told him she enjoyed looking at him when he wasn't aware she was doing so, so he decided to let her. He had plenty of time on his hands, which was one of the reasons he had decided to paint this storage shed.

The building wasn't an eyesore. Far from it. In fact, he figured it had been painted just a few years ago and had done a good job of withstanding the Louisiana weather. However, while out jogging, he had wondered what he could do during the weekends to stay busy. He liked boating but he didn't want to spend an entire day out on the water when the object of his attention, desire and affection would be here at this house on Blueberry Lane.

Last night, he'd tossed and turned for most of it. Eventually, he'd rolled onto his back and stared up at the ceiling, remembering the day he and Velvet had met. He'd thought about that day a lot lately.

He knew from talking to Vaughn this week that Sierra had invited the women who were part of her wedding party to meet today at the Green Fig. That meant Velvet would be attending since she was a bridesmaid. By the time she returned, he would have the grill fired up and the meat cooking. He loved to grill and Velvet hadn't been able to turn down any Colfax grilled bar-beque ribs yet.

He recalled the first time she'd bit into one. The look on her face had totally turned him on. But then it hadn't ever been difficult to get turned on by Velvet. They'd had a perfect sex life and he knew she assumed during the three years they'd been together that he'd only seen her as a sex partner. For a long time, he'd thought the same thing. The person who said *you don't miss your water until the well runs dry* knew exactly what they were talking about.

The one thing Jaye knew was that the way Velvet had left—just picking up and leaving without so much as a goodbye—meant she didn't believe he could change. She saw him as a hopeless case, that he would always be incapable of falling in love, settling down and marrying.

And he would be the first to admit that had been true. He recalled often seeing the pain in his father's eyes, especially around the holidays. Pain that Jaye had felt for his father. It was years before his father opened himself up to love someone again. Jaye was glad when Arlene had come into not only his father's life, but his three adult sons' lives as well. He would admit they'd been cautious, but it didn't take long to see that Arlene was just what Jack Colfax, Sr., had needed in his life. He was glad his father had been able to see it as well and hadn't refused love like Jaye had done.

He knew that he had several people rooting for him—his father and brothers, and the entire Steele family who was like a second family to him. They'd tried to warn him of the mistake he'd been making by taking Velvet for granted and not admitting to himself what she'd come to mean to him. Losing her was his fault and he rightly took the blame. Just like he would do everything in his power to get her back.

He had started on the final side of the building when he saw Velvet walk out of the house to get into her car. He refused to pretend not to see her and when he glanced over at her—even at a distance of what had to be a good twenty feet—he could pick up on the sizzle between them when their gazes connected.

She looked good in a pair of slacks and a pretty blouse. Because it was January and the air was rather cool, she'd thrown a shawl around her shoulders. Shoulders he loved touching, kissing, caressing...

"Hello, Velvet," he said. He had gone along with her formality BS yesterday, but he wouldn't today.

Jaye could feel her slight hesitation before she said, "Hello, Jaye. You are busy this morning."

He smiled. "Yes, I like working with my hands." Of course, she knew that.

"Well, I'm sure Delisa will appreciate it."

"I'm sure she will."

"Well, have a nice day," she said, getting in the car. "You, too."

He watched her drive away and swore even with the distance that had separated them, he could inhale her heated scent. He recalled other days when he had watched her leave and how he would wait anxiously for her to return.

Like he would be doing today.

"I LOVE THE way you're wearing your hair today," Ashey Sullivan complimented Velvet as she took the chair across from her at the table. The meeting had ended and now they were enjoying the desserts, compliments of LaFreda McEnroe who had moved to town almost a year ago and opened Catalina Cove Bake Shop.

Velvet smiled. "Thanks." On most days, it was just easy to wear her hair pulled back in a tight bun. Of course, her wearing it down today had nothing to do with the fact that Jaye always liked it that way.

"I understand the hottie banker is your neighbor."

This wouldn't be the first time someone had mentioned that she and Jaye were neighbors. Nor was this the first time some woman, married or single, had referred to Jaye as the *hottie banker*. "Yes, but I rarely see him."

"It still must be nice. I heard he's turned a lot of the brazen women in town away, letting them know he was a man who didn't like being chased."

"That's what I heard," Velvet said. Ruthie swore that the reason Jaye had been so taken with her was because she hadn't gone after him. He had gone after her.

Velvet decided to change the subject before the other women, who'd attended the meeting and were now gathered around the dessert cart, joined them. The last thing she wanted or needed was a continued discussion of Jaye. "How are the twins?" she asked. Ashley and her husband, Ray, had adorable twins, a boy and a girl.

"They are two-year-old busy beavers," Ashley said with a huge grin on her face. "I can't take my eyes off them for a second, but I'm loving every minute of motherhood."

"Obviously," Vashti Grisham said. She smiled, taking a seat next to Ashley. Vashti's husband, Sawyer.

was the cove's sheriff. A man Velvet thought was a very likable guy.

When Ashley gave Vashti a Cheshire grin, Velvet felt like she was missing something. Evidently, she wasn't the only one. Bryce Witherspoon Chambray joined them at the table and asked, "Okay, Ashley and Vashti, what gives?"

Before anyone could answer, Sierra, who approached the table with a plate of brownies, called out, "Wait, don't leave me out."

"We want to hear, too," Sierra's sister, Dani, said, as she, Donna Elloran and Vaughn's sister, Zara, hurried over to the table. Dani and Zara had arrived in town for the weekend to attend Sierra's bridal meeting.

Velvet scooted over to make room for them. When everyone was seated and looking at Ashley expectedly, she beamed and said, "Ray and I are having another baby."

There were cheers, clapping and hugs. And because there had been an emotional catch in Ashley's voice when she'd made the announcement, Velvet figured there was a lot more to Ray and Ashley increasing their family than Velvet was privy to. But it didn't matter. She was happy for Ashley. Velvet pushed the thought from her mind that just like she would forever be a bridesmaid and not a bride, chances were she would never be a mother, either.

An hour or so later on the drive back home, Velvet gave herself a pep talk. At some point the conversation had shifted to the wonderful men the women were married to. It seemed that she and Zara were the only single ones in the group. Sierra didn't count since she was engaged to marry Vaughn soon.

Velvet knew that she was the only person who controlled her destiny. She could understand not wanting to get involved with anyone when she'd first moved to the cove, but there was no reason she shouldn't be dating now, was there? Like she constantly told Ruthie, she'd gotten over Jaye and there were a number of nice single guys in town. However, it seemed after being turned down several times, they no longer asked.

At least, none of them but Webb Crawford, who thought he was the hottest bachelor around. Granted, he wasn't bad-looking, but Webb seemed to feel entitled to have any woman who suited his fancy. She believed the only reason for his persistence in wanting to date her was because he saw her as a challenge. He couldn't figure out why any woman wouldn't want to date one of the wealthiest men in town.

Pulling into the driveway, she noticed Jaye had finished painting the storage shed. Since his car was in the driveway that meant he was probably home, upstairs, tackling some other kind of handy work.

The moment she opened her car door the aroma hit her. She breathed in deep and licked her lips. There was nothing like the taste of Colfax barbeque ribs. It wasn't just his family's own special blend of ingredients that could get to you but knowing the ribs bathed in the sauce would practically fall off the bone.

As if in a trance, she followed the aroma and rounded the corner to the back of the house. Jaye was using the freestanding grill Delisa kept stored in the shack. He was standing in front of it, turning over the meat.

As if he sensed her presence, he turned around and smiled. "Hello, Velvet."

The sound of her name off his lips made a stirring in the pit of her stomach. Instead of returning the greeting, she said, "You're grilling?"

His smile widened. "Yes, I'm grilling. I also cooked corn, potatoes, and I made a salad."

Velvet felt her mouth water. He was so wrong for this. So completely wrong. She of all people knew how well those Colfaxes—Daddy Jack, Jaye and his brothers, Dean and Franklin—could grill and prepare all the delicious side fixings. "It smells good."

"It is good and, of course, you're welcome to join me, Velvet."

CHAPTER SIX

JAYE'S INSIDES TIGHTENED, hoping Velvet would accept his invitation. He knew he wasn't playing fair but there were times when a man had to do what a man had to do. After realizing his mistakes, he was working like hell to correct them. She was eyeing the ribs and the ones on the grill were juicy, well-done, but not tough. Just the way she liked them.

She moved her gaze from the meat back to him. "Are you sure you have enough to share?" she asked.

He chuckled. "Trust me, I have enough to share. I also have a few beers in that cooler over there."

She nibbled on her bottom lip for a moment and then said, "In that case, yes, I'll join you."

He forced the smile from spreading over his face. "Okay."

She looked at the picnic table he was using and since he had covered it neatly with a tablecloth, the last thing he wanted her to do was get ideas that he was expecting someone, namely some woman, to join him later. "I found that table in the shed and tried making it look decent by covering it with a tablecloth."

"You did a good job." She switched her gaze from the table to him. "What made you decide to grill today?"

He had expected her question. "You know how muc

I like using my hands and had decided earlier in the week to paint this shed. When I finished painting, I looked inside and saw the grill, picnic table and a few other things that would be perfect for a cookout or a day at the beach since the weather is so nice today. You know how much I enjoy grilling, so the cookout won over the beach."

He flipped over the meat and said, "Of course that meant going grocery shopping but that didn't take long. Besides, it was nice getting out and meeting some of the locals. It seems a number of people do their grocery shopping on Saturdays."

She nodded. "Yes, they do. That's why I avoid grocery shopping on Saturdays."

Without looking, he knew that her eyes were glued to the meat when he began removing some pieces from the grill. "How did you find out about this town?" he asked.

He handed her a plate and a fork, knowing she knew the drill. He cooked and she served herself. Velvet was not a finicky eater. She took the plate from him and grabbed the piece of meat he knew she'd been eyeing— the one he'd cooked just for her.

"Reid Lacroix. He and my father were on the rowing team together at Yale. When Reid attended my parents' memorial service, he said if I ever needed to get away, this would be the place to come."

"I see." And he actually did see. Thanks to him, she hadn't just felt the need to get away, she'd been driven to do a full escape. "He was right. In the month I've been here, I've discovered Catalina Cove is a pretty nice place."

"It can grow on you, that's for sure," she said. "How did you find out about it?"

He didn't say anything for a minute as he filled his own plate with food. There was no way he would tell her he'd hired a private investigator to find her and relocated here to win her back. He would confess everything to her one day, but not now.

"You know how it is in the banking industry. We're always looking for expansion and a way to grow our brand. When the Barrows Bank came up on my radar, I knew taking it over would be a good investment and moved on it quickly."

When she walked over to the table to sit down, he joined her. "How are you adjusting, Jaye? Colfax National Bank offers a number of services that Barrows Bank didn't. You're bringing everyone into the technology age."

He chuckled. "I might as well since that's the way things will be moving forward. Most people have smartphones and they're getting smarter by the day. A week ago, we held a class at the bank on how deposits can be made from home or just about anywhere using your cell phone."

She lifted a brow. "You actually held a class?"

"Sure did. You'd be surprised how many older people don't use the advanced services or features because they feel intimated by them. Our class was for the sixty-five and older group and was taught by banking and technology experts from the same age group. That increased the participants' comfort level tremendously. The last thing an older person wants is a millennial trying to show them anything. Needless to say, the class wer well, and those who attended discovered all the added features my bank has to offer that will save time."

"I'm glad."

"The results of a follow-up survey we did show those who took the class are using some of the new banking features already. They especially like being able to check their bank balances at any time. Next week, we're hosting a class on the benefits of direct deposit. There are a group of people who feel they need to look at their check, cash it and then take the money to the bank. Colfax National Bank is working with the major employers in town to implement benefits that will come with direct deposit."

"Such as?" she asked, biting into her meat. When she licked sauce off her bottom lip, he felt the lower part of his body harden and was glad he was sitting down so she had no idea how aroused he was.

When she looked at him, waiting for his response, he said, "One benefit is having your funds available to spend a day early. That means those who would normally wait for Friday to get paid, now will be able to spend their money Thursday. They like that."

"I can see why."

She then tackled the corn. He loved seeing her eat and it was obvious that she was enjoying the food. To avoid staring at her mouth, he asked, "Yesterday, you said you had your challenges. How so?"

She shrugged. "Just the regular challenges most teachers face." Then she asked, "How's your dad and brothers?"

He was surprised she'd asked, especially since she'd made it clear she didn't want people to know about their past. But he figured she was only asking because they were alone.

"Everyone is fine. Dad got married last year, Dean got engaged at Christmas and Franklin is still Franklin."

A beautiful smile spread across her face. "I'd heard about your dad's marriage, but Dean really got engaged?"

He wondered how she'd known about his father and figured her best friend, Ruthie, must have told her. "Yes. Dean met Sherri a year and a half ago and didn't waste time putting a ring on her finger."

"I'm happy for him."

It was on the tip of Jaye's tongue to say that he was glad his brother had had a lot more sense that he'd had. In fact, Dean had come right out and said that he didn't intend to make the mistake Jaye had made with Velvet.

"Not sure if you knew there aren't any more *Bad News Steeles*. Every last one of them is now married. Gannon and his wife had a baby last year and Mercury and his wife are expecting."

"I'm sure their mother is extremely happy."

"Yes, Eden is very happy. All six of her sons have tied the knot and are producing grandkids."

Deciding to change the subject, he told her how he enjoyed jogging through the blueberry field behind their house. "I'm beginning to like blueberries, especially in muffins."

"Then I guess you've become quite acquainted with the Witherspoon Café."

He chuckled. "Yes. I've had breakfast and lunch there a few times with some of the guys Vaughn introduced me to. Ray, Sawyer and Kaegan Chambray." Kaegan owned a huge shipping company in town.

She nodded. "All nice guys I've gotten to know since moving here. Their wives, Ashley, Bryce and Vashti are pretty special, too."

She sipped her beer, then pushed her empty plate aside. "That was good, Jaye. There's nothing like Colfax ribs." She wiped her mouth, then stood to throw her scraps in the trash. "Thanks for the invite. That was right neighborly of you."

Jaye knew her statement was deliberately letting him know they had enjoyed the meal together as neighbors and nothing more. "You're welcome. In fact, why don't you fix a to-go plate? I have plenty of leftovers."

"You sure?" she asked with a hopeful look on her face.

He smiled. "I'm positive."

"In that case…" She prepared another plate and wrapped it in foil. "Thanks, Jaye."

"You're welcome, Velvet."

"Well, I'll be seeing you."

"Okay."

He watched her walk away in that sexy stroll of hers, hoping she would look back.

But she didn't.

VELVET PRACTICALLY HELD her breath until she had rounded the corner of the house where Jaye could no longer see her. Sitting across from him while eating had stirred up a lot of memories that should be dead and buried.

Just seeing him eat—nibbling on a rib bone—and

drinking beer from the bottle had been a total turn-on. She'd always loved the shape of his full lips and thought they were inviting and sensually hot. More than once, her gaze had moved from one corner of his mouth to the other and lingered in the center, the very place her tongue would enter whenever they kissed.

Feeling her breathing was getting out of control, she drew in a deep breath as she entered her house. She needed a drink and it needed to be stronger than the beer she'd had. If she didn't know better, she would think the grilling and the food had been premeditated on his part, but there was no way that it could have been. He'd had no idea when she would be returning home today. For all he knew, she might have made plans to be gone most of the day. Besides, why would he deliberately plan anything to include her?

She placed her cross-body purse on the end table and carried the plate of leftovers to the kitchen to put in the refrigerator. She returned to the living room and sat on the sofa, thinking of how she had studied Jaye when he hadn't realized she'd been doing so. This was the closest she had been in his presence in the daytime, and more than anything she wanted to see what, if anything, about him was different. He had aged two years but had done so well. His features were still striking, from his dark eyes to his enticing lips and dimpled cheeks.

His outfit that she'd first observed through her bedroom window was even more compelling up close. During the day, he usually wore his tailor-made suits. However, today he was dressed casually in jeans and a T-shirt. He was still built, with muscles in all the right places. She had seen those muscles up close. Had touched them. In fact, she had tasted every inch of his body.

And he had tasted every inch of hers.

The one thought she couldn't dismiss from her mind was their ability to satisfy each other in bed. She was feeling a throbbing sensation between her legs just thinking about it. So why was she? Mainly because seeing him in the flesh couldn't be helped. She had been a virgin at twenty-five when they'd made love together for the first time. Her body knew him as the man who'd introduced her to sexual pleasures and, at that moment, it was reminding her of that.

More than once over the last two years, she had awakened in the middle of the night after dreaming of one of their lovemaking sessions. Now, with him here in the flesh, it was even more challenging for her. Today, she not only saw him, but she smelled him, too. No man had a more sensuous scent. She would admit she had been turned on by it. Today.

Stretching her legs in front of her, she was about to grab her e-reader off the coffee table when her cell phone rang. Recognizing the ringtone, she reached into her purse and pulled it out. "Sierra?"

"Yes, I just wanted to thank everyone personally for coming to the meeting today, and also for agreeing to be in my wedding."

Velvet smiled. "I feel honored that you asked me. Are you getting excited?"

"Yes, I am. Granted this will be my second wedding, but for Vaughn it's his first and he wants to go all out. So I'm treating it as my first as well, since my marriage to Nathan was a huge mistake."

Velvet had met Sierra's ex-husband one time when he'd come to town to make trouble. Luckily, his plan had backfired. "And I am happy for the both of you."

"Thanks. And there's another reason I called."

"Oh?"

"To make sure that you're okay. We'd barely finished eating desserts and you rushed out rather quickly."

Velvet didn't say anything for a moment and figured, of all the people who'd attended Sierra's meeting today, she would be the one to home in on her emotions. Deciding to be honest with her friend, Velvet said, "I needed to rush off for a pity party of one. I guess being around so many happy people in love got the best of me."

"Not everybody at the meeting is happy and in love, Velvet. I told you about Zara and how she and her boyfriend broke up a couple of years ago. Probably around the same time as you and Jaye."

Velvet leaned back on the sofa. "Okay, that's two out of the eight women who were there. Whoop-de-do."

"Sounds like your pity party is still in full swing, girlfriend. Should I come over with some more of these brownies? I could also bring a bottle of wine."

That made Velvet chuckle. "Okay, I get your point. Besides, I can't eat a single thing more. I just finished off a big plate of barbeque spareribs."

"Barbeque ribs? From where?"

She hesitated, nibbling on her bottom lip. She might as well tell Sierra since there was no reason for her not to. "Jaye. When I got home, he was outside grilling and invited me to join him. I saw no reason for me not to, especially since I knew they weren't just any spareribs, but Colfax ribs."

Sierra chuckled. "There's a difference?"

"Trust me, there is. Jaye's paternal great-grand-mother had her own special sauce. It's been passed down through generations and it is so delicious."

"That was kind of him to invite you to join him. How was it?"

"Like I said, the ribs were great."

"That's not what I'm asking, and you know it."

Yes, Velvet knew it. "I thanked him for being neighborly. Nothing has changed, Sierra."

"I think it has. Obviously, you didn't mind being seen with him today."

Velvet pursed her lips and then said, "Have you forgotten I live on Blueberry Lane where there's only six houses on the block? In addition, this house is the only one in the cul-de-sac and Jaye and I were sitting at a picnic table in the backyard." She stood when she felt the need to stretch. "Besides, I'd think people would expect me and Jaye to get to know each other, given the proximity of our residences. The last thing I want is for people to assume Jaye and I have any romantic interest in each other."

"Who gives a royal flip what anyone assumes? You know the mistakes I made with Vaughn in caring what anyone assumed or knew. It's your life and you should live it for you and nobody else. And you still haven't answered my question, Velvet. How was it? How was it spending time with Jaye, the man you once loved?"

Velvet eased back down on the sofa as she thought

about Sierra's question. "I was hoping it wouldn't feel like old times, Sierra, but…"

"But what?"

"Some parts of it did, although I think we were both trying not to let it. I might have placed him in an awkward position."

"How so?"

"Jaye doesn't love me, I know that. On the other hand, he knows why I left and I don't want him to pity me. That's why I've decided to start dating. The last thing I want is to give Jaye the impression that I haven't gotten over him."

"And you're honestly going to start dating?" Sierra sounded surprised.

"No reason why I shouldn't enjoy some fun dates. I'm not looking for any serious involvement, but it would be nice to go to the movies or out to dinner with a guy occasionally. Only problem is that no one has asked me out in months. Do you think I've scared the guys off?"

Sierra paused before answering. "No, but I believe someone else has."

Velvet raised a brow, confused. "Who?"

"Webb Crawford. I heard he's made it known around town that he wants you for himself and has pretty much told the other guys to back off. That means they won't be approaching you for dates."

That angered Velvet. "Webb had no right to do that when I made it clear over a year ago that I'm not interested in him. I don't like his entitled attitude, and he would be the last guy I'd go out with."

"I don't blame you for feeling that way, but I've

known Webb a lot longer than you have, and he was the same way in school. He felt he had a right to have whatever he went after. I guess he figures with none of the guys asking you out, eventually he will be your only prospect and you will go out with him."

"When hell freezes over."

"Well, I'm just telling you how he thinks. Vaughn is at the door, so I will chat back with you later. And promise me no more pity parties."

"Okay, I promise."

"Good."

Velvet clicked off the phone, angry at what Sierra had told her about Webb. If the men in Catalina Cove were such wimps that they would do whatever Webb told them, then they weren't worth going out with, anyway.

Velvet stood and was about to go into the kitchen when she heard a noise outside in the back. Moving to the dining room window, she saw Jaye was cleaning up the grill site. She drew in a deep shuddering breath and let it out slowly as she watched him.

Well, she knew at least one man in Catalina Cove who wasn't a wimp. Too bad he was off-limits to her.

CHAPTER SEVEN

JAYE STOOD AT the window in his office and looked out. Although this was the middle of the week, memories of last weekend still dominated his thoughts. And he figured that they would for quite some time. Just the idea that he and Velvet had shared a meal together still overwhelmed him because it was something he'd feared would never happen. Hopefully, that meant he was making progress.

Once she'd gone inside her home, he hadn't seen her again until Monday morning when she'd left for work. As usual, after his morning jog, he had stood in his kitchen and drank a cup of coffee, waiting to watch her leave before he jumped into the shower. She always looked good, although he wished she would wear her hair flowing around her shoulders more. However, he understood that she preferred wearing her hair up in a bun while in the classroom.

The buzzer on his desk sounded and he crossed the room to press it. "Yes, Ms. Carter?"

"Webb Crawford is here to see you."

Jaye lifted a brow. He recalled meeting the man the night of the town hall meeting a few months ago. He also recalled that Webb was Laura Crawford's brother. The same Laura Crawford who'd shown up at Shelby

by the Sea to see him, basically saying she was interested in him and for that reason they should date. He'd
had no problem letting Ms. Crawford know he pur-
sued women and was put off by any woman who pur-
sued him. She hadn't liked what he'd said but he didn't
care. And that night at the town hall meeting, the one
thing he had picked up during his short conversation
with Webb was that both he and his sister had an en-
titlement complex. Jaye was always put off by people
like that. "Does Mr. Crawford have an appointment?"

"He said he doesn't need one."

Jaye shook his head. Obviously, Larson Barrows had
had an open door, a visit-anytime-you-want, come-and-
sit-a-spell policy. Jaye didn't. Sure, he wanted to get to
know his customers, but this was a financial institution
and there were guidelines and protocols to be followed.
Respecting his time was one of them.

"I'm busy right now but if Mr. Crawford wants to
wait twenty or thirty minutes, then I'll be able to see
him then."

"Yes, sir."

Jaye ended the call and went back to stand by the
window.

WHEN VELVET ARRIVED at school that morning, a note
had been placed in her teacher's mailbox. It said that
the principal, Fred Dunning, wanted to meet with her at
ten thirty. She wondered what the meeting was about.

She glanced at her watch as she walked the hall toward Mr. Dunning's office. It was hard to believe today
was the first of February and it had turned out to be a
rather nice day. Granted, the air was cool, but she rather

liked the temperature. Evidently, Jaye had liked it as
well because he hadn't bothered to put on a jacket when
he'd gone jogging this morning.

As usual, she had stood by her kitchen window and
sipped her coffee when he had appeared, leaving for his
morning jog. Those muscular legs and thighs always
held her attention until he was no longer in sight. By
the time she showered and was dressed for work, he
would have returned. Then she had the pleasure of seeing him—with all that glorious sweat streaming down
his body—before he went inside his house.

Their paths hadn't crossed since they'd shared a meal
on Saturday. Had he deliberately stayed inside on Sunday so he wouldn't see her again? But then hadn't she
done the same thing? With nothing to do and nowhere
to go, she had lounged around and watched a few movies on television.

"Ms. Spencer?"

Velvet blinked upon seeing she had reached the principal's office and was standing next to his personal assistant's desk. "Yes."

"Mr. Dunning is expecting you. Please go on in."

"Thanks, Ms. Taylor."

Mr. Dunning stood the moment she entered his office.
He was an older man, probably in his sixties. She'd heard
he'd been principal of the high school for a good ten
years. "Come on in, Ms. Spencer. I hate to interrupt your
day but a matter has come up that we need to discuss."

"Alright." She took the chair across from his desk
and looked at the man expectantly.

"I received a call from Allen Bordeaux, Lenny Bordeaux's father."

When she didn't say anything, he continued, "He's upset. Claiming his son is being treated unfairly."

Velvet tilted her head. The official warning letter she had sent to Lenny's parents had gone out last week. "Treated unfairly in what way?" She was curious to hear the answer.

Mr. Dunning leaned back in his chair. "First, I need to tell you something about Allen Bordeaux."

"Alright."

"Al, as most people call him, was Catalina Cove Senior High School's star baseball player, and I was his coach at the time. Recruiters from professional teams would show up at our games just to see him play. He was on his way to the pros and was set to make millions after signing on after high school with the Dodgers."

Velvet nodded. "What happened?"

"Car accident. Two weeks before his first game, he and some of his teammates went out partying. There was an accident. Al was the only one who got hurt with a broken wrist. None of the intensive therapy he went through helped. He was eventually released from the team a year or so later."

Mr. Dunning paused. Then said, "He returned to the cove and everybody welcomed him back, but it was hard for Al to accept the downfall. Then on top of that, the woman he'd met and married from New York divorced him after their baby was born."

"Lenny?"

"Yes, Lenny. There are those saying Lenny is a better ballplayer than Al ever was. However, that won't mean anything if Lenny isn't allowed to play varsity baseball or if he's held back. Al sees you as the one standing in the way of Lenny playing ball."

Velvet shook her head, thinking the man's rationale was totally ridiculous. "First of all, such an expectation is a lot to put on Lenny's shoulders. Second, it's up to Lenny to do the class work to bring his grades up. It's not up to me."

"We both know that, but Al doesn't see it that way."

"That, Mr. Dunning, is not my problem. How is Lenny doing in his other classes?"

"He's a C student. However, he probably dislikes math as much as Al did. In high school, he barely passed to play."

Velvet lifted a brow. "Then how did he?"

Mr. Dunning hesitated. "Al had teachers who were willing to work with him."

Velvet frowned. "By willing to work with him, you mean they gave him passing grades he hadn't deserved." No wonder Lenny's father had told him he didn't need algebra to play ball. "Now he expects the same thing to be done for his son?"

When Mr. Dunning didn't respond, Velvet knew she'd gotten her answer. "Well, unlike those other teachers, I refuse to give any students a grade they don't earn. I'm willing to tutor Lenny to help him get his grades up and offered to do so, but he needs to do the work, the same as all my other students. Giving him a free pass wouldn't be fair."

There was a long pause. "I just want you to know Al won't make things easy for you."

"For merely doing my job? Lenny either does the work like my other students or he'll fail. It's that simple." And because Mr. Dunning had yet to say he supported her position, she felt the need to say, "And if I ever feel pressured to do otherwise, then I will submit my resignation."

Mr. Dunning rubbed his hands down his face. "You won't have to submit your resignation, Ms. Spencer. I will abide by your decision."

When Velvet left the man's office, she recalled he'd said that he would abide by her decision, but at no time had he said he agreed with it or would support her on it.

"You can send Mr. Crawford in now, Ms. Carter," Jaye said.

"Yes, sir."

Jaye remained standing when his office door opened, and Webb Crawford walked in. From the look on the man's face, it was obvious he'd gotten annoyed at having been kept waiting. "Mr. Crawford," Jaye said, offering the man his hand in a firm handshake. "What can I do for you?"

"First of all, Mr. Colfax, you can make sure I'm seen whenever I arrive."

Jaye had to keep from laughing. Who in the hell did this man think he was? "I don't see anyone without an appointment, Mr. Crawford, unless there's an emergency. One that's life or death." He decided to add the latter just in case Webb Crawford figured his very existence constituted an emergency.

"Do you think the Crawfords aren't important customers at this bank?"

Jaye shoved his hands into his pockets. "As far as I'm concerned, every individual who has an account at

the Colfax National Bank is important. If you're looking for preferential treatment because of the amount of
funds in your account, then I suggest you transfer those
accounts elsewhere."

To prove he wouldn't tolerate the man's bullshit, Jaye
walked behind his desk and sat down. "Now. Is there a
reason you're here or do you prefer to begin processing
the paperwork to transfer your funds to another bank?"

Webb Crawford was staring at him as if he didn't
believe Jaye's audacity. Well, he might as well not only
believe it but get used to it. Respect was earned and not
entitled. Evidently, somewhere along the way no one
had ever told Crawford that.

Suddenly, a smile appeared on the man's face. Then
he sat down in the chair across from Jaye's desk. "I like
you, Colfax."

It was on the tip of Jaye's tongue to tell the man that
he honestly didn't give a royal damn if he liked him or
not since the jury was still out as to whether Jaye liked
him. So far, he didn't. Steepling his fingers, Jaye studied the man and was tempted to suggest that he dispense
with the bullshit. Instead, he prompted, "And the reason
for your visit, Mr. Crawford?"

He noticed the man's hesitation before he finally
said, "I understand you're living in one of the houses
on Blueberry Lane."

Jaye frowned, wondering where this conversation
was going. "That's correct. What of it?"

Again, the man paused. "You're new in town so you
might not be aware of how the single men in the cove
handle our business."

How the single men in the cove handle their business? Now Jaye had heard everything. "Such as?"

"Such as my ability to claim any woman that catches my interest and it's understood that no other male can intrude into my territory."

His territory? Jaye stared at the man, convinced he was joking. When Crawford's expression indicated he was dead serious, Jaye said, "Maybe you should cut to the chase and tell me exactly what you are referring to."

Webb Crawford leaned forward in his chair as if assuring he had Jaye's absolute attention. "I understand you're living in a duplex that's under the same roof as a woman by the name of Velvet Spencer."

Jaye kept his body from showing any reaction at the mention of Velvet's name. However, he felt every nerve poised to snap. "And?"

"And I'm very interested in Ms. Spencer."

Welcome to the club, Jaye thought while holding Crawford's gaze. "Are the two of you engaged? Seriously involved? Dating?"

"None of those. However, I've let my interest be known to her."

Jaye didn't say anything for a minute and then he said, "I understand she's been living here for a couple of years. At least that's the information I received from the woman who is our landlord. I'd think you would have swept her off her feet by now…if you're that interested in her." He knew from Webb's expression that he didn't like anyone bringing up the fact he'd apparently struck out in pursuing Velvet.

"Currently, she's playing hard to get, but eventually, I'll wear down her resistance."

Good luck with that, asshole, Jaye thought. With that kind of entitled attitude, no wonder the man hadn't even gotten to first base with Velvet. Just like Jaye detested pushy women, Velvet loathed cocky and arrogant men. "So, what is it you want from me?" he asked.

He knew the look he was giving Crawford. Some referred to it as the Jaye Colfax glare. After all, he was the oldest of Jack Colfax's sons, the one destined one day to head the family dynasty his father had built. Jaye was the least likely to put up with foolishness. He practically wore a sign that said Leave Your Bullshit at the Door.

"What I want, Colfax, is a gentlemen's agreement between us that during the time you're here in Catalina Cove, you won't try pursuing Velvet Spencer yourself."

There was no way in hell Jaye would agree to something like that when his sole purpose was to win back Velvet's love. And did Crawford honestly assume his directive would be followed? Obviously, he did because other men were apparently doing so.

"First of all, Mr. Crawford, I don't make deals with men when it concerns a woman. They aren't property to be bartered or negotiated on. A woman has the right to choose but no man has the right to claim. At least, without her permission. What you're suggesting is as asinine as it could get and is nothing a true *gentleman* would even consider doing."

Webb Crawford narrowed his gaze at Jaye. From his expression, it was obvious Jaye's insult had not been

taken well. "Good day, Mr. Crawford, and to avoid waiting, next time please make an appointment."

Then the man stood and walked out of his office.

VELVET HAD WIPED down the chalkboard and was getting
ready to pack up to leave for the day when her classroom
door opened and a tall man walked in. A man she didn't
recognize. "Yes, may I help you?" she asked, standing.

"You are Velvet Spencer, I presume?" he said, approaching her with an unreadable expression on his
face.

"Yes, I'm Velvet Spencer. And you are?"

"Allen Bordeaux."

So, this was Lenny's father. "Yes, Mr. Bordeaux?
How can I help you?"

"You can make things easier for Lenny. He plans
to go to the pros after high school. He doesn't need algebra."

"That's not your decision to make, Mr. Bordeaux.
It's a school board policy. Every student must pass the
core classes to move to the next grade."

"I don't care about that. Lenny needs to ace this
class."

"I will be glad to give him makeup assignments and
even tutor him after school. But Lenny has to do the
work."

She could tell the man didn't like what she was saying. "Why are you being so difficult?" he asked her.

Velvet placed her palms on her desk. "I'm not being
difficult. I'm merely doing my job. I will not give Lenny
a grade he doesn't deserve."

"And I'm not asking you to do that."

"Then what are you asking?"

"For you to give him extra credit when you can. Even colleges do that for their athletes."

"So, I heard, but a dedicated teacher wouldn't do such a thing. She would treat all her students fairly and only give them the grade they deserve."

The man stared at her and then turned and walked out, slamming the door behind him with enough force to rattle the windows. It's a wonder they didn't break.

Just because his teachers had given Mr. Bordeaux *extra credit* that he didn't deserve, he was expecting the same thing for his son? It wouldn't be happening. And since she was the only ninth-grade math teacher, transferring Lenny from her class wasn't an option.

Velvet drew in a deep breath, angry at Principal Dunning for trying to play both sides with Mr. Bordeaux. He was the principal for heaven's sake and should have his teachers' backs in such a situation.

During her drive home, the more she thought about it the angrier she got. When she turned into the driveway, it wasn't unusual to see Jaye's car already parked there. What was unusual was to see him sitting on the steps of her porch, as if he were waiting for her. *What in the world?*

When she parked the car and got out, he stood and walked toward her. There was an intense look on his face. But that didn't keep her gaze from roaming all over him, appreciating how he looked in his business suit. "Jaye? Is anything wrong?"

He came to a stop in front of her. "Were you aware that Webb Crawford is claiming you as *his* and warning other men away from you?"

She shrugged as she closed the car door. How had he heard about it? "What of it?"

"And you're okay with that?"

"I didn't say I was okay with anything, Jaye, and why does it concern you?" she asked, walking around him toward the steps. After a day dealing with Principal Dunning and the likes of Allen Bordeaux, she really didn't need a discussion with Jaye about Webb Crawford's foolishness.

"It concerns me when the man shows up at my office wanting me to agree to keep my distance from you."

His statement made Velvet stop and turn around. "He did what!"

"You heard me. The man is outright interfering in your love life?"

Her love life? Now that was a laugh. However, the last thing she wanted Jaye to know was that she hadn't dated anyone since leaving him. Instead of answering, she said, "There's no need for you to be concerned with my love life, Jaye. In fact, you could have simply let him know that you had me for three years and after all that time, I didn't come to mean anything to you then, and that I don't mean anything to you now."

She was turning to head up the steps when Jaye reached out and grabbed her shoulder. She was about to read him the riot act when she met the intensity of his gaze. There was anger in the dark depths, and she wondered why he was mad when she'd spoken the truth. Suddenly, his anger was replaced by something else, something she knew and recognized—*desire*.

She drew in a sharp breath, wondering why here and why now? She didn't know who made the first move, but suddenly her body was pressed to his, and she felt her nipples stiffen and poke him in the chest like they usually did when she was aroused.

And she *was* aroused. There was no way to deny that. Just like there was no way to deny he was aroused as well. The firm hardness of his erection pressed against her middle reminded her how things used to be between them and what usually came next.

The intensity she saw in his eyes made her shudder before releasing a throaty moan. Velvet felt his presence in every part of her, and for the first time in two years, her body was responding to a man. But then standing before her wasn't just any man. He was the man who had taught her body to sing in the most sensuous voice possible. The man who had the ability to make her come, just from his kiss.

His kiss…

He began lowering his head and automatically, she moved her mouth toward his. She felt a jolt of sexual energy, and it dawned on her just how much she'd missed this.

Their mouths were mere inches from touching and she was about to use her tongue to trace a path over the lips she knew so well when suddenly the sharp ringing of her phone made them quickly step back from each other, although their gazes remained locked. Velvet recognized Ruthie's ringtone and appreciated her best friend's timely interruption. Just seconds ago, she'd felt vulnerable to her desires and her needs for the first time in two years. No man could have made her feel that way other than Jaye. He could make her sizzle just from a look or a glance.

Feeling intense heat flow all through her, it was at that moment she realized his hands were still on her. At some point, they had moved from her shoulder to her waist. "Please let go of me, Jaye," she said in a soft voice.

He immediately dropped his hands to his side. Without saying anything else, she turned and hurried up the steps, unlocked the door, went inside the house and closed the door behind her.

CHAPTER EIGHT

JAYE LET HIMSELF inside his home, tossed off his jacket and nearly ripped off his tie before heading toward the wine cabinet and straight to his bottle of scotch. He needed a shot. If things hadn't been real before, they were pretty damn real now. The moment he had touched Velvet, desire and need had been as real as it could get.

It had been two years; two years since he had been with a woman, refusing to sleep with anyone after Velvet had left him. At first, he'd told himself he'd needed time to adjust but then after a year he'd known it was more serious than that. He needed and wanted Velvet and no other woman would do. He didn't want a substitute, and he found the thought of sharing his body with another woman became downright nauseating.

Finding out where she'd gone hadn't been easy, especially when her best friend, Ruthie, refused to even talk to him. Velvet had also given orders to her executive staff at the Spencer's Corporation that her whereabouts were not to be shared. For the longest time, Jaye had assumed she was living somewhere under an alias or had even moved out the country. He'd almost lost all hope of seeing her again when he'd finally gotten word from the private investigator he'd hired of where she was.

If nothing else, what had just happened proved the

still had the hots for each other, but he wanted more than just desire and need connecting them. He wanted love. He needed to prove to her that he loved her above all else. And he did love her, with every beat of his heart and with every breath he took. Mentally, she consumed his entire being. However, today upon touching her, he was reminded that physically she consumed him entirely as well.

He'd come close to kissing her, rekindling that taste that had once been as much a part of him as the feel of blood rushing through his veins and drawing air in his lungs. He had wanted to hear her moan his name, break apart in his arms and to come—to have an actual orgasm—from the mating of their lips. That had happened between them more times than he could count.

He downed a shot of scotch and flinched when the strong liquid flowed down his throat. He had forgotten just how addictive Velvet Spencer was. He had desired her on Saturday but not like this. Not with an intensity that made him want to go downstairs, knock on her door and pull her into his arms and finish what might have happened had her phone not interrupted.

And then, he recalled she was wearing his favorite color. Yellow. When she got out of her car wearing that yellow wrap dress with a flattering scoop neckline and a hem that hit just above her knees—which emphasized her shapely legs—he was reminded of just how much he loved those legs. Whether they were walking or wrapped around his waist while they made love.

He rubbed a hand down his face, needing to regain some semblance of that control he'd had with her on Saturday. His true mission in coming to Catalina Cove was not to regain Velvet as a bed partner, but to get back inside her heart.

He sat down at the table to recall when they'd first begun dating. After their spontaneous dinner at Captain Scampi, he had been determined to get her in his bed and make her a one-and-done. But no matter how many dates they'd shared after that, Velvet wasn't having it. She'd made him earn a place in her bed, something he'd never had to do with any woman. She hadn't been easy, had stood her ground and in the end, he had given her what she wanted—an exclusive relationship.

Jaye's thoughts shifted to Webb Crawford and the sheer audacity of the man. Gentlemen's agreement, his ass. It had sounded more like an order Crawford expected to be followed. Well, he had news for Crawford. Velvet *was* off-limits but in a way the man would soon discover was *not* in his favor. Crawford's intention was clear. He only wanted a spot in Velvet's bed, whereas Jaye wanted a lot more than that. He wanted a place in her heart just like she had a place in his.

"YES, RUTHIE, SORRY I missed your call," Velvet said, easing down on her sofa and trying to get her heart rate back to normal. She could not believe that she'd been just seconds from kissing Jaye in their front yard. How could she?

"I was returning your call from earlier today," Ruthie said.

Yes, she had called her best friend and immediatel remembered why. "I need to get away, Ruthie. Rea bad. How does a girls' weekend in New York sound?

"This weekend?"

"Yes," she said, hoping Ruthie and her fiancé, Todd, didn't have anything planned.

"Short notice, but yes, this weekend will be great since you know what weekend this is."

Velvet frowned. She honestly didn't have a clue. "No. What?"

"Super Bowl weekend. Every sports enthusiast will be glued to a TV, so this weekend is perfect."

Velvet was glad to hear that. "Thanks. I desperately need to get away."

"Why? Being so close to your sexy-hot neighbor is getting to you?"

Velvet drew in a deep breath. "If only you knew just how much."

"Do tell."

She knew that she might as well, or Ruthie would hound her until she did. She spent the next ten minutes telling her everything.

"Aww, heck. It would have to be my phone call that interrupted things," Ruthie said, chuckling.

"Ruthie, did you hear everything I said? What part did you find amusing? Jaye and I were standing outside, in broad daylight about to kiss. Anyone could have seen us. And had we kissed, it wouldn't have stopped there. We would have been rolling in the grass in no time."

That visual got a laugh out of Ruthie. "Knowing how much sexual chemistry the two of you have, I'm surprised you two haven't kissed already and been done with it."

Velvet rolled her eyes. "Because there can't be a *done with it* with a Velvet-and-Jaye kiss. It always leads to more."

"Then do more. If you recall, I suggested you take him as a lover."

"I can't do that."

"Why? You claim you don't love him anymore."

"I don't love him anymore."

"Then what's the problem? The way I see it, it will serve Jaye right by letting him think that you're now the new more sophisticated and liberated Velvet. And since all those single men in Catalina Cove seemed to have been run off by that Webb guy, it's up to you to show Jaye."

"Show Jaye what?"

"That a man isn't the only one who can engage in meaningless affairs. You can prove your point on that end while satisfying your need to get laid on the other. Stock up on all Jaye Colfax's lovemaking so when he leaves Catalina Cove, at least he'll be out of your system."

Velvet frowned. "Who say he's in my system?"

"I do. And don't deny you are in dire need of a sexual fix. There's no way a woman who was as sexually active as you and Jaye were, and who's gone without sex for two years, isn't."

"I am not addicted to sex, Ruthie."

"No, but you're addicted to Jaye. Admit it."

Velvet refused to admit anything. Ruthie's suggestion to take Jaye as a lover was crazy. "Jaye will think I'm trying to get back with him and he wouldn't want that."

"Then spell things out for him. You control the narrative and make sure he knows this is the *new* you."

The new her. Velvet kind of liked that. But still. " don't know, Ruthie."

"Well, I do. Think about it and we'll talk about it some more this weekend. So, what else had you in a bad mood today? The voice message you left indicated something about a parent who raised your blood pressure."

Velvet blew out an exasperated breath. "Yes." She spent another twenty minutes telling Ruthie about her meeting with Principal Dunning and then her meeting with Lenny's father.

"I can't believe your principal is taking that approach. The man sounds like he doesn't have a backbone."

"I agree and, like I told him, if he expects me to fall in line, he can forget it. I will resign first."

"Good for you, but I hope he'll have your back if things escalate between you and Mr. Bordeaux."

"I would hope so. I can't believe people expect athletes to get a free pass."

"Unfortunately, some people do, but it's up to us to remain fair and objective."

After she and Ruthie had finalized their weekend plans, she hung up the phone and headed to the kitchen. This was the last day for her leftovers from Saturday. As she sat down at the table to eat, she pushed thoughts of Jaye and Allen Bordeaux from her mind. But there was another man who was now front and center. Webb Crawford. The nerve of him telling men to stay away from her. He really had a lot of gall to approach Jaye with that nonsense. She knew Jaye and could just imagine how that had gone. Jaye might not be interested in her, but he wouldn't appreciate someone like Webb telling him to keep his distance. She intended to seek

Webb out before the week ended and tell him a thing or two. No man had a claim on her, especially not him.

Later that night, Velvet couldn't sleep and for the longest time she stared up at the ceiling. Why was her body tingling all over? In truth, her body really hadn't stopped tingling since the moment Jaye had reached out and touched her shoulder.

All she had to do was close her eyes and recall other times when his touch had been the catalyst to drive her desire. Not only his touch, but the look that would always appear in his eyes when he was aroused. He'd had that look today.

Velvet hadn't been joking when she'd told Ruthie had they kissed, she and Jaye would have been rolling in the grass in seconds. It wouldn't have been the first time. That had happened when they'd been at his vacation home on Lake Tahoe. Good thing his cabin was in a secluded area.

She wished three years' worth of memories of lovemaking weren't stored in her brain. That kind of archive had kept her up many nights when she'd first moved to Catalina Cove. Now that he was here, in her space, her intense desire for him was trying to take over again.

She felt hot and there was a deep constant throb between her legs. Why did she have to remember how Jaye would take care of that inconvenience with his mouth, his hands or, even better, his shaft. Jaye had always been the kind of lover women dreamed of. He'd never sought his pleasure before first making sure she'd had hers, or that they shared it together.

Velvet shifted in bed.

A part of her wished Ruthie hadn't put that though

into her head, about her and Jaye becoming lovers if for no other reason than to prove she had moved on and was no longer looking…or expecting…a forever kind of love.

Jaye had taught her a valuable lesson. No matter how much a woman could love a man, you couldn't make him love you back, no matter how good the sex was or how well the two of you complemented each other. If both hearts weren't in it, none of it meant anything.

"MAY I HELP YOU?" The attractive woman sitting behind the lobby desk gave Velvet a friendly smile.

"Yes, I'd like to see Webb Crawford."

Still smiling, the woman said, "Certainly, and who may I say is visiting?"

Visiting? Velvet wouldn't call this a visit but she answered, anyway. "Velvet Spencer."

The woman nodded, then picked up her phone and said, "Mr. Crawford, there's a Velvet Spencer here to see you."

Before the woman could disconnect the call, the office door opened. "Velvet, to what do I owe this visit?" Webb came out of his office with a huge smile on his face.

"Hello, Webb. I need to talk with you about something."

"Certainly." He glanced at the woman and said, "Marla, hold any calls and appointments." He then escorted Velvet into his office.

After he closed the door behind them, she turned on him. "How dare you go around town and tell other men to back off from me, Webb!"

Instead of frowning, his smile widened. "Has anyone ever told you that you're beautiful when you're angry, Velvet?"

"You haven't seen anything yet."

He shrugged. "I didn't tell other men to back off. I merely let them know I was interested in you, because I am." He leaned against his desk. "What has you upset? Have I shown up at your house unexpectedly again since you told me not to? Have I called you or sought you out for a date?"

"No, but you're making sure no other man does, either."

"Are you saying you're ready to start dating now? I recall you told me a while ago that you weren't. If you are, then that's good to hear. And as far as those other guys, I'm not holding a gun to anyone's head. However, they seem to know what you obviously refuse to acknowledge."

She crossed her arms. "Which is?"

"You can't do any better than me here in the cove. I give those guys credit for looking out for your best interests."

She glared at him. "For your information, you aren't the best I can do."

His smile was dropped to a frown. "I hope you're not holding out for your neighbor, the banker, to show any interest in you. Take my advice, Velvet. Don't waste your time because you don't stand a chance. If my own sister, who has the same pedigree as Colfax, struck out with him, then there's no hope for you."

Velvet was surprised he would admit that his sis

ter had struck out with Jaye. "So, Laura didn't interest him?" She knew her question would strike a nerve.

He frowned. "His loss. I told Laura not to worry
about him. He will only be around temporarily, anyway. Besides, I heard he has a serious girl back in Arizona, which would be the only reason Laura isn't the
woman on his arm."

The one thing Velvet had learned about the Crawford
siblings was that they had no problem putting each other
on pedestals and honestly thought the world revolved
around them. "Like I said, Webb, stop giving people the
impression we're an item because we aren't. And as for
whether or not I'm ready to start dating, it's no concern
of yours. You're still not welcome to visit or call." She
turned and walked out of his office.

Later that night, while trying to relax with a glass
of wine, she told Sierra of her meeting with Webb. "It
was as if what I said went in one ear and out the other.
I don't think he's taking me seriously and just assumes
I'm playing hard to get."

"Well, if he starts harassing you, then you need to
tell Sheriff Grisham."

"He's not harassing me. He's just annoying."

"What do you plan to do about Webb telling other
guys to stay away from you?"

Velvet shifted to a more comfortable position in the
chair. "I doubt there's anything I can do. If those guys
meekly do whatever Webb says, I wouldn't be interested in them, anyway. I'd want someone who would
stand up to Webb."

"Like Jaye probably did?"

Although Jaye hadn't shared any details of his conversation with Webb, knowing Jaye like she did, there was no doubt in her mind that he put Webb in his place. "Yes, like Jaye did."

"Well, put all negativity out of your mind and enjoy your weekend in New York."

"Thanks, Sierra, and I will."

ON FRIDAY MORNING, Jaye looked out the window as usual to watch Velvet leave for work. On this particular morning, he noticed her placing an overnight bag in the trunk of her car. Was she going away for the weekend? Where? With whom?

Their paths hadn't crossed since Wednesday, when they'd come close to kissing. He'd deliberately made sure their paths didn't cross yesterday, thinking the best thing to do was give her space to deal with what almost happened between them. They were still fiercely attracted to each other, and he hoped it was an attraction they could build upon.

Thoughts of where she'd gone and whom she was with plagued his mind the rest of the day. He decided to eat light that evening and stopped at the Green Fig. Usually, he got takeout but there was no need to rush home. He was feeling lonely just knowing the house was empty below.

"Welcome to the Green Fig, Mr. Colfax."

Jaye glanced at the man he knew to be the café's assistant manager, Levi Canady.

"Hello, Levi, and remember, you can call me Jaye."

"I'll try to remember that, and you're in luck. W have several tables empty now. This is usually our bus hour."

"Thanks, and I'll grab one." Jaye headed for a booth in the back.

It wasn't long before a waitress came to take his order. He requested the soup of the day, a sandwich and a beer. No sooner had the waitress walked off, a voice said, "Mind if I join you?"

Jaye looked up and smiled. "Of course, you can, Vaughn. I guess you have a taste for soup tonight as well."

Vaughn Miller slid into the seat across from him. "Yes. Besides, this place has become my favorite hangout."

"I don't have to guess why," Jaye said, grinning. The waitress delivered his beer, then took Vaughn's order. After she walked off, Jaye asked, "How's the wedding plans coming?"

"According to my future bride, they're coming along great. I think Sierra would have been just fine had we eloped to Vegas since this isn't her first rodeo, but I wanted it all. My first and final."

Jaye nodded. Vaughn looked happy and he knew that he would look the same way once he'd recaptured Velvet's heart. "Congratulations again."

"Thanks. Some of the guys and I will be hanging out at my place on Sunday for the big game. You want to join us?" Vaughn asked. "You might as well, since I understand your ladylove is having a girls weekend in New York with her best friend."

Jaye's head snapped up. "She is?"

Vaughn nodded, grinning. "Yes. Sierra mentioned it to me this morning. Velvet and her best friend are going shopping and attending a Broadway play."

A smile spread across Jaye's face. "Is that so?"

Vaughn leaned back in his seat and chuckled. "Yes, it is so. When I saw you walk in with a long sour-looking face, I figured you either had problems at the bank or at the house on Blueberry Lane. I went for the latter."

"You were right."

After the waitress served Vaughn his beer, Jaye said, "There's someone I need to ask you about, though."

Vaughn lifted a brow. "Who?"

"Webb Crawford. Is the man for real?"

Vaughn chuckled. "I guess you got the don't-get-interested-in-Velvet warning."

"Yes. Who the hell does he think he is?"

"A man who honestly believes he can have any woman he wants. He figures he's a prime catch. Velvet isn't into him, like a lot of the women are, so I think he sees her as a challenge."

Jaye snorted. "Men like Webb Crawford turn Velvet off."

Vaughn took a huge sip of his beer and then laughingly said, "Since she hasn't given him the time of day, I figured as much. Sooner or later, Webb will discover that fact."

Although Jaye didn't comment, he knew he would make sure of it, in case Webb didn't get the hint.

CHAPTER NINE

IT WAS SUNDAY evening when Velvet returned home. Although she had enjoyed her weekend in New York immensely, she was glad to be back. The first thing she'd noticed when she pulled into the yard was that Jaye's car wasn't there. This was the first time she could recall him not being home on a Sunday evening. That made her wonder if he had a date.

As she strolled toward her bedroom, pulling her carry-on luggage behind her, she knew she couldn't discount that possibility. It certainly wasn't any of her business what he did and with whom. Jaye had been a womanizer when they'd met. Had she honestly expected him not to go back to his old ways? She'd even mentioned to Ruthie about Webb's claim that Jaye had a steady woman back in Phoenix. Ruthie staunchly claimed that wasn't true. But could Ruthie be certain of that?

Leaving her luggage in the corner of the room to unpack later, she paused to look at her bed. The three nights she'd spent in it before leaving for New York had been hell and all because of Jaye's touch. Whenever possible, Ruthie reminded Velvet that she could go to bed every night and dream of having Jaye in her bed, or she could take the bull by the horns—or the man by the crotch—and do something about it.

Velvet hated to admit it, but the more she and Ruthie discussed it, the more sense it began to make. She no longer loved Jaye, that was a given. So why couldn't she have casual sex, just like he could? It would only be temporary since he'd be leaving in a few months. In the end, it would prove she was over him, while at the same time she would satisfy her body's craving. And her body *was* craving him. Just the thought of a roll between the sheets with Jaye had the tips of her nipples getting hard and the area between her legs throbbing something fierce.

For her plan to work, the first thing she needed to do was get him interested in her again. Granted, their reaction to one another the other day showed their sexual chemistry was still there, but she needed to raise the bar even higher. Then, when it got to the right level, she would reveal the new Velvet Spencer to him and deliver her terms.

A short while later, she was sitting at her kitchen table, going over her lesson plans for the week and enjoying a glass of wine. She wished she could stay focused and not allow her thoughts to drift to Jaye. But now that she'd made a decision, she needed to map out a course of action. It was time to draw on everything Jaye had taught her during the three years they'd been together—which meant seduction.

He liked the chase, and she would give him that— up to a point. She wasn't totally immune to him, after all. The man was sex on legs and that appendage in the middle could deliver pleasure with a capital *P*. She of all people knew that. There was a chance that no matter how hot things got between them, he might not want to get involved with her again, thinking once was enough. Especially since she'd taken their relationship more seriously than he had—even after his repeated warnings for her not to—she needed to convince him she was no longer that woman.

When she heard a car pull into the driveway, she figured it was Jaye. What if he had brought a date home with him? She got up and, as discreetly as possible, peered out the window. It was dark but when he opened the car door, she saw he was alone.

Quickly coming up with an idea, she removed one of her hoop earrings, then grabbed the flashlight from the counter and headed for the front door.

THE MOMENT JAYE pulled into the yard he saw Velvet's car parked in the driveway. He did not have to question why he felt all kinds of sensations riding low in his gut. It didn't matter that he wouldn't see her tonight. All he needed to know was that she was back. Hopefully, he'd get a glimpse of her tomorrow morning when she left for work.

Jaye saw the curtain in her kitchen move and figured she'd heard the car and glanced out to check who was pulling up. He was headed toward his side of the house when suddenly Velvet's front door opened and she walked out with a flashlight in her hand.

It was dark but the soft glow from the porch light illuminated her. She was wearing jeans and a pullover top. She looked beautiful, causing his heart to miss a few beats.

"Hello, Velvet."

She jerked and looked at him. "Jaye, you scared me. I didn't hear a car pull up."

He forced himself not to raise a brow. Strange she would say that since he knew for certain she had. "What are you doing out in the dark with a flashlight? Are you looking for something?"

"Yes. My other loop earring," she said, tapping her right earlobe. "I must have lost it in or around the car because I'm certain I had it in my ear while driving home from the airport."

"Do you need help looking for it?"

"No, thanks. I got this," she said, walking past him. Her luscious scent followed in her wake and his nostrils took it all in.

He turned to watch her shine the flashlight on the ground near her car, then opening the door to look around inside. She might not need help looking for her earring, but he wasn't going to leave her alone outside and unprotected.

He walked over and saw she was leaning over the car seat, checking the cushions and the areas between the consoles. He wished her ass weren't all up in the air like that. Remembering how many times he'd ridden it was too much temptation. "I know you said you didn't need help, but four eyes are better than two."

She peered over her shoulder at him and nodded. "You're probably right."

He leaned inside the car, and she suddenly moved, bringing their bodies into contact. When he drew in a sharp breath, she looked up at him. "Jaye, are you alright?"

It was on the tip of his tongue to tell her that no, he

wasn't, and hearing her say his name wasn't making him any better. He always thought her pronunciation had a sultry kick to it.

"I need to look under the seats where it's dark. Could you shine the flashlight there for me, Jaye?" She pushed the driver's seat back and got on her knees to peer underneath.

He was about to say it probably would be easier if she held the flashlight herself, but he had offered his help so he needed to make himself useful any way he could. "Sure thing."

He leaned down close to where she was, maneuvering his body almost alongside hers to hold the flashlight at the angle she needed. It was torturous watching her stretch her body. And why were her nipples hard and pressing against her shirt? Then there was her perfect rounded ass being hugged by a pair of skin-tight jeans. Lordy.

"Jaye?"

He blinked. "Yes."

"Where are you shining the light? It's not in the area I'm looking."

No, it wasn't since he'd been shining it on her backside. A direct hit if ever there was one. "Sorry about that." He adjusted the flashlight in the direction she needed him to.

A few minutes later, she decided to search the back seats. He didn't know how her earring could have gotten back there but decided to keep his mouth shut since he was enjoying being so close to her.

"How was your date?" she asked casually, without

looking at him. He was surprised she hadn't noticed he'd slipped back to shining the flashlight on her ass again.

"My date?"

"Yes. I noticed you weren't here when I arrived and figured you'd gone out on a date."

Boy had she figured wrong. Was she asking for conversational purposes or was she fishing for information? Either way, he had no problem answering her. "No date. This is Super Bowl weekend. Vaughn gave a party, and I was invited."

"That was nice of him."

"Yes, it was. I got to hang out with some of the guys."

"Oh, like who?"

If he didn't know better, he'd think she was stalling about finding her earring. Hadn't she searched that area already? Not that he had any complaints. In fact, it reminded him of the time they'd made out in the back seat of his car. It hadn't mattered that the car was parked in the garage at the time. She said she'd never made out in a back seat, so he'd shown her how it was done.

"Jaye?"

Hearing her say his name reminded him that he hadn't answered her question. "The sheriff, for one."

"Ah, Sawyer Grisham is nice. Were Ray Sullivan and Kaegan Chambray there, too?"

"Yes."

"I'm not surprised. Those three are close friends."

"I know."

When the car got quiet, she asked, "Who else?"

"Who else, what?" Jaye had lost focus when he noticed she was rubbing her hands all over the seat cushions the way she used to rub her hands all over him. He was convinced it was with the same measured strokes. Was she deliberately trying to arouse him?

"Jaye?"

He blinked. "Yes?"

"Who else was at the party?"

Did she want a list? And why was she interested? "Isaac Elloran, the two Witherspoon brothers—Ry and Duke—the fire marshal, Brody Dorsett and a guy, who grew up here and recently moved back to town to work at LaCroix Industries, by the name of Evans Toussaint. Kaegan invited all of us to go night fishing on his yacht next month. I told them I'd loved to join them if I'm still here."

Her head whipped up so fast it was a wonder she didn't get whiplash. That bit of information was of interest to her apparently. And was he seeing panic in the depths of her dark eyes?

"You're leaving Catalina Cove?"

He was tempted to tell her no, not until he won back her love, proved that she had his. "Not sure yet. Things are doing better at this branch than I thought they would. That means I'm not needed here as long as expected. Dean is interviewing a bank manager for here. And we break ground on a new bank in Birmingham in a week."

"Oh."

Was that disappointment he heard? Or was it too much to hope? "I'll take stock of how things are looking in another month," he decided to add.

She nodded as she glanced around and then back at him. "I guess I've looked enough tonight for that earring. Maybe it dropped out of my ear near the porch."

"You want us to look there now?"

"No. I'll look in the morning when I leave for work."

"And I'll be sure to look around when I leave for my morning jog," he said.

"You don't have to do that, Jaye."

"I don't mind." He offered his hand to help her out of the car. He braced himself for the impact he knew he'd feel from their hands touching. He noticed she hesitated only a moment before taking his hand, and his body began to sizzle. Her touch had him all ablaze.

Still holding her hand, he pulled her closer to him, not caring if their bodies touched in a way that would tell her he was aroused. His erection was a dead give-away. But then there was truly nothing dead about his hard-on. It was very much alive and, at the moment, had a life of its own.

He recalled his decision to keep things nonphysical between them. She needed to know that he loved her and how much. But with her staring into his eyes and standing this close—even closer than they had the other day—it was messing with his common sense.

It was dark but there was a soft light from the porch, which meant they could be seen if anyone was looking. At the moment, he really didn't give a royal damn. All he wanted to do was ease his mouth closer and capture hers with his.

"I think I need to go inside now, Jaye. Thanks for helping me look for my earring."

"Anytime." He swallowed and then said, "Vel?"

Too late, he'd said her nickname, which she didn't want him to use. He braced himself for her sharp retort. Instead, she surprised him when she answered, "Yes?"

He wanted to tell her that he loved her, wanted her, needed her and, more than anything, wanted to marry her, but he knew now was not the time. She wouldn't believe him. So instead, he said, "Good night, Velvet. Pleasant dreams."

She smiled at him when she said, "Trust me, tonight they will be pleasant."

She turned toward the house. He watched as she walked up the steps and entered her home. He decided right then and there that the next time their mouths came that close to kissing, they would.

CHAPTER TEN

VELVET WOKE UP the next morning with a huge smile on her face. Just like she'd told Jaye, she'd had pleasant dreams—more than pleasant—they'd been downright scandalous, naughty even. Last night, she hadn't been able to get into her house quick enough to take a cold shower. Her goal had been to semi-seduce Jaye, but in the end she was the one who'd gotten all hot and bothered. Just knowing they were in such close proximity had nearly overpowered her.

She had deliberately done things that would get his attention, like twisting her backside in the air, rubbing her hands over the car's interior and placing her body in positions where he couldn't help but notice her. She was pretty certain that he had.

Glancing at her watch, she saw it was ten minutes past the time Jaye usually jogged past her kitchen window. What was up with that? Should she be concerned when she knew the man had an internal clock? When they had been a couple, she'd had a hard time convincing him there were times when it was okay to be fashionably late, and that you didn't have to be the first to arrive each and every time.

She put down her coffee cup, deciding she couldn't

worry about Jaye's no-show when she needed to get ready for work. She was about to walk out of the kitchen when she saw him jog across the yard. Instead of leaving, it appeared he was returning. That meant he'd gone jogging before she'd gotten out of bed.

He paused right outside her window to bend over. Her heart rate kicked up a notch when she saw him doing his cooldown exercises. Even from where she was standing, she could see drops of perspiration trickling off his face and rolling down his neck, shoulders and back. Lordy, his sweats were low on his hips, and why on earth was he bare-chested? It was February for heaven's sake, and since Catalina Cove was so close to the water, mornings tended to be cool. But the weather didn't seem to faze him. And if jogging hadn't been enough, now he was on the ground doing crunches.

Intense desire surged inside her, and she moved closer to the window. She didn't want to get too close, since she didn't want to be seen. Velvet stood with her gaze fixed on Jaye until he finished his crunches. When he stood and began running in place, even more perspiration covered his face and barreled down his chest to disappear in the waistband of his sweats.

She placed her hand at the center of her throat and felt her erratic pulse. Not only that, her body was growing hot and a slow throb began right between her legs. Moments later, he stopped, grabbed his water bottle, uncapped it and tipped his head back. He took a huge gulp, then lifted the bottle and poured the rest over his head and face. Dang, she could just imagine lapping up every drop that touched his skin. Licking him was something she'd always enjoyed doing, and from the way her tongue was twitching in her mouth, it was also remembering, and itching to do it again.

Suddenly, his head snapped toward her window, and she quickly jumped back. Had she made a sound? A deep moan that might have carried out to him? She closed her eyes, hoping she had moved quick enough and he hadn't seen her. He didn't need to know just yet that he could still make her body sizzle.

She shook her head, knowing he already knew. There was no way he didn't when on two separate occasions they'd come close to kissing. Jaye used to read her well and could tell just what she wanted and how much of him she needed. There was never a time he had disappointed her in the bedroom. He had always gone above and beyond, which made him a hard act to follow.

Honestly, he had never disappointed her once they had gone exclusive. Over the years, they'd received many comments on how good they looked together and how well they complemented each other. He often told her that himself. What he'd never told her was that he loved her. For some reason, she'd begun thinking he did. At least she had until she'd overheard what he told his best friend one night he thought she was still in the shower.

That was why no matter how much she desired Jaye for her it was about satisfying her needs and not anything else. As long as she remembered that, Jaye could not wiggle his way into her heart again.

Satisfied she had gotten her thoughts and her hormones in check, she left the kitchen to get dressed for work.

JAYE STOOD IN his kitchen and watched Velvet leave for work. He wondered if she'd had pleasant dreams. If she had, then she was the only one. His night had been torturous as hell. He had dreamed they'd made love...or attempted to. Each time, just before their bodies were to join, they'd been interrupted, and the deed was never done. He'd had very little sleep. That was why he'd gotten up at the crack of dawn and gone jogging.

He hadn't expected to be watched while working out his sexual frustration by exercising and cooling down after his run. He had detected Velvet's presence by her kitchen window and, more than once, he'd seen the curtain move. He'd even swear he heard a moan. Had he known she'd be watching, he would have made it worth her while and given her something to think about today—which reminded him of last night.

A few things just didn't add up. Had she deliberately tried to tempt him? Although she had searched for her earring with the flashlight, he'd expected her to look again this morning. However, she had gotten into her car without even a glance around for the lost earring.

If he didn't know Velvet, he'd suspect she had looked for her earring deliberately to get him next to her. But he *did* know Velvet and one thing he knew was that she didn't play those kinds of games. When her car was no longer in sight, he turned to get his cup of coffee...and to think.

He loved Velvet. That was a definite. He didn't want to rush her into anything. That was a definite, too. But being around her was hard, making him impatient. Maybe it was time to level with her and tell her everything. Exactly what had brought him to Catalina Cove in the first place.

His chest tightened at the thought that she wouldn't buy it. She would think he'd just missed the sex and not her. He needed time to court her properly, but he didn't think he had that kind of time. According to Delisa Mills, Velvet's lease would be up soon. The older woman had mentioned that Velvet wasn't sure if she would renew it. Why? Was she thinking of moving to another part of town? For all he knew, she might have plans to move away from Catalina Cove altogether. If she did either, where would that leave him? Maybe it was time for him to take his chances and level with her.

Frustrated, he rubbed a hand down his face. Tomorrow, he was leaving for a business trip to Birmingham. He decided he wouldn't keep things from Velvet any longer and would tell her everything today. Hopefully, while he was away, she would think about how far he'd gone to regain her love and prove that he loved her. More than anything, he wanted them not to dwell on the past, but to move forward. If she wanted to take things slow, he'd agree to that. Hell, he'd agree to just about anything to get her back into his life.

He headed to the shower, knowing he was making the right decision.

VELVET SLID INTO the booth opposite Bryce at Spencer's. Bryce had called when she was en route to work, inviting her to lunch to discuss plans for Sierra's surprise bridal shower and thought this would be the perfect place.

"Vashti is on her way," Bryce said, smiling. "She

had to wait on the babysitter. Ashley won't be able to make it since she has a doctor's appointment. She and Ray will get to listen to the baby's heartbeat today."

Velvet nodded and knew that had to be exciting for them. "Where's your little one?" she asked. Bryce and her husband, Kaegan, were the proud parents of a nine-month-old, Kaegan, Jr., whom they called K-Gee. From what Velvet had heard, K-Gee had been Kaegan's nickname while growing up. Bryce had given him the name in elementary school when she couldn't pronounce the name Kaegan correctly.

"I dropped K-Gee off at the office to spend time with his dad. All Kaegan has to do is crank up K-Gee's swing and place him in it, and you won't hear a peep out of him. Our son loves that thing."

Velvet glanced around. Whenever she came here, she noticed how well-kept and clean this Spencer's was, and that made her feel good. She'd been here a number of times and had to give credit to whoever was the manager. The food was always delicious, and the employees were always friendly. At her annual meeting with the corporate team, she knew this particular Spencer's consistently got high customer rankings for service, food delivery and management. She also knew there wasn't a lot of employee turnover, which meant people liked working here.

Her parents had always been the face of Spencer's, which was why a large portrait of them hung on the wall of every Spencer's restaurant. The photograph was taken when they were in their early thirties. They'd been young, in love and determined to build a hamburger empire. The picture showed them in the kitchen of their very first restaurant in Seattle. Her dad was standing in front of the hamburger grill and her mother stood beside him with her order pad. Both were smiling and dressed in their Spencer's aprons and sailor caps. Seeing that portrait always reminded her of what she'd lost.

"Are you okay, Velvet?"

She switched her gaze from the portrait over to Bryce. "Yes. Why do you ask?"

Bryce shrugged. "For a minute there, you looked sad."

Since Bryce didn't know of her connection to the Spencer's restaurant chain, she would have no idea what had bothered Velvet. "I'm fine. I was just thinking of something."

Velvet liked Bryce and had from the beginning. She was the realtor who had found the Blueberry Lane rental property.

She loved where she was staying and always knew it was temporary. She had considered moving when her lease was up and had even mentioned to Delisa that she was thinking about it. But now she figured she would wait since she was interested in possibly buying property in Reid's new development on the waterfront. When she did, everyone in town would discover her association with the Spencer's restaurant chain, since there was no way she could afford the house she intended to build on a teacher's salary.

"Here's Vashti now," Bryce said, breaking into her thoughts. When Bryce waved to get her attention, Vashti smiled and headed their way.

Just like Bryce, Velvet thought Vashti, who'd she met through Sierra, was beautiful on both the inside and outside. And she was enjoying getting to know the better. She'd heard that Vashti, Kaegan and Bryce had been best buddies since elementary school and the three even have a nick on their fingers from when they'd become blood sisters and brother.

"I am starving and so glad one of you picked this place." Vashti gave them both hugs. "I hate to admit it, but I'm happy the girls talked their grandfather into opening a Spencer's here. I remember those days when we would drive all the way to New Orleans just to eat at one."

Velvet knew the *girls* Vashti referred to were her twin daughters, who were also Reid Lacroix's granddaughters. Vashti had told Velvet the story herself, calling it Catalina Cove's *fifteen-year scandal* where she'd played a starring role.

"I hope my lateness doesn't cause you to rush back to school after lunch, Velvet," Vashti said.

"It won't. I have no class period after lunch, so I'm good. I wish I could go home and take a nap. I did a girls trip to New York this weekend with my bestie."

"I bet that was fun," Bryce said.

"It was fun and exhausting."

A friendly young lady came to take their order and they all ordered the same thing. Cheeseburgers and fries. Velvet ordered a strawberry shake and Vashti and Bryce ordered vanilla shakes.

They began making plans for Sierra's bridal shower. "We can have the party at my place," Bryce said excitedly. "We'll tell Sierra that it's one of Kaegan's usual parties. That way, the guys will be invited, too. She won't suspect a thing."

"What will the guys be doing?" Velvet asked.

Bryce grinned and leaned forward, conspiratorially. "Here's the part that will make it really fun. I think we should keep the details of the shower from Vaughn as well. Like Sierra, he'll assume he's coming to one of Kaegan's parties. So, in a way this will be a groom-and-bride shower. I've talked to Sierra's sister, Dani, and Vaughn's sister, Zara, and they both plan to fly in to attend. While the ladies are inside with the bride-to-be doing typical bridal shower stuff, the guys will be outside helping Kaegan prepare and grill all the food. Plus, afterward, we'll have all that muscle power to load the gifts into the car."

"I think that's a great idea," Vashti said.

Velvet thought it was a great idea, too. She had been invited to one of Kaegan and Bryce's parties before. It had been nice with *plenty* of food. Kaegan was in the seafood-shipping business, and he had cooked everything fresh.

"And," Bryce said, still grinning, "I've already talked to Ashley and Ray, and they've agreed to be in charge of the guest list."

Less than an hour later, they had finished planning the surprise shower. "We covered everything in good time," Velvet said happily. Then she looked around the restaurant and noticed Allen Bordeaux. He was restocking some of the supplies at the main counter. "Does Allen Bordeaux work here?" she asked.

"Yes. He's the manager," Bryce answered.

"The manager?"

"Yes," Vashti said. "And, I have to admit, he's don a great job. The service is always excellent. Since opened, I understand this Spencer's restaurant has wo a number of awards. Just look at all those plaques on the wall."

Velvet did. There were quite a number of them. "It's odd that I've never seen him here before."

"He was probably in the back in his office or something," Bryce said. "I guess you heard about him being one of our hometown heroes. Like when Vashti put Catalina Cove on the map for her baton twirling, Al became known for baseball when he signed on to play for the Dodgers."

"Did he attend school with you guys?"

"He graduated a few years after we did. I think he was in the same class as Sierra and Zara." Bryce looked at Velvet, curious. "Do I hear feminine interest in your voice? He's rather cute and considered a hottie around town."

Velvet shook her head. "No feminine interest. His son is in one of my classes." She was glad when the subject changed—namely to how great business was at Vashti's bed-and-breakfast inn, Shelby by the Sea.

A short while later as Velvet got into her car to return to school, she couldn't get over the fact that Allen Bordeaux was employed by the Spencer's Corporation. That meant he worked for her.

CHAPTER ELEVEN

JAYE CHECKED HIS WATCH. Although there was still some daylight left, it was getting late. He'd expected Velvet to be home by now. Granted, he wasn't privy to her comings and goings but being home before dark was usually the norm for her.

He was about to check his watch again when he heard her car pulling up. He had decided to tell her everything tonight. Not wanting to keep it from her any longer, he left his house and headed toward the front when he saw her getting out of the car. That's when he noticed she wasn't wearing what she'd had on that morning but a pair of tights and a matching hoodie top. He then recalled that someone had mentioned she taught gymnastics a couple of days a week. Her classes must have started up again.

"Hello, Velvet," he said, knowing she hadn't seen him yet.

Her head jerked in his direction. "Jaye? What are you doing out here?"

"Waiting for you."

Her expression showed she was surprised. "I hope you're not here to tell me something else about Webb Crawford."

"No, that's not it."

"Then why were you waiting for me?"

"I need to talk to you about something."

She tilted her head and looked at him. "What?"

"I'd rather we do it inside. My place or yours. It doesn't matter." Too late, he remembered those had been his exact words the first night they'd made love. He had a feeling she would remember as well.

"Why can't we talk out here?" she asked in a soft voice.

"I'd rather we didn't."

She studied her sneakers for a moment, then looked up at him. She nibbled her bottom lip before she said, "Fine. We can talk inside my place because I need to talk to you about something as well."

Jaye could tell she was nervous about whatever she wanted to discuss with him, which made him somewhat uneasy. Was she going to tell him that she'd decided to move out because their close proximity had gotten uncomfortable for her? Or, even worse, she was moving away from Catalina Cove altogether? He couldn't forget the only reason she had moved here was to get away from him. A knot formed in his stomach and he asked, "What do you want to talk to me about?"

"Like you said, it's best we talk inside."

Velvet walked past him and he followed, trying to keep his gaze off the way her tights emphasized the shapeliness of her hips and thighs. Then there was the sensuous sway of her curvy backside. He recalled how when they slept, that very same backside fit perfectly snug against his groin.

She glanced over her shoulder at him. "You said something?"

Had he? What she probably heard was a deep, guttural moan. "No, I didn't say anything."

When she opened the door and stepped aside for him to enter, it hit him that the only other time he'd been inside her place was the night he'd visited her after the town hall meeting. When she closed the door behind them, he couldn't help but hope that whatever she had to talk to him about would be the start of their new beginning and not the finality of their end.

The latter was unacceptable to him.

Velvet set her duffel bag and purse on the table and turned to face him. "You said you wanted to talk to me about something," she said, deciding to get things over with.

"And you wanted to talk to me, too. Ladies first." He stood in her living room, wearing dress slacks and a white shirt—missing the tie and jacket. He wore basically the same thing the night he'd taken her to Captain Scampi. She could remember the exact moment he'd taken off his jacket and removed his tie to help her pack up the boxes. And just like then, tonight he took her breath away.

She inhaled, determined to get a grip. Although he offered for her to go first, she wondered what he wanted to discuss with her. Was he going to tell her that their last two encounters had gotten too heated for him? That he was in an uncomfortable situation since he knew she'd once loved him? If that was the case, maybe it was a good idea for her to go first, after all. She figured she had nothing to lose. Jaye was a man who enjoyed sex especially when there were no strings attached, and she definitely wouldn't be giving him any strings.

"Okay. Let's sit and talk, then. Would you like something to drink? I have beer and wine."

"Thanks, and yes, I'll take a beer."

"One beer coming up." She headed for the kitchen. Was she misreading him, or did he seem nervous or uncomfortable? She wanted him to be relaxed and have a willingness to keep an open mind about her proposal. One she hoped he would accept.

When she returned a short while later, he was staring out the window with his hands shoved in his pants pockets. She was convinced that no other man had such a gorgeous physique and backside as Jack Colfax, Jr. "Here you are, Jaye."

At the sound of her voice, he turned around and their gazes met. It suddenly occurred to her that she and Jaye were alone and the sexual chemistry between them was more electrifying than ever.

He crossed the room and took the beer from her, and their hands touched in the process. The energy between them intensified. He cleared his throat. "You got our favorite brand," he said.

She slid her gaze from his eyes to the bottle. She never was a fan of beer until she'd met Jaye. She'd always been a wine girl. But one night, he had been drinking beer and offered her a sip of his.

"I like a beer every once in a while, to unwind."

"So do I," he said, opening the bottle and taking a huge gulp.

Watching him raise the bottle to his lips, tilt it up

and swallow was still one of the most erotic things she'd ever witnessed.

"Where's yours?" he asked her, holding her gaze.

Her chest tightened from the look she saw in the depths of his eyes—desire and lust. She swallowed and said, "I don't want anything to drink now. I'll have a glass of wine before bedtime." She needed to operate with an undiluted mind, so the last thing she needed was alcohol in her system.

He nodded. "Okay, you're ready to talk?"

"Yes, I'm ready." She sat on the sofa and he took the wingback chair across from her. He looked at her expectantly.

"You were right, Jaye."

He lifted a brow. "About what?"

"All those times you would tell me that love wasn't for everybody. It took me two years, but I finally get it."

"You do?"

"Yes. And just like it wasn't for you, I can now accept it's not for me."

Something flashed in his eyes. She wasn't certain what, but he tilted his head and looked at her for a moment, then said, "No, Velvet, I believe love is for you."

"Maybe, but I'm not going to lose any sleep over it. What I am going to do is continue to move on." She leaned forward to make sure he heard her next words clearly. "I don't love you anymore, Jaye, so if the thought that I do makes you uncomfortable, then don't let it. It took me a while, but I've gotten over you. However, what I haven't gotten over is the good times I spent with you. Especially in the bedroom."

"What are you saying?"

"I'm saying that I believe I can do just like you."

"Do what like me?"

She was glad he'd asked since she had no problem telling him. "Engage in loveless, insignificant, inconsequential, not to mention irrelevant, affairs as long as the sex is good."

He shook his head. "No, Velvet, you need more. You deserve more."

She chuckled. "There was a time I honestly believed I did, but now I've taken the blinders off and see that I don't. It's been a little over two years since we broke up, Jaye, and it was time I needed for my heart to heal. It has and it won't ever be hurt again by any man, because I won't let it. I'm no longer interested in an ever-after. I'll just take *the now*."

"The now?"

"Yes. I'm going to start listening to my body and not to my heart. And lately my body has been going through some things."

He frowned. "Some things like what?"

She decided to be blunt. "It's craving sex."

"Sex?"

Why was he saying that word like he'd never heard it before? "Yes. You know, that loveless act you introduced me to." That should remind him she'd been a virgin until that night they'd made love for the first time... just in case he'd forgotten.

What she was about to tell him might come as a surprise, and some might consider it too much information, but she needed him to fully understand her dilemma and her position. "I haven't slept with a man since you, Jaye. And the way I see it, since you are responsible for my present state, my sexual cravings, I think it's only fair that you and I get it on a few times and then I should be good for a while."

He stared at her for the longest time before saying, "Good for a while?"

"Yes, good until any sexual aches return. Hopefully, that won't be for another two years. By then I should have decided who my next sex partner will be after you."

JAYE COULDN'T BELIEVE what he was hearing. The woman sitting across from him looked like Velvet, but she sounded nothing like her. The Velvet Spencer he knew would never engage in meaningless sex. But then, he had to painfully remember what she'd assumed was meaningful sex had only brought her heartache.

He recalled every time she'd told him that she loved him, but he'd never said it in return. He'd been convinced he hadn't when deep down he truly had. If he told her that now, chances were she wouldn't believe him. Nor would she care because the bottom line was that she didn't love him anymore. That was something she had so eloquently stated. In essence, Velvet was giving him a taste of his own medicine. She was willing to engage in affairs that went nowhere, too. He was getting just what he deserved.

However, it was not what he would accept.

"So, Jaye, will you accept my proposal or offer whichever one you want to think of it as?"

He drew in a deep breath. Whether she knew it o not, just knowing that no other man had shared her be and her heart since him gave him hope. Regardless

what she said, he was considering what she *wasn't* saying. Yes, he would accept her offer but it was not with
the intent she had in mind. He was a strategic planner,
and his mind was already working on one to counter-
act her proposal.

Jaye had no intention of engaging in an insignificant,
inconsequential or irrelevant affair with her. Just the
opposite. He intended to make things so good between
them that their affair would become as meaningful as
it could get. Meaningful and permanent.

"Because what you're proposing is so unlike you,
Velvet. Regardless of everything you've said, I want
you to sleep on it and think hard about it."

She shrugged. "I'll sleep on it and think about it as
you've insisted, but I won't change my mind. Like I
said, Jaye, I'm a different person now. I don't see things
through rose-colored glasses. I see things a lot more
clearly than before, and what I don't see happening is
for me to ever fall in love again. Love and marriage are
no longer in my future."

He couldn't believe she was actually saying that.
Hell, he hoped not when his prime reason for being here
was for her to fall in love again. With him. He knew regaining her love wouldn't be easy, but with her current
mindset, it would be a lot harder than he'd expected.
Somehow, he had to convince her that love and marriage were still a part of her future—and his.

"And another thing, Jaye, there's one stipulation to
this arrangement."

Her words had intruded his thoughts. "What is that?"

"I don't want to go public with our affair."

She actually wanted them to sneak around? "Why not?"

"Mainly because you'll be leaving in a few months to return to Phoenix. I am a teacher in this community and prefer not to become the subject of small-town gossip over having an affair with the banker who ultimately dumps her to return to the girl back home."

He frowned. "I'm not involved with anyone back in Phoenix."

"That's what the rumor mill is saying whether it's true or not. After you leave, I want to retain my level of respectability."

He didn't say anything for a moment. "Is that what you truly want, Velvet? For us to sneak around?"

"Honestly, I don't see it as sneaking around, Jaye. I just see it as not broadcasting our business. Especially when we both know how things will end."

Jaye stood and crossed the room to her. "I hope you know what you're asking of me, Velvet. Just so you know, you aren't the only one who's been celibate for the past two years. I haven't shared a bed with anyone since you." He saw the shocked look on her face.

She tilted her head back to look up at him with disbelief in her eyes.

"It's the truth," he said.

"Why?" she asked.

"I only wanted you."

She didn't say anything for a moment, as if trying to make sense of what he'd admitted. Finally, she said "Then we agree your want of me is merely a sexua thing. In that case, I really don't understand what's th big deal of us having an affair. You act as if you' be doing something you're not used to doing, anywa

You'll be going back to how you operated before agreeing to an exclusive relationship with me."

That reminder didn't sit well with him. "And what about you, Velvet? Have you forgotten why I agreed to exclusivity with you? I wanted you in a bad way and you were not the type of woman to engage in casual affairs. Are you sure you can now?"

She broke eye contact with him and stared down at the floor for a moment before returning her gaze to his. In a quick instance, he saw the pain in her eyes. Pain she was trying to shield. Pain he knew he was responsible for. "Yes, I'm sure," she answered. "Like I said, I fell in love once and don't intend on ever doing it again. Besides, sex-only affairs are something you always enjoyed, so maybe it's time for me to give them a try."

Jaye felt he needed to get her to understand. "I just don't think you realize what you're asking of me," he said, holding her gaze with an intensity he wanted her to feel.

"Yes, I do. I know more than you'd ever realize. And since I know you don't love me and that I could never love you again, I feel comfortable with what I'm proposing. A sex-only affair. Maybe I need to demonstrate just how comfortable I am with it."

Then, standing on tiptoes, she leaned in and pressed her lips to his.

VELVET WAS CONVINCED the moment her lips touched Jaye's—everything within her suddenly came to life. And when he slid his tongue between her parted lips and began tangling with hers, every cell was bombarded with sensations she hadn't felt in two years.

It amazed her how easily and effortlessly he could make her moan. With Jaye, it had always been about pleasure of the most intense kind. Pleasure that was so deep and hot it could overwhelm her senses and push her body into a need that was all-consuming.

When he changed the angle of his mouth and pulled her closer to fit against him, she felt his hard erection, which was a telltale sign of how aroused he was. She was just as aroused.

Together, their tongues began mating in the sensuous way that was so familiar. This is what she had gone without for two years and four months and…fourteen days. Her lips and tongue knew his and were fully aware of the pleasure Jaye could deliver.

Like he was doing now.

When he suddenly broke off the kiss, dropped his hands from her waist and took a step back, she tried to keep the disappointment out of her expression. "What's wrong?" she asked, after pulling in a much-needed breath.

"Nothing's wrong, Velvet. I just want you to be sure about this, because if I agree to your offer, there's no turning back."

No turning back? Did he think she hadn't accepted that the sole purpose of their affair would be for her to share his bed and for him to share hers while she got her fill of him? "Like I told you, Jaye. I'm not the same person. From now on, it's about satisfying a physical need for me just like it's always been for you. Besides, it's not like you're going to remain in Catalina Cove. You'll be leaving in a few months, anyway."

He didn't say anything for the longest moment. H

just looked at her in the way he always had when trying to figure out something about her. Honestly, what was there to figure out?

"Regardless, I still want you to think about it, to make sure you're making the right decision," he finally said.

There was nothing for her to think about when her mind was made up. If she'd had any doubts before, they'd been eradicated by that kiss they'd just shared—the one she had boldly initiated.

"Fine, I'll think about it, Jaye. And I suggest you do the same. I want you to be sure that getting involved with me again, even for just a short while, is something you want to do."

When he remained silent—as to whether he needed to think about it or not—she figured that could only mean one thing. "If you're worried that I will become attached, then don't. I learned my lesson and, like I said, falling in love is not part of the equation this time for me." Hopefully, what she just stated would assure him that he had nothing to worry about.

He looked down at the floor as if he were considering her words. She knew at that moment that she'd been right. The only reason he was hesitant was because he needed to make sure she didn't fall in love with him again, especially when he knew that he wasn't capable of loving her.

Then she remembered something. "What was it you needed to talk to me about?"

He finally looked up at her. "I wanted to let you know 'll be leaving town on a business trip in the morning nd wanted to kiss you before I left."

She blinked. "Why would you want to kiss me?"

He took a step closer, and with his gaze locked on hers, he said in a low husky voice, "The same reason you kissed me just now. You and I generate a lot of sensual heat, Velvet. Nothing has changed about that. Besides, I've always enjoyed kissing you."

Yes, he did. But then, she'd always enjoyed kissing him, too. "Well, you got your kiss. Please have a safe trip, Jaye."

He shook his head. "No, I got *your* kiss, Velvet. The one you gave me. Now I want you to have mine. The one I'm about to give you."

The next thing she knew, Jaye drew her into his arms and took her mouth with an intensity she could feel in every part of her body. When she had kissed him earlier, he had let her be in control. Now he was. There was just something about a Jaye Colfax kiss, and when he deepened it, fierce desire surged through her to settle deep in her bones.

Velvet sensed a flare of heat between her legs at the same moment her breasts felt full and sensitive, and her nipples hardened. Their lips were fused together while his tongue tangled with hers in a way that had her senses spinning. Pressure began building up, and it was as if her entire body below the waist was on fire.

Then it happened. Her body exploded in an orgasm so intense, she saw stars and felt as if she'd been rocketed out of this hemisphere.

He didn't let up until the last spasm had flowed from her body. When he released her mouth, he swept her into his arms. Was he carrying her to the bedroom now?

Would he make love to her tonight? Multiple orgasms had always been their specialty.

She moaned in protest when instead of taking her to the bedroom, he placed her on the sofa. She felt weak as she fought to recover from the first orgasm she'd had with a man in two years. Ironically, it had been with the same man.

She was about to say something but was too drained to speak. He hunched down beside the sofa and stared at her with penetrating dark eyes. "Are you, okay?"

She still couldn't speak so she just nodded.

He reached out and touched her ear. "I'm glad you found your earring."

What he said registered. Had he figured she'd lied about losing it? "Me, too," she managed to say, refusing to own up to it now.

"We both have a lot to think about while I'm gone. We'll talk when I get back." He leaned in and placed a kiss on her lips before standing. "Good night, Velvet. I'll lock the door behind me."

She watched him cross the room to leave, knowing when they did sleep together, they wouldn't just burn up the sheets—they'd burn up each other as well.

CHAPTER TWELVE

"You want to talk about it, son?"

Jaye looked over at his father. All the Colfaxes had arrived in Birmingham for the groundbreaking ceremony. It was in an ideal location for the newest Colfax Bank and tonight they would celebrate. Dinner reservations had been made and they were seated, waiting for his brothers, Dean and Franklin, to arrive. Although his dad had retired, he still liked giving his advice on any bank acquisitions. Jaye always welcomed whatever his father had to say.

He recalled when he'd told his father about his desire to purchase a bank in Catalina Cove, his father had questioned why that location instead of another highly populated Louisiana city. That's when Jaye had told him the reason. He would be acquiring more than a bank, if things worked out the way he hoped, he would be getting back the woman he loved. His father had wished him the best.

His father and his brothers had adored Velvet. They, too, had seen what Jaye had refused to see. That she was a keeper and the woman he'd fallen in love with even when he'd sworn that he hadn't.

There was no way he would talk to his father about

Velvet's proposal, but he would bring him up to date on how things were going with them.

"There's not a lot to talk about, Dad. Regaining Velvet's love isn't as easy as I thought it would be."

His father took a sip of his wine as he gazed at him. Jaye knew that look. It was one of those I-told-you-so stares. His father had warned him there was a chance that Velvet had moved on with her life and he was someone in her past she preferred to stay there.

"What's really sad is that you honestly thought that it would be easy, Jaye."

No, he hadn't thought that, but he figured he had a plan and time on his side. What he hadn't expected was the proposal she'd offered him, where she made it clear all she wanted from him was sex. Just like he'd assumed in the beginning that that had been all he'd wanted from her.

"I didn't think it would be easy, Dad. I just assumed if she truly loved me, she would still have some feelings for me. Feelings that I could rekindle."

"And you've discovered she doesn't."

He took a sip of wine. "That's what she says." But there was no way he could accept that. "I still plan on getting her back, Dad."

"You can only do so if she lets you, Jaye. The worst thing you can become is a nuisance."

No way he would tell his dad that Velvet didn't see him as a nuisance but the man she wanted to scratch her sexual itch. "I won't become a nuisance, but I'm determined more than ever to regain her love and her trust."

Jaye swirled the wine in his glass and then looked at

his father. "How did you do it? You sent Arlene away at first."

"Yes, but not for two years. That's a long time. I came to my senses about Arlene in less than two weeks. Even then, I had to prove to her just how much she meant to me. I thought that was your plan for Velvet."

"It was and still is, but she's convinced that she no longer loves me."

"If that's true, then what do you plan to do? I know how much you love her, Jaye, and for you, giving up and walking away is not an option, is it?"

"No, it's not. I love her too much and already I might have competition."

His father lifted a brow. "She's involved with someone?"

"No. In fact, it's my understanding she hasn't dated since ending things with me."

"Just like you haven't dated since things ended with her," his father said. "So, who is your competition?"

Jaye told his father about Webb Crawford's visit. Not surprisingly, his father shook his head and said the man had a few screws loose if he thought his arrogant attitude was a way to win over Velvet.

Jaye thought so, too. At least the old Velvet wouldn't tolerate such foolishness. However, this new Velvet concerned him. She claimed she wasn't looking for forever anymore, just a bed partner. That was all Crawford wanted as well. Jaye knew he had to convince Velvet she was much more than that to any man. "I made a mess of things and intend to fix it."

"So, I'm going to ask you again, Jaye, what are you going to do?"

Jaye released a frustrated sigh, when he thought of his last conversation with Velvet. Maybe giving Velvet what she wanted, or thought she wanted, wouldn't be a bad idea. Especially if it would give him time to convince her they would be sharing love and not just lust.

He would make things so good between them that the little *fling* she wanted would become something more meaningful and permanent. "Nothing has changed. I intend to repair the damage I caused, but with a new strategy."

"And what strategy is that?"

"Not anything specific, but nothing is off the table."

And Jaye meant *nothing*. He didn't like the idea of them not going public because of possible small-town gossip, but he had to remember they weren't in Phoenix. They were in Catalina Cove, Louisiana. From the short while he'd lived there, he knew most of the people were good and not judgmental. However, there were those who thought they had a right to know everything that went on. They were the same people who expected high morals and virtuous behavior even if their own were questionable.

For that reason, he could understand Velvet's concern. Maybe keeping out of sight of prying eyes was a good thing for now, especially when he intended to make sure the house on Blueberry Lane became the place when their love would blossom again.

"I wish you success, Jaye. You know how I feel about Velvet. She was the best thing to ever happen to you. I'm sorry you let what happened between me and your mother be the reason you refused to fall in love. But then I did the same thing for years." Jack Colfax, Sr., took another sip of wine. "Now that I know what it's like to have a good woman in my life, I want the same thing for my sons. I honestly hope things work out between you and Velvet."

Jaye nodded. He was hoping for the same thing.

"AND JAYE DIDN'T tell you when he'd be back, Velvet?"

Dressed in her pj's, Velvet sat at the kitchen table talking to Ruthie. She'd finally gotten around to calling her best friend to tell her how things had gone down between her and Jaye Monday night. Of course, Ruthie had been pleased Velvet had taken her advice to have a fling with Jaye. Especially since she'd admitted to Ruthie months ago, before Jaye even arrived in town, that she was going through sexual withdrawal. Now, after experiencing her first orgasm in two years, she was convinced what she was now facing was an addiction. To her detriment, those wants, needs and desires were only for Jaye.

"No. All he said was that he was going away on business."

"I'm a little disappointed," Ruthie said. "I would have thought that once you told him what you wanted and needed, he would have acted immediately. Why is he giving you time to think about anything?"

"I told you why. He's not comfortable in accepting this *new* Velvet because she's the total opposite from the old. He wants to make sure my mind is in the right place for a sex-only affair. He needs to be certain since he doesn't love me and at no time wants me to think that he does."

"And he told you that?"

"No, but what other possible reason could there be? I could ruin things by falling in love with him again and Jaye and I both know that. I'm hoping that I pretty much convinced him that it won't happen, but he's probably worried that it might. That means all through this process, I need to keep reminding him it's sex-only."

She immediately stopped talking when she heard a sound outside. "I heard a car pull up. Do you think it's Jaye returning home?"

"Honestly, Vel, how would I know? It's Wednesday night and according to you, he left yesterday morning. I'd think he would have been gone at least two days. That's how it was whenever he traveled before when you were together, right?"

"Yes."

"Then chances are it's not him. Could it be someone else? Sierra perhaps?"

"She would call before just dropping by," Velvet said.

"What about that guy who wants you? Webb what's-his-name?"

"It better not be him."

"What if it is?" Ruthie countered.

Velvet got up from the table and discreetly peeked out the window. "It's him, Ruthie!" she said, excitedly.

"Him who? Jaye or Webb?"

"Jaye. And I hear the sound of footsteps on my porch. He's coming to my door. What do you think?" Velvet glanced down at herself. Her pj's were a cutesy pair of leggings and a top that didn't reveal anything.

"I'd rather not say what I think, but I have a feeling there might be some action at your place tonight. Maybe you'll finally rid yourself of all those sexless hours you've accumulated over the past two years." Ruthie chuckled.

When there was a knock at the door, Velvet said, "He's knocking."

"Aren't you going to answer it?"

"He probably just wants to let me know he's back," she said, walking to the door.

Ruthie laughed. "If you say so."

"Hold on, Ruthie," she said, placing her cell phone on the foyer table. She called out, "Who is it?"

"Jaye."

She opened the door and he stood there. The soft porch light seemed to highlight everything about him. He was dressed in a business suit that fit him perfectly and emphasized the successful businessman that he was. That she always loved. She quickly reprogrammed her mind to mean that she *used to* love.

"I'm back, Velvet."

Did he appear at her door just to tell her that? In the old days whenever Jaye returned from a business trip, the moment she opened the door he would sweep her into his arms and carry her to the bedroom. "Thanks for letting me know. Good night."

Velvet was about to close the door when he said, "Wait."

She raised a brow. Could he not see the longing in her eyes? Seeing him standing there, looking all tall, built and hot was having an effect on her, reminding her of the orgasm he'd given her the other night. "Yes?"

"Did you think about the offer you made to me, Velvet?"

She could tell him there was no need for her to think

about her offer. Instead, she said, "Yes, I thought about it and nothing has changed, Jaye. Did you think about it?"

"Yes, I thought about it."

She tilted her head. "And?"

"And I cut my trip short to come back. May I come in?"

Velvet nodded and took a step back. The look in his eyes was dark and intense and she nervously licked her lips. Just because he cut his trip short, it didn't mean he was in favor of her offer. What if he wasn't?

After closing the door behind him, she remembered Ruthie was still on the phone. "Excuse me a second," she said, quickly scooting past him to grab her cell phone off the table. "Ruthie?"

"I heard, girlfriend. Now go handle your business."

Ruthie's words were followed by a resounding click in Velvet's ear.

CHAPTER THIRTEEN

"SORRY. I DIDN'T know you were on a call." Jaye looked at Velvet with his hands shoved into his pants pockets. He needed to keep them there. Otherwise, he would reach out and pull her to him and give her the kiss he needed. What he'd told her was true. He had cut his trip short. What he hadn't said was that he'd returned early because he hadn't been able to get her off his mind.

"No problem. It was just Ruthie telling me how her wedding plans were coming along," she said. "Do you want something to drink?"

"Sure, a beer would be nice."

"Okay. One beer coming up."

He watched her head for the kitchen. One thing he remembered well was that Velvet liked wearing some of the cutest pj's, although he would eventually take them off her. She said pj's always made her feel sexy and she'd always looked the part.

When she had opened the front door and stood there and his gaze had roamed over her, appreciating her in a pair of pink leggings and a printed pinkish blouse, he'd almost been speechless because it looked so good on her shapely body.

Last night, when he couldn't sleep, he'd ended up sitting out on the hotel's balcony and remembering all the time they had spent together after they'd first met. For three years, he had assumed everything between them was perfect. Deep down, a part of him had known she'd meant the world to him, but he'd never been able to admit that to himself.

"Here you are," she said, returning with a beer. He could tell from the way her nipples were pressing against the fabric of her top that she wasn't wearing a bra. Chances were she wasn't wearing underwear, either. Just the thought riled his libido.

"Thanks," he said, standing. He uncapped it and took a huge gulp, knowing she was watching him. He lowered the bottle and licked his lips. "That was good."

"Glad you like it."

She was looking at him in a way that sent tingles up and down his spine. "You want some of my beer?"

"Yes." She accepted the bottle from him.

She looked at him as she tipped the beer to her own lips, and a wave of desire flooded his insides.

She handed the beer back to him. "Now I wish I hadn't done that."

"Why not?" He finished off the rest, liking the thought that his mouth was where hers had been just seconds ago.

"It brought back too many memories."

It had for him, too, but he wouldn't complain. Nor did he have any regrets. They had been good together, both in and out of the bedroom. Now he was determined to get her to see there was an out-of-the-bedroom for them, even while keeping her in the bedroom. The chemistry between them seemed stronger than ever, and he'd honestly thought such a thing wasn't possible.

"It brought back memories for me, too, Velvet."

The room got quiet for a moment and then she broke the silence. "You said you thought about my offer." As if those memories were overpowering her, she moved to sit down on the sofa.

"Yes, I gave it a lot of thought."

"And what did you decide?"

He gripped the empty bottle in his hands and joined her on the sofa. "I decided that I will give you whatever you want. No matter what it is."

He saw a flash of something in her eyes and recognized it for what it was. Skepticism. Knowing she doubted his words made him more determined than ever to prove he meant what he said.

"Are you sure about that, Jaye?"

"I'm positive. So, tell me what you want, Velvet."

Their gazes held for the longest time, and the way she was looking at him made him more aware of her than ever. If she could read the look in his eyes, then she would know the depth of his love for her. His desire and his need.

"Do you really want me to tell you?"

"Yes, I really want you to tell me what you want," he said.

She nodded and said in a soft voice, "I want you to take care of my sexual cravings, Jaye."

Standing, he extended his hand to her. She took it and he gently pulled Velvet to her feet and then swept her into his arms.

SHE GAVE HIM directions to her bedroom and after he placed her on the bed, he stepped back, and she watched as he removed his jacket and tie.

"The only question I need to ask you is how you want it, Velvet? Hard or easy?"

She swallowed. Jaye hadn't done it easy with her since that first time when he'd discovered she was a virgin. After that, they'd gone straight into hard. And hard was the way she preferred it. "You know how I like it, Jaye."

"Yes, but I want you to tell me. I won't assume anything with you."

She wondered why. "Physically, my needs are the same, Jaye. Emotionally, they are not. Unlike before, I know what not to expect from our intimacy." She'd tacked on the latter as a reminder that he didn't have to worry about her wanting and expecting more like she had before.

And just in case he needed further clarity, she said, "Sex is all I want from you." Was she mistaken or had something just flashed through his eyes? It was as if what she'd said had disturbed him. There was no reason it should have so she must have been mistaken.

"If hard is the way you want it, sweetheart, then hard is how you'll get it."

Sweetheart? Now why did he have to go there and use that term of endearment? He'd used it when they were together before, but in the end he'd proved he hadn't meant anything by it. Her biggest mistake was in thinking he had.

He came close to the bed and pulled her to her feet. She wrapped her arms around his neck and pushed to the back of her mind the fact that she was about to do something with him that—since the day she left Phoenix—she thought she'd never do again.

He leaned in and slanted his mouth over hers, and the moment their lips touched, her entire body came alive. Although they had kissed twice Monday night, and one of those had resulted in her first orgasm in two years, she knew sharing a bed and getting the total sexual experience with Jaye was different.

His tongue was moving inside her mouth so seductively and with painstaking precision. He deepened the kiss, just the way she liked, and wound his tongue around hers, reminding her just how well Jaye could kiss.

Then there came the part when he totally possessed her mouth. He locked his lips to hers and she barely remembered to breathe. And with a mind of their own, her hips began moving, grinding passionately against his hard erection.

When the intensity of his kiss had her stomach trembling, he suddenly broke off and stared down at her with enough hot desire in his eyes to melt her bones.

Heat simmered through her veins, his masculine scent flooded her nostrils, and the throbbing sensation between her legs grew so intense she moaned. Why was he just standing there, looking at her that way? The look in his eyes only made her hotter.

"Why did you stop kissing me, Jaye?" She didn't want to sound needy, but she desperately wanted to know.

"Because I know where the kiss was headed and there are other parts of you I ache to explore besides your mouth. Like I told you, Velvet. It's been two years for me, too, and I'm having sexual cravings as well."

UNABLE TO WAIT any longer, Jaye took a step back and began removing his shirt, knowing she was watching his every move. When he heard her breath catch, he met her gaze and the sexual chemistry between them was as explosive as it had ever been.

He sat down in a nearby chair to remove his shoes and socks. Then he stood and their gazes held as he began unzipping his pants. It didn't take long to ease them down his thighs and legs, along with his briefs. He heard her moan when he stood before her totally naked.

When she made a move to take off her top, he said, "No. I want to undress you, Velvet." He wondered if his words made her remember all those other times that he had undressed her and all the things he would do to her while doing so.

When she nodded her consent, he slowly moved to the bed as his gaze roamed over her, wondering where he should start. By the time he reached her bed, he had decided to begin at her feet and work his way up, saving the middle for last.

Lifting each leg, he removed her slippers, and then slowly began massaging first one foot and then the other. She had such dainty feet and she'd always taken good care of them. Her toes were painted a bright coral to match the color of her fingernails. Then while she watched, he licked her toes. She knew what that meant. There was no part of her body he didn't intend to taste tonight.

He wouldn't say he had a foot fetish, but he would say that he hadn't desired to get intimate with a woman's feet until Velvet. There was just something about nibbling her heels and ankles that was a huge turn-on for him. From her prior responses, it had been one for her. He wanted to see if it still was.

He took his time and tasted her feet while holding her gaze. He knew when her breathing pattern changed and how she was clutching the bedspread, she was close. One night, he'd made her come just from sucking her toes.

"Jaye…"

"Humm?"

"I—I…"

"You what, sweetheart?"

"I won't be able to last."

He smiled. She'd always said that like there was a limit with the time he spent on any part of her body. "Yes, you will. I'll make sure you do."

Not to torture her too much, he placed her legs on his shoulders to ease off her leggings and, just as he thought, she wasn't wearing undies. The moment her womanly core was exposed, his shaft hardened even more at the thought of pumping hard inside her. Refusing to let those thoughts distract him, he quickly whipped her top over her head. Just that quick, she was completely naked.

He focused on her breasts. Those two luscious mounds he enjoyed licking so much; he recalled a couple of nights he'd dozed off with her nipple in his mouth. He licked his lips just looking at them and, as if they knew what they were in for, the nipples appeared to harden even more, right before his eyes. He met her gaze, knowing she knew what he wanted. And just like she'd done many times in the past, she lifted one up and offered it to him.

Lowering her legs from his shoulders, he moved toward her and took what she offered.

CHAPTER FOURTEEN

JAYE HAD EASED her nipple into his mouth, and before he could get in more than a few hard sucks, an orgasm ripped through her and she nearly bucked off the bed.

Velvet was convinced she was losing her mind when suddenly her world began spinning again and a throb pulsed anew between her legs. Was this happening because she hadn't had sex for two years? Deep down, she knew it had nothing to do with her lack of getting laid, and everything to do with the man staring down at her. And when his gaze roamed down her body, she knew his intent.

"Your scent is calling my name, Velvet. I have to taste you."

His voice was deep, rich and sensual. She knew Jaye Colfax's tongue well, and knew what all it could do. He slid off the bed and pulled her close to its edge. Lordy, this man who claimed he was just as sex-craved as she was, intended to make a feast of her.

As if he'd read her thoughts, he said, "This is what going without the only woman you want for two years will do to you."

Velvet was tempted to ask him why he hadn't moved on, then decided not to bother. It really didn't matter because he was letting her know his need and desire for her was just as intense as hers for him. She watched as he went to his knees in front of her spread legs. He didn't say anything as he stared at her womanly folds. It was as if he was drinking in the sight of her while thinking about all he intended to do to her.

Her inner muscles began quivering and she could feel her sex clench in anticipation, waiting for his next move. Then he looked at her and said, "I'm going to give you as many orgasms as possible while getting my fill. Okay?"

All she could do was lay there with her legs spread open in front of him and nod.

When he lifted her legs to his shoulders again, the chemistry flowing between them became primal, raw and elemental. Their gazes held, transfixed for the longest time until, finally, he widened her legs a little more. Licking his lips, he said in a deep, guttural voice, "If only you knew how much I miss tasting you, Velvet. Loving you this way."

"Show me," she said, barely breathing out the words.

"I intend to." And then he lowered his head between her legs.

THE MOMENT JAYE'S tongue had its first taste of Velvet, after going without for two years, he was convinced this, like every other part of her, belonged to him. He loved her taste and he loved her. How on earth could he have thought that he hadn't?

Her moans made all kinds of sensations nearly overwhelm him. He'd missed the sound of her getting pleasure as much as he'd missed giving it to her. He'd never been sure what it was about her that made his need to taste her like this so intense. What it was that could fill him with so many emotions. He stroked her with his tongue and sucked her clit. When he pressed his tongue deeper inside her, he wanted to clamp his mouth down on her, lock in and taste her forever.

She screamed and her thighs began trembling, but he didn't let up. Like he'd told her, he intended for his tongue to stay inside her until he'd gotten his fill.

After she experienced another orgasm, he finally pulled back and looked at her. He smiled at the thought of just how satisfied she appeared, lying there spread out before him.

"God, you're beautiful, Vel," he whispered and meant it. Even down to the polished fingertips that were gripping the bedspread. He had pushed her over the edge a number of times already, and he'd barely just begun.

At that moment, he felt a closeness to her that their two years of separation couldn't diminish. He was connected to her in a way he knew he'd never be to any other woman. He hadn't meant to fall in love with her, but he had. Now he had to prove to her the depth of that love.

"Now for the icing on the cake," he said, scooting her body to the center of the bed. His eyes roamed over her as he said, "Like I told you, I haven't been with a woman since you, Velvet. I'll put on a condom if you want me to."

She shook her head. "There's no need, Jaye. I still get injections. Besides, I want the feel of you exploding inside of me."

Her words made him want her even more. She was the only woman he'd ever shared his essence with and intended for her to be the only woman that he ever would. "Then I won't use a condom."

Moments later when his body was positioned over hers, she unclutched the bedspread and gently caressed his back and shoulders a few times before reaching up to cup his face in her hands. "You do things to me, Jaye," she said in a low voice.

"We do things to each other." He leaned close to her ear and said, "I'm going to make love to you, Velvet."

"We will have sex," she countered, releasing his face.

In all the many times their bodies had joined, it had always been about making love—even though he hadn't realized it. It had never been about just sex and that, he knew, would be his challenge. In making her see what he now knew, what had been true all along.

Jaye wouldn't waste his time arguing with her. Especially not now. Instead, he would show her. There was no doubt in his mind that over time, his demonstrations would be convincing. He captured her mouth and slid his tongue between lips that easily parted for him. Both passion and greed took over his senses, and he wanted to absorb everything that was Velvet into every part of him. She kissed him back with just as much hunger.

While still kissing her, he reached down and began massaging her clit. Instantly, he felt her body buck beneath his fingers. He felt her grip on his shoulders and didn't wince when her fingertips dug into his skin. He felt no pain. Instead, he felt pleasure of the most intense kind.

Breaking off their kiss, he whispered against her moist lips. "I can't wait any longer. I need you and I want you."

She opened her mouth but whatever she'd intended to say was replaced with a moan when his fingers continued to stroke inside her. "Tell me what you want, baby. Tell me."

She held his gaze as he slowly pumped his fingers in and out. Instead of answering, she began moaning again. He didn't intend to let her off with not telling him what he wanted to know. "Tell me, Velvet."

She released a deep breath and said, "I want you inside me, Jaye. Real deep."

"And I will give you what you want," he whispered huskily, pulling his fingers free and then licking them as she watched, seeing desire darken her eyes.

He eased inside her and when he was halfway there, he pushed deeper with a powerful thrust.

"Jaye!"

When he was as deep as he could go, he began moving and threw his head back to breathe in her scent. Her inner muscles began clenching him hard, then harder.

"Velvet…"

He was thrusting deeply and became wrapped up in passion of the most intense kind. Jaye pounded into her, making sure he hit the right spot, the exact location, to give her ultimate pleasure. Suddenly, she cried out, screaming out an orgasm, and he kept going, going and going.

The sound of her coming apart fueled his need and he thrust even harder. She asked for it hard and, like he told her, he intended to give her everything that she wanted. When she screamed again and her body began bucking beneath him, his own body exploded in what felt like an intense ball of sensuous fire.

It seemed to take forever to conclude their orgasmic high. And when she moaned out his name again, it threw them into another sexual frenzy, which propelled him to take her all over again.

CHAPTER FIFTEEN

VELVET SLOWLY OPENED her eyes when she heard the sound of her alarm going off. Then, when she felt a warm hard body pressed against her naked one, she recalled everything about last night and before dawn.

Jaye had stayed the night.

That realization had her pulling herself up in bed to turn off the alarm. She pushed hair back from her face to look down at the man still sleeping. She wasn't surprised that he'd slept through the alarm. That was a Jaye thing. She'd discovered early in their relationship that he had his own built-in alarm. That's what he went by and had the ability to tune out any others.

She eased back down, deciding another thirty minutes of snooze time wouldn't hurt. Turning to face Jaye, she studied his features. No man should look this good while sleeping, and she was convinced the older he got, the more handsome he looked. But then all the Colfax men were totally gorgeous. Even Jaye's father had a debonair and distinguished look about him.

Velvet's thoughts shifted to last night. Jaye had said something about getting his fill—well, she'd certainly gotten hers. After the last seven hours, he should be out of her system, and she hoped he was. She recalled once telling Sierra how her hormones had gotten out of whack so bad one night that she'd considered going back to Phoenix for a one-night fling with Jaye just to get a sexual fix and then disappear again.

She wouldn't need a short-term affair with him, after all. Because of the intensity and frequency of last night's roll between the sheets, she was confident all her sexual needs and desires were taken care of for another two years. Maybe even more. Jaye had been just that thorough. Now she could begin functioning without her hormones getting the best of her. If that were true, then why was an ache forming between her legs just from laying here, looking at him? And why could she explicitly recall all the times last night when her legs had opened wide and he'd slid inside her, giving her body what it wanted, needed and desired.

While she was staring intently at him, his eyes suddenly opened and her breath caught. She was reminded of other times she had awakened before him and he'd caught her staring. She also recalled what always happened next. He would pull her into his arms, give her a kiss that curled her toes and then make love to her all over again.

"Good morning, Velvet."

"Good morning, Jaye."

She didn't want Jaye to begin thinking that waking up in her bed would become the norm. Last night's sex marathon had been different. It had been needed, and although she should feel tired, she felt energized and rejuvenated.

"We need to talk, Jaye."

"First, we need to do this," he said, pulling her close and taking control of her mouth.

Velvet knew she should say something, but discovered she was unable to say anything—nor did she want to. She rather enjoyed the way Jaye was working his mouth over hers, taking her tongue like he had a right to claim ownership. Because it felt so good, she would let him do it. This one time.

When he released her mouth, they were both panting, and when he reached out for her, to pull her closer into his arms, she regained her senses and pushed back against his chest. "We need to talk, Jaye, and then I need to get ready for work."

"Okay."

Okay? When had he ever agreed with her whenever it was about being turned down for sex? And why was he looking at her like that? With a degree of hunger reflected in his gaze that should be outlawed.

"Is something wrong, Velvet?" he asked, taking her hand and lifting it to his lips to kiss her knuckles.

"What make you think something is wrong?"

He shrugged. "You said you wanted to talk but you aren't saying anything."

She rubbed her hand down her face. "You're confusing me, Jaye."

"I don't mean to. So, what do you want to talk about?"

"Moving forward, I don't want you to assume we'll automatically become bed partners. In fact, last night was it for us. I'm good."

He smiled, showing those dimples she loved. "Yes, sweetheart, you are good, and I'm glad last night was it for us."

She frowned. That honestly wasn't what she'd expected to hear. "Why?"

"Because I'm not into *sex-only* relationships anymore. Last night, I made you an exception."

He had to be kidding. "Why aren't you into sex-only relationships anymore?"

He paused as if collecting his thoughts, so she said, "No need to answer. I already know."

He lifted a brow. "You do?"

"Yes."

"And what do you know, Velvet?"

"That some of the people you hang out with, namely those Steele Brothers, are no longer single. So now you figure maybe it's time to take a social break before moving forward and getting back into the game."

When he didn't say anything, she asked, "Well, am I right?"

He frowned. "No, you're totally wrong. If anything, you should know that I am not influenced by what others are doing. I am happy for the Steeles and think the women they've married are worthy of their love, but my decision to end my sex-only relationships is not about that."

"Then what is it about?"

"It's about me facing the reasons why I had done it in the first place."

She'd known the reason, although he'd never shared it with her. She knew it had to do with his mother's desertion. That had always been one subject he'd made off-limits. Was it something he would share with her now? Maybe not at this second but at some point? "And have you faced the reasons, Jaye?"

"Yes."

She would have loved to hear the full details, but she

knew if he wanted her to know anything more, he would eventually tell her. Deciding to change the subject, she said, "We didn't finish talking about Webb Crawford."

"No, we didn't."

"Well, just so you know, I went to see him to reiterate my position. I can't believe he's going around telling guys that I'm off-limits. Webb is the last man on earth I'd go out with. He's too full of himself and not worth my time."

"Now that's something we both agree on," Jaye said, swinging his leg over the edge of the bed. He looked back at her. "Ready?"

She lifted a brow. "Ready for what?"

"To go jogging with me."

She couldn't hide the shock on her face. "You want me to go jogging with you?"

"Sure. Why not?"

Why not? Was she missing something here? "You've never asked me before. In fact, it's always been understood that jogging is your private time to think, strategize and plan."

"Not anymore. I want your company."

"Why?"

"I'd like to know what's been going on with you since you left Phoenix."

"You know all you need to know, Jaye." She stood to grab her robe from the back of the chair. "Besides, we shouldn't be seen together."

He chuckled. "And who's going to see us in the blueberry fields behind our house?"

Probably no one and he knew it. Plus, hadn't she made a New Year's resolution to get more physically fit? Granted, teaching that gymnastics class helped, but she wanted to do more. She hadn't imagined doing it with Jaye.

Velvet thought about what he'd said about using their jogging time to find out what had been going on with her since they parted ways. She wondered if he knew that meant she would inquire into what he'd been doing as well. Jaye never liked sharing anything about his work with her—or anything personal, for that matter. He'd had the position that their time together was about pleasure and not business.

"Velvet?"

She realized he'd been waiting for an answer, one way or the other. "Fine, I'll start jogging with you, but not today. I want to go shopping for jogging clothes. I'll start jogging with you tomorrow."

"Okay."

She sighed, thinking that this *agreeable* Jaye was going to take some getting used to. It wasn't that he'd made it a practice to be disagreeable, but he had liked ruffling her feathers only to take her to the bedroom to unruffle them. Seeing him standing in the middle of her bedroom naked wasn't helping matters, either.

Finding her voice, she said, "When you get dressed, I'll walk you to the door." She moved to walk around him to the bathroom.

He reached out and took hold of her hand and their eyes met. Instantly, heat began radiating between them. She wasn't sure who made the next move, but they tumbled back on the bed. In no time at all, he'd removed her robe and she was straddling him.

"We shouldn't be doing this again, Jaye." She stared down at him.

"No, we shouldn't."

There he was being agreeable again. "But we will," she said, easing down on his ramrod straight erection.

She watched his eyes darken with desire and he replied in a deep throaty voice, "Yes, we will."

JAYE LOOKED UP from studying the pile of documents on his desk when his intercom buzzer sounded. Pressing the button, he said, "Yes, Ms. Carter?"

"Your two o'clock appointment is here."

"Thanks. Please send Mr. Sullivan in."

Jaye had been surprised when he looked at his roster of appointments that morning and saw Ray Sullivan's name. Ray had made national news a few years ago when the man—who everyone believed to be dead— was found living in Catalina Cove with retrograde amnesia. It was his wife who'd found him, when she came to the cove to deal with the grief of losing said husband.

Although Reid Lacroix was the wealthiest man in the cove, very few people knew that Ray was a close second. Before Ray's memory loss when he'd become the jeans-and-T-shirt-wearing, bearded ship captain of a touring boat business, he'd been Devon Ryan, a Harvard-educated, tailor-made-business-suit-wearing suave wealthy tycoon. Although one and the same, Devon Ryan was the total opposite of Ray, even after his memory had returned. He'd told his family and friends he preferred to be Ray. That might be the case, but he still had the wealthy tycoon instinct of Devon Ryan. In other words, whatever Ray touched turned to gold.

Like the water-taxi service that would soon be opening in Catalina Cove.

When the door opened, Jaye stood from behind his desk and Ray Sullivan walked in, smiling. Jaye liked Ray as a businessman and as someone he'd gotten to know as a friend after moving to the cove. "Ray, what brings you here today? Another money-making venture?" he asked, shaking the man's hand.

"No. Something else altogether," he said, taking the chair Jaye offered him.

Jaye nodded as he took the seat behind his desk. "And before it slips my mind, I want to say congratulations. I heard the news from Vaughn that you and Ashley are expecting."

Ray's smile widened. "Yes, we are, and we're happy about it. We waited long enough to have kids and now it seems we can't get enough of the darlings."

It was obvious that Ray, with his growing family, was a very happy man. That was something else Velvet would see was different about him—he'd always liked kids, but figured he wouldn't have any since he hadn't planned on ever marrying. Now, not only did he plan to get married, but he couldn't wait to see Velvet pregnant with his child.

"I'm here to invite you to a party."

Ray's words brought his thoughts back to the present. "A party?"

"Yes. It's a surprise groom and bridal shower for Vaughn and Sierra. Kaegan is hosting it at his and Bryce's place on the Bayou and you're invited."

Kaegan Chambray, who owned a seafood shipping company, was another guy Jaye had met since living in Catalina Cove. He'd heard about Kaegan's parties and all the good food that was served. The man liked to entertain and usually held an annual party for his employees, and during the year he held others for his friends. Jaye felt honored to be invited. And what made it doubly nice was that he knew Velvet was part of the wedding party, so chances were she would be there, too.

"Thanks for the invite, Ray, and I'd love to attend."

"Good."

After Ray left, Jaye leaned back in the chair, knowing he needed to get back to work but he'd rather just sit there and let memories of last night and this morning consume him. He had needed Velvet as much as she had needed him and all that need had been fiery and, at times, out of control. He didn't want to think about all they'd done, how many sexual positions they had enjoyed and how many orgasms they'd shared. Just thinking about it was making him aroused again.

He stood and walked to the window to look out at the water. Now, this was something he could definitely appreciate, the view of the gulf from this window. Another thing he could appreciate was being in Velvet's bed again. Although she'd let him know not to assume anything, that was fine with him. The one thing he needed for her to see was—just like he'd told her—he was no longer into sex-only relationships.

Now, it was time he told her the reason. The subject of his mother had always been difficult for him. The only people who knew how deeply her desertion had affected him were his father, brothers, Mercury and the other Steele brothers. He figured no one else needed to know. He'd been wrong, because Velvet *had* needed to know. Hopefully, when he explained things to her, she would understand why he'd built that wall around his heart. A wall she had eventually torn down.

Jaye checked his watched. Since he'd worked through lunch, he might as well go grab something now. He smiled at the thought that Velvet had agreed to go jogging with him and was even buying outfits to do so. She was right when she'd said jogging had always been his private time to think, strategize and plan. Little did she know all those efforts were now centered around one thing, more specifically, one person: her.

VELVET LOVED SHOPPING at the stores on Main Street, which was a stone's throw away from the pier. Today had turned out to be a nice day. That was the one thing she loved about Catalina Cove's weather in mid-February. It was always comfortably cool. However, since she was close to the pier, it was a little cooler.

She had found the jogging gear she wanted and was excited about it—although a part of her knew she shouldn't be. Just because Jaye had invited her jogging with him, it meant nothing. Still, she couldn't get over the fact that he had. Nor could she dismiss the other thing he'd said, namely, that he was no longer interested in sex-only affairs. She'd left him because she'd given up on that ever happening.

"Velvet!"

She turned and smiled when four women with strollers walked toward her. Ashley had her twins, Bryce had little K-Gee, Donna had her son Ike and Vashti's two kids, Cutter and Shelby, were in a two-seater that resembled a police cruiser. Velvet laughed, thinking it was the cutest thing since the toddlers' daddy was the sheriff. She walked over to meet the group. "Well, hello, everyone. What's up?"

"Nothing much," Donna said, grinning. "Looks like you've been shopping."

"Yes, I needed more athletic wear," she said, deciding not to be more specific than that.

"Daddy's there!" One of Ashley's twins pointed at the sparkling blue water of the gulf.

Velvet followed the little boy's finger and saw what he was talking about. Tugboats were delivering the first of Ray Sullivan's water taxis. They were large, spacious and elegant, which was different from what Velvet had imagined. She'd thought they would resemble a ferryboat, but she should have known better since she'd heard Ray had personally designed them.

"They're beautiful," she said, and noticed a crowd had gathered on the pier to look at the water-taxi boats as well.

There was a buzz of excitement in the air as people were finally seeing what Ray's dream of a water taxi would look like. Velvet noticed Ashley watching her husband in the distance as he talked to the men who'd delivered the boats. It was obvious that Ashley was proud of her husband's accomplishments and was happy for the man she loved.

"How many will there be?" Velvet asked.

"Two for now, but another is under construction. We're planning an open house to kick off the first one that will provide service during Mardi Gras."

"That's perfect timing," Vashti said, lifting her daughter out of the stroller to hold in her arms. Velvet agreed that having a water-taxi service from the cove to New Orleans during Mardi Gras would be perfect timing.

A short while later, she'd declined the women's invitation to join them at the Witherspoon Café. After all the sleep she'd lost last night by being with Jaye, she intended to get to bed early tonight.

Less than an hour later—after stopping at the Green Fig to grab a take-out order of soup—she was pulling into her driveway. The first thing she noticed was Jaye's car already there, which meant he was home. Would he come out to greet her? Why should he when she'd made it clear that what had happened last night was a one-time deal. He'd let her know he had no problem abiding by her wishes, because they were his as well. She should be pleased by that, but for some reason, she wasn't.

That thought was still on her mind hours later when she'd gotten in bed. Regardless of what he had told her, she honestly had expected Jaye to knock on her door tonight, sweep her into his arms and head for her bedroom. He hadn't and was clearly playing by the rules she'd established. When had Jaye ever done that? Especially when it came to their time in the bedroom. Probably because she'd never established any such rules before.

Shifting positions in bed, she knew they would at least spend time together tomorrow when they went jogging. That thought made her smile as she drifted to sleep.

CHAPTER SIXTEEN

JAYE KNEW HE was in trouble the moment Velvet opened the door. In all the years they'd been together, they'd never gone jogging together, so he hadn't known what to expect. He wasn't prepared to see her fully awake, dressed, all smiles and ready to go. It was, after all, five in the morning. And if he recalled, she was not a morning person…unless it was to wake up to make love.

Before, whenever he would leave bed to go jogging, she wouldn't even stir. But then it could have been that he'd pretty much worn her out the night before. Last night had been different. He had slept in his own bed and she in hers.

They had agreed to meet earlier than his usual routine, since she needed to be at work at seven thirty. He had no problem with that since he made his own hours at the bank and any appointments weren't until after ten o'clock. He had figured, although she had agreed to the time, that today would be a challenge for her. Evidently, it hadn't been.

"Good morning, Velvet."

"Good morning, Jaye."

His gaze roamed over her, and he thought she looked good in her jogging suit. Curvy in all the right places. Sexy as hell. But then, he thought she looked good in anything she put on her body. And he noted she had a good pair of running shoes on her feet. They appeared new. "You look nice."

"Thanks, and so do you," she said, coming to stand out on her porch as if testing the temperature. Then as if satisfied she'd dressed appropriately, she closed the door behind her.

"Thanks." He also thought she smelled good. Who did that to go jogging, knowing they would eventually get all sweaty?

"I hope you remember that I'm not a jogger and give me some slack, Jaye."

He grinned at her as they headed down the steps. "You'll do fine, but I promise to let you set the pace."

"Thanks, but I don't want to slow you down."

"You won't. There's a path I usually jog that goes the full diameter of the blueberry field. I usually cover it at least four to five times each morning, but today we'll run it only once so you can get used to it. In no time at all, you'll be doing four or five easily."

"Please don't hold your breath for that to happen."

He threw his head back and laughed as they headed toward the back of the house. "Before we start, we should do a few warm-up exercises."

"Okay."

Of course, she would be familiar with doing those since she taught gymnastics. He'd been surprised to hear that because, in the three years they were together, he hadn't known her to ever frequent a gym. "When did you get into gymnastics, Velvet?" he asked as they began doing stretches.

She peered over at him. "I've always been into gymnastics, Jaye."

He couldn't help the dumbfounded expression that appeared on his face. "I never knew that."

"Well, I have been. Since a child. I almost made the Olympic tryouts but a tendon strain did me in." She smiled. "How do you think I was capable of doing all those crazy positions in the bedroom?"

He honestly hadn't thought about it—all he'd known was that she could and that had been good enough for him. No questions asked. Now he wished he had.

"I'd never thought about how you did it, Velvet," he said.

"Well, now you know."

He wondered what else he didn't know about her because he'd deliberately kept her on her back between the sheets most of the time. They did several other kinds of stretches for ten minutes or so and then he noticed something. "Where's your water bottle?"

She shrugged. "I didn't know I needed to bring one."

"You do. But that's no problem, I got mine and we can share."

She didn't say anything, but he was aware she knew that meant drinking from the same bottle. They'd done so in the past without thinking about it, and he was glad to see she didn't have a problem doing so now.

"Okay, Velvet, let's go."

VELVET NEVER HAD a reason to walk the blueberry field, so she'd been surprised by how large it was. And just to think that Jaye ran around it five times? Amazing.

She would be lucky if she completed one lap. She was huffing and puffing already.

The field was beautiful with some of the blueberry bushes growing as high as eight feet tall. This was Reid Lacroix's land and on the other side of it, beyond several acres of thick woods, was where Vashti's inn, Shelby by the Sea, was located. She wondered if the place was full of occupants this week. Why should she care if it was or wasn't?

Mainly because thinking about anything was better than concentrating on the man running by her side. The man whose body made sweat a total turn-on. The temperature had dropped a little overnight and the morning air was still rather cool and, like her, he was dressed for the weather. He looked good in sweats, and they emphasized what a great body he had. Nothing had changed about him when it came to staying in shape.

It was obvious he'd adjusted his pace for her and more than once she suggested he run on ahead. She hadn't promised to catch up because there was no way she could. But he never took her up on her offer to leave her side. He stayed right with her. If she slowed her pace, then he slowed his as well.

"How do you like teaching at the junior school you're at now?"

She glanced at him as they continued jogging. "It's great. The other teachers are all nice and of course I love my kids, but…"

"But what?"

Velvet didn't say anything because when they'd been together before, Jaye had this thing about not discussing work—only if there was good news to share. He didn't like discussing anything about work that he thought of as unpleasant. That's why one would imagine he'd always had good days at work since he never discussed the bad ones. The few times she'd tried to tell him about her unpleasant days, he would cut their conversation short or deliberately change the subject. After a while, she'd known to only share good news with him about her work, just like he did with her.

She would tell him how well her students were doing, especially when they received any national mathematics achievement awards. However, she would never tell him about any problems she encountered. She wondered what he would do if she told him now. Would he change the subject or cut the conversation short like he was known to do? There was only one way to find out.

"I have this slight problem at work." She waited, fully prepared for him to do what he'd normally do.

"You want to tell me about it?"

She almost missed a step. Looking over at him, she saw he was watching her, waiting for her response. "There's this great student who's letting his grades slip because he honestly doesn't think math is important. He plans to become a professional baseball player one day and believes that as long as he has the basic math, he'll be able to count the millions of dollars he intends to make."

Jaye shook his head. "I'd think he'd want to understand other aspects of math that include investing. As a sports agent, Mercury would share with me the number of young professional athletes who end up broke before they hit thirty. But I'm sure you're going to do whatever you can to help bring his grades up, right?"

"I'm going to try. My biggest obstacle is his dad. He feels his son should get special treatment because of his potential as an athlete."

He looked at her, frowning. "That's not how it works."

"I know that, but evidently when his father was in high school here in Catalina Cove, he was a great baseball player, destined for the pros. He wasn't a great student, and the teachers gave him extra credit and passed him, anyway."

"And now he wants you to do for his son what those teachers did for him?"

"Obviously."

"Unfortunately, I see that kind of stuff all the time in my profession. You wouldn't believe how many people assume we should give their son or daughter a loan for a car, although their credit is bad, because some bank did the same for them."

She nodded. "How do you handle those type of customers?"

"I stick to my guns and let them know I'm a banker who goes by the rules. I bend them when I see a need to do so and not because they feel that I should. In your case, the bottom line is that you can't give the kid a grade he doesn't deserve. Have you talked to your principal about it?"

"Yes, but there's no help there. The principal used to be the father's coach when he was in senior high school, the one who boosted him for the pros. They see the son as a future pro baseball star who will achieve what his father did not."

"Why didn't the father make it in the pros?"

"He got signed up by the Dodgers, but he was released after a wrist injury."

"That's too bad, but you're doing the right thing in sticking to your guns. The father shouldn't expect special treatment. I don't give a damn if the kid has a golden arm. He should do the work. And if you ask me, the principal isn't doing his job if he doesn't have your back on this."

Velvet thought basically the same thing. "I agree."

They slowed and then came to a stop when they had finished the first lap and were back where they'd started. "This is where we part ways," he said.

His words surprised her. "It is?"

"Yes, I have four more laps to run, and you need to shower and get ready for work."

Yes, she did. She was surprised that he hadn't suggested they shower together. The Jaye Colfax she knew would have jumped at the chance. Not only would he have insisted on showering with her, but he would also have made love to her before she got dressed for work. "Okay. Thanks for inviting me to jog with you today and listening to my problem."

He pushed a strand of hair back off her face. "Don't thank me, Velvet. One of the things I realized after you left was that during the time we were together, we failed to communicate. It was all about the physical with us."

She frowned up at him. "That's the way you wanted things."

"Yes, that's the way I wanted things and I've come to regret it."

She was surprised he'd admitted that. She was about

to ask when he'd reached that conclusion when he asked, "What are your plans for the weekend?"

She wondered why he was asking and hoped it wasn't because he intended to intrude in any way. "Tomorrow is Sierra's goddaughter, Teryn's birthday and there's a big sleepover at Sierra's place with ten of her friends. I'm spending the night to help Sierra with everything,"

"Ten little girls? That sounds like fun," he said, grinning.

Velvet couldn't help but grin back. "Yes, it will be. Sierra's sister, Dani, is flying in to help as well."

"Well, have a good day, Velvet, and enjoy your weekend." He leaned in and brushed a kiss across her lips, and then added, "And about that problem we discussed. Like I said, don't worry about it. You're doing your job and that's what matters."

And then he took off jogging again. This time without her.

JAYE STOOD AT his kitchen window to watch Velvet leave for work. He had pushed himself to jog those four additional laps so he could be here, standing in this same spot as usual. He would have to say that he'd enjoyed jogging with her this morning and, more than once, he'd had to catch himself when his body reacted to seeing her run beside him.

There had been a gracefulness in her stride, and whenever he looked over at her, an electric charge would hit his heart. And then if she smiled, too, he'd have to fight to keep himself from tripping over himself while jogging.

Bottom line was that she looked amazing. It didn't

matter if she was in running attire, or what she was wearing to work today, as he watched her get into her car—a pair of black slacks, a brown button-up shirt and a beige, brown and black colored tweed jacket. She looked both classy and sexy.

When she drove off, he moved away from the window, pleased with how their first jog had gone. Jaye was about to pour a cup of coffee when his cell phone rang. It was his brother Franklin. Clicking on, he said, "What's up, Franklin?"

"I was thinking."

Jaye rolled his eyes. Whenever his youngest brother got to thinking that usually meant trouble of the female kind. However, when it came to business, Franklin was an ace, always on top of his game. He successfully managed the construction company they'd inherited from their paternal grandfather, as well as being a pinch hitter when needed with the family's banks. You could say Franklin was a jack-of-all-trades. Sometimes, Jaye wondered how he managed it all, and so efficaciously. But Franklin's personal life was another matter. His younger brother was more of a womanizer than Jaye had ever been.

"And what were you thinking, Franklin?"

"About putting in a bid for that housing project that Reid Lacroix is developing in Catalina Cove."

There was no reason to ask Franklin how he'd heard about the development. His brother made it his business to keep his finger on the pulse of any major construction projects.

"I think that will be great, Franklin." He was glad his brother wasn't calling him with women issues. Jaye couldn't have helped him there since he was trying to undo his own major screw-up.

He talked to Franklin a few minutes more. "I wish you luck with that Lacroix bid."

"Thanks."

Jaye ended the call, not sure if Catalina Cove was ready for the likes of Franklin Delano Colfax.

CHAPTER SEVENTEEN

"ALL THE LITTLE darlings are asleep. So is Dani," Sierra said with a quiet laugh as she joined Velvet at the kitchen table for a glass of wine.

"Dani did say her flight had been one from hell," Velvet said, grinning.

Sierra rolled her eyes. "That's any flight for Dani. She hates flying and her hubby, Emory, wasn't with her to hold her hand. She claims Crane wasn't any help. Honestly, what did she expect? My precious niece is only six." She took a sip of the wine Velvet had poured. "Thanks, I need this."

Velvet took a sip of hers, too. "So do I," she said, then asked, "When will Vaughn be back?"

"Tuesday before noon. He's been gone almost a week and I miss him so much. I plan to be at Zara's Haven, and the minute he opens the door, I'll jump his bones." Sierra then burst out laughing. "Good grief, I'm sounding like Dani."

"But that's all good because you're happy and in love," Velvet said, recalling a time she'd been happy and in love. Unfortunately, her guy hadn't fallen in love with her the way Vaughn had fallen in love with Sierra. Why was she unlucky when it came to love?

"Don't do that, Velvet."

Velvet looked up at Sierra. "Do what?"

"Dwell on the past."

Velvet took another sip of wine. "It's not hard to do when the man from my past is living next door."

"And how's that going?"

Velvet breathed out a deep sigh. "You recall that time when I told you about my hormones and how they'd almost gotten the best of me once?"

Sierra nodded. "Yes. That was the time you thought about flying back to Phoenix for a one-night stand with Jaye and then disappear again, right?"

"Yes. Well, I did it, Sierra, and I didn't have to fly to Arizona for it."

Sierra's mouth dropped open. "Are you saying that…"

"Yes, that's what I'm saying. Jaye and I had a one-night stand. And it was just what I wanted, and definitely what I needed. After, I made it clear it was a one-and-done with no continuation."

Sierra studied her over the rim of her glass. "He agreed to that?"

"Yes." She leaned closer and said, "That's the way he preferred things, too. But now, according to Jaye, he no longer engages in sex-only affairs."

Sierra lifted a brow. "Since when?"

"Not sure. He did say he hadn't had sex with a woman since me."

"He actually admitted that?"

"Yes."

"Hmm, what do you think of that?"

Velvet shrugged. "I honestly don't know what to think, Sierra. Granted, given his womanizing reputation, nobody could believe it when he agreed to an exclusive relationship with me. But when we broke up, there was no reason for him not to go back to his womanizing ways."

"What if he's changed?"

Velvet didn't say anything for a minute. "He has changed, Sierra, but not the way you think. I figure since all his close friends have gotten married, for the first time ever he probably feels out of his element and is merely taking a social break. I'll give him a few months and he'll be back to sex-only affairs again."

"Do you really think that's what it is?"

"I have no reason not to think so. I suggested that reason to him and he claims that's not it, and that he's merely giving himself time to explore his inner self to determine why he engaged in those kinds of affairs in the first place. Honestly, what's there to figure out? He's a man who enjoys sex and women."

"So, the two of you haven't had any other contact since sleeping together that one time?"

"Not sexually, but he did ask me to go jogging with him, which I found very odd."

"What's so odd about it?"

"For one thing, during the three years we were together, Jaye never invited me to go jogging with him. Not once. He always said that it was his private time."

"Did you go?"

"Yes."

"Hmm…now he's including you in that private time?"

"I guess you can say that. And another thing, he didn't freak out when I told him unpleasant news."

"Freak out how?"

"In the past, whenever I would bring up unpleasant news from work, with my corporation or if I tried discussing our future, he would either end the conversation or immediately change the subject. Yesterday, when we were jogging, he actually listened when I told him about that situation with Allen Bordeaux." Velvet took another sip of wine. "And there's something else."

"What?"

"He hasn't tried taking me to bed again."

"But didn't you tell him it was only a one-night stand?"

"Yes, but the Jaye that I knew would see that as a challenge and would have seduced the hell out of me by now."

Sierra laughed. "You seem disappointed that he hasn't."

Was she? Maybe she was a little. "I just don't understand him anymore."

Sierra reached out and touched her hand. "What's there not to understand, Velvet? I think he's changing for you."

Velvet shook her head as she picked up the wine bottle and poured herself another half glass. "Jaye doesn't change for anyone."

"But what if he's doing it to get you back?"

"That's not it, trust me. But whatever is driving Jaye to do what he's doing will eventually come out."

"You look busy."

Jaye turned around upon hearing Velvet's voice. Removing his safety glasses, his eyes roamed over her. Every single inch. He liked how she looked in a pair of skin-tight jeans and a pullover green sweater. When his gaze returned to hers, he asked, "When did you get home?"

"Thirty minutes ago. When I was unpacking my overnight bag, I noticed you out here from my window." She looked at the worktable, lumber and electric saw. "What did you do? Turn Delisa's shed into a workshop?"

He couldn't stop the smile from spreading across his lips. "Something like that. I figured she wouldn't mind."

"I'm sure she won't." She paused. "So, what are you making?"

"Rocking chairs."

She lifted a brow. "Why?"

He gazed toward the house and said, "Because they will complement the style of house. I can see them on the porch. Besides, it gives me something to do."

"Oh, I see."

No, she really didn't, and Jaye decided now was not the time to let her know he was building the chairs for them. He recalled her telling him once that for years her parents had his-and-hers rocking chairs, and how in the evenings they would sit out on their porch and watch the sunset, rock in the chairs and talk. She'd said that had been their private time together and that's what he wanted for him and Velvet. A private time that wasn't connected to the bedroom.

"Well, I'll let you get back to what you were doing."

He wasn't ready for her to go yet. "How was the sleepover?"

She smiled. "It was great. The girls were wonderful, and Sierra, Dani and I really enjoyed them. Of course, Teryn thought it was the best birthday ever."

"I'm glad things turned out great for Teryn. She seems like a swell kid."

"She is." Then Velvet asked, "How long will it take you to build the chairs?"

He leaned against the worktable. "Not long. I plan to work on them every chance I get. My goal is to have them finished in a couple of weeks."

"Then you will."

He chuckled. "Why are you so sure of that?"

She shrugged. "Because you're the type of person who'll accomplish anything he sets his mind to doing."

Jaye certainly hoped so because right now winning back her love topped the list. "You can help."

"I can? How?"

"By deciding on what color the chairs should be."

She tilted her head to look up at him. "You want me to do that?"

"Yes."

"You might not like the color I pick."

"I'll like it. I trust your judgment."

She hesitated. "You're sure?"

"I'm positive."

A huge smile touched her lips. "Thanks, Jaye."

It occurred to him at that moment the number of times she had volunteered to help him with his home-improvement projects, and he would turn her down, preferring to do it himself. Now he could see how doing so had shut her out of things when they'd been together. Yet, she had remained in their relationship for three years, hoping he would change. When she saw he wouldn't, that's when she'd determined he was a lost cause.

"Okay, I'll start looking at colors next week. I already have an idea of what will blend in well with the color of the house."

"Okay."

"Aren't you going to ask me what that color is?"

"No. Surprise me."

She nodded, grinning. "I'll do that." She glanced at her watch. "You don't have much more daylight left so I'll let you finish up."

"Have you eaten dinner?" he asked her.

"No, but I'm not hungry. Sierra prepared a special brunch of soup and sandwiches for everyone, including the parents, when they came to pick up their girls. I'm still stuffed from that."

"Just asking. I'm going to grab dinner at the Witherspoon Café and wanted to see if you'd like me to bring you back anything." There was no need to invite her to dine with him since he knew her position on them being seen together.

"Thanks for asking, Jaye, and I'll see you later." She turned to leave.

"You will see me in the morning."

She turned back to him. "Excuse me?"

"I said you'll see me in the morning. We're going jogging, remember?"

"Are you sure you want to do it again with me?"

"Vel, I'll do anything again with you at any time."

Jaye could see the darkening of her eyes and was glad she knew he wasn't just talking about them jogging together.

"I'll see you in the morning, Jaye."

"At five."

"Okay, at five." And then he watched as she quickly walked back inside the house.

"OKAY, RUTHIE. YOU'RE BEGINNING to sound like Sierra," Velvet said later that night as she curled up in bed. She had just finished telling her best friend the same thing she'd shared the other night with Sierra at the girls' sleepover.

"And maybe you ought to listen to what we're saying. If you recall, I told you whenever I saw Jaye around town, he was never with a woman. He was hanging with Mercury or his brothers. He'd pretty much become a loner after you left him. That's why I believe what he told you about taking a break from sex-only affairs."

"Well, it honestly doesn't matter to me."

"And I honestly think it does. I hope you know that the one-night stand you two shared will have the opposite effect. You're going to want Jaye now more than ever."

Velvet frowned. "How do you figure that?"

"Because whenever you get a sexual itch that needs scratching, he's right next door. You won't have to talk yourself out of flying to Phoenix to make a booty call."

She rolled her eyes. "Another roll between the sheets with Jaye won't be happening. I'm good for another two years, maybe even three or four."

"We'll see."

"Goodbye, Ruthie."

"And before you go, I just need to tell you that I read somewhere that making out in a blueberry field is out of this world."

Velvet knew Ruthie had read no such thing. "Bye." She clicked off the phone.

After getting up to go to the bathroom, she was sliding back in bed when she heard a noise outside her window. It was close to ten at night. Surely, Jaye wasn't still outside working on those chairs. She went to the window and discreetly looked out. He had erected a huge bright light in the shed and was still at it. His profile was to her, and she saw he was still wearing his safety glasses and work gloves.

Leaning over the worktable and measuring a slab of wood, she liked how his jeans stretched tight across his rear end. Instead of thinking of what a great tush he had, she should have been concerned that he was still outside working at this hour when they were supposed to go jogging at five in the morning. Did he not believe in getting eight hours of sleep at night? But then when did he ever get that many hours of rest? Although they'd maintained separate households during their three years, they had slept together most nights at his place or hers. Even then he would wake up during the wee hours of the night and make love to her.

Slipping the curtains back in place, she knew Jaye was a grown man who could take care of himself. When he got tired, he would call it a night.

Yawning, she moved back toward the bed, determined to get her proper rest, even if he didn't.

Hours later, Velvet found herself caught in the throes of one heated dream. She and Jaye were in this house together, in this bed. Again. He was kissing her all over, and every touch of his lips to her skin was precise, perfect, on point. And the wet licks to her flesh magnified her desire for him. Jack Colfax, Jr., knew what to do and how to do it to make her come apart and she was doing it now. She could feel herself thrashing around in the bed, eager for what was to come.

She almost came, and each time she did, Jaye would do something to stall it, make her that much more greedy and needy. Finally, he was positioned above her and was lifting her hips, getting ready to thrust deep. Her body was ready, excited, hungry for this. Only from the only man it knew.

Velvet could feel him begin to ease inside her, and then suddenly...

Her clock's alarm went off.

"ARE YOU READY, VELVET?" Jaye asked when she opened the door for him early the next morning. He'd always loved that I'm-still-sleepy look she was wearing now or those times he would wake her up in the middle of the night to make love to her.

"Yes."

"You might want to grab a jacket. It's cooler outside than it was on Friday."

"Okay. Come in while I grab one."

He entered as she hurried toward her bedroom. The last time he'd been here was when they'd made love and the memory of that night was making him aroused. He wished he could say it was too early for that, but when it came to Velvet, the time of day never mattered. He always wanted her.

"I'm back and ready."

Jaye had news for her. He'd never left and was still

ready. He was grateful for the looseness of his jogging pants that adequately concealed one hell of an erection.

"Then let's go. Early morning jogging is a great way to start your day." He escorted her to the door, noticing she smelled good. Her scent always had a way of filling his nostrils.

"And your week, I hope. Progress reports go out this week, and I know that parent I was telling you about won't be too happy. But then he was sent an official warning of what could happen if his son's grades didn't improve."

"Well, at least he's been put on notice," Jaye said, opening the door and following her out.

As they walked toward the back to do warm-ups, he said, "Let's try to do a couple more than we did last week, in the same amount of time."

"Okay."

Ten minutes later, they were jogging off toward the blueberry fields. "I forgot to mention that Dad told me to tell you hello. So did Dean and Franklin," he said, gazing over at her.

"When did you talk to them?"

"Last week on that business trip. The four of us were together then. In Birmingham. We officially broke ground for our new bank. The first in Alabama."

Jaye figured she was surprised he'd told her that. Usually, she never knew when another Colfax Bank was opening until he asked her to join him for the grand-opening celebration. He was seeing more and more how he'd deliberately shut her out of his life when he should have been including her in it.

"I like your dad and brothers," she said as they began

jogging at a comfortable pace for the both of them. He liked that their movements seemed in sync with each other. Just like their movements in the bedroom.

"And they like you."

She didn't say anything for a minute and then said, "Deciding to leave Phoenix was hard for me. I had to give up friendships I'd cultivated because of my relationship with you."

It had been hard for him, too. His brothers had given him hell. So had the Steele family. "Everyone missed you, Velvet, and blamed me for your leaving."

"They should not have blamed you, Jaye, and I regret that they did. My expectations of your feelings were my doing and not yours. You'd told me upfront and several times in between that our relationship was built on sex and nothing more. I was wrong to hold out for more."

"I did tell you once that I loved you."

"Yes, but in the same breath you made it clear what you really loved was all the time we spent in bed having sex."

Jaye didn't say anything for a moment because he could clearly recall that night. The words *I love you* had slipped out while they'd been making love. He had been buried deep inside her and emotions he had never felt before for any woman had consumed him, and before he knew it, he had blurted out the words. When he realized what he'd done, he quickly decided to take the true meaning of them back. The last thing he'd wanted was to fall in love and admit it to anyone.

"So tell me about your new bank."

Was she making the request because she figured he wouldn't tell her anything because he never had? If that was the case, then he would surprise her. "It's going to be nice. The community it will serve is big. It will be one of our biggest banks."

"Even larger than the one in Phoenix?"

They had several branches in Phoenix, but he knew which one she was referring to. "Not larger than our corporate office but definitely larger than any of the other branches."

By the time they had finished the first lap, he had discussed a number of things with her, and she definitely seemed interested in what he'd told her about Franklin submitting a bid to Reid Lacroix regarding that housing development.

"It's going to be a nice place. I want one of those lots on the ocean and plan to purchase one when they go up for sale."

He lifted a brow. "You do?"

"Yes. I like it here and have always wanted to own oceanfront property."

"I thought you liked Phoenix."

She hesitated. "I still do, but I'm not sure I'd consider Phoenix my home again. I have no reason to do so."

He was silent as they came to a stop at the spot where they had begun. He heard what she'd just said, and more than anything he intended to give her a reason. "This is where we part ways for now. I hope you have a good day. I'm stopping by LaFitte Seafood House on my way home to grab takeout. Would you like anything?" He saw her eyes light up. Seafood was her favorite, and he knew it.

"Are you sure you don't mind? I have a community

committee meeting after school, and it would be nice if I didn't have to stop anywhere before I got home."

"I don't mind at all, Velvet. Just tell me what you want."

"A number twenty-two. It has an assortment of everything, including their crab cakes, which are to die for."

"Okay a number twenty-two it is." And just like the last time, he leaned in and brushed a kiss across her lips. "I'll see you later, Vel." It seemed she didn't have a problem with him using the shortened version of her name when they were alone.

"Okay, I'll see you later, Jaye."

He took off to finish his other laps and although it was hard, he didn't look back.

CHAPTER EIGHTEEN

VELVET HAD JUST finished preparing the math problems for this week's test when she heard a car pull up outside. She knew without looking that it was Jaye. She stood, placing the files in her briefcase. Lenny hadn't come to her class so he hadn't been there for the review. She'd seen him earlier in the halls, so he had been at school today, and she hoped he didn't think that skipping her class was the answer.

She knew a lot of students detested math and struggled with algebra. However, instead of seeking the extra help she'd offered, he honestly believed he would pass her class because his father said he would. And what was sad was that Lenny seemed to be a nice kid. He was always well-mannered and respectful. His other teachers concurred with that.

When she heard the knock on her door, she wondered if accepting Jaye's offer for dinner had been the smart thing to do. At the time, it had seemed convenient, knowing she had that community committee after school.

It didn't help matters when at the end of the meeting, Robin Dyer, one of the single teachers in town, who was also on the committee, asked how it was having such a gorgeous hunk for a neighbor. Other women had overheard Robin's question and had been interested in hearing Velvet's answer. She had shrugged and said with their schedules she and Jaye rarely saw each other, which wasn't the truth now that they jogged together. What she should have done was tell Robin it really wasn't any of her business.

She opened her door to find Jaye with several bags. "Come in, Jaye."

"Thanks. Do I get to join you?"

"Join me?"

"Yes, eat with you. Share this meal with you?"

Since he had been kind enough to bring her food, the least she could do was share dinner with him. "Sure."

Velvet headed toward the kitchen, and as he followed, she swore she could feel the heat of his gaze on her backside. He'd always said he loved every part of her body but liked her ass the best. "What would you like to drink, Jaye?" She opened the refrigerator.

"Iced tea will be fine."

She peered over her shoulder at him. "When did you become an iced-tea drinker?"

"After you left."

Lifting her brow, she turned to face him. "It took me leaving for you to try iced tea?"

"No, it took you leaving for me to realize all the things I resisted were probably good, as well as good for me."

Velvet honestly didn't know what to say to that. She turned back to the refrigerator and grabbed the pitcher of tea. It sounded like he had regrets. Unfortunately, it was too late and didn't change a thing.

Placing the pitcher on the counter, she leaned up on

tiptoes to grab glasses from the top cabinet. Usually, she would use plastic cups but felt the least she could do was service him tea from a glass.

"I can get that for you," he said, and suddenly she felt the heat of Jaye's breath on her neck and the front of him resting against her rear end.

She eased off her tiptoes and immediately wished she hadn't. Doing so made her backside fit more snugly against him and she had to take deep breaths to calm her raging hormones.

"Are you okay, Velvet?"

Velvet could tell him that no, she was not okay and that being this close to him, inhaling his scent and feeling his erection were doing all kinds of salacious things to her. That wasn't good, considering the unfinished dream she'd had last night.

When he took a step back, she could no longer feel him, but she still felt his heat. "Yes, I'm okay." She concentrated on filling the glasses with iced tea while trying to get her mind and body under control.

When she finally turned around with both glasses in her hands, she saw he was standing at the kitchen window and gazing out. Apparently, he'd needed to get his mind and body under control as well. Without saying anything, she walked over to the table and started pulling the food containers out of the bags.

"The food smells good," she said.

That's when he turned around and his gaze locked on hers. At other times whenever he'd looked at her that way, he would cross the room, sweep her into his arms and carry her to the nearest bedroom…or table or floor. Whenever the urge hit to make love, they did it. All over the place.

"Where can I wash my hands?" he asked, breaking the stretching silence.

"The hall bath." There was no need telling him where it was since he had passed it that night when he'd taken her to her bedroom.

"Okay. I'll be back in a minute."

And then he was gone, and she hoped by the time he returned that she would have pulled herself together.

JAYE LEANED AGAINST the closed bathroom door and drew in a deep breath. No help there because her scent was even in here. She loved jasmine and this bathroom with the scented candles placed on the vanity smelled like her. Except when they made love. During those times, her pheromones dominated and intermingled with the scent of them making love.

He knew Velvet and the one thing he was certain about was that she wanted him as much as he wanted her. Desire was something she could never hide from him. Nor him from her. For three years, it had ruled his mind and his senses, which was why he was in the predicament he was now.

Regardless how much he wanted her, he would not make love to her. If they made love again, it would be because she wanted it and asked for it. Hell, he wouldn't have a problem if she seduced him. Bottom line, like he'd told her, he was no longer into sex-only relationships. His only relationship would be with her, and if she felt the need to have her desires filled, then it would be up to her to let him know.

Moments later after washing his hands, he returned to find the table set in the dining room. Velvet had removed the food from the containers and arranged it on plates that looked like costly dinnerware. How easily he had forgotten how she liked to do things formal at times. He had gotten used to it and after she left, like so many other things, he had missed it.

"Food is still hot," she said, not looking at him.

"Okay."

She was already sitting down, and he moved to join her at the table. He had eaten at LaFitte's Seafood before with Vaughn but had never gotten the number twenty-two. Since that was what she'd wanted, he had gotten it as well and the food looked good.

"How did your committee meeting go today?" he asked her, mainly to get her to look at him. She did.

"It was great. We're making plans for the Blueberry Festival in May."

Jaye nodded as he began eating. He hoped to be married to her by May, and if not married, then definitely engaged. He had the ring already. He had purchased it right before coming here in November. "How many festivals are held in the cove each year?" he asked in between bites of food. The meal was delicious. He'd had crab cakes before, but these were the tastiest he'd ever eaten.

"In addition to the Blueberry Festival, there's the Shrimp Festival. Whereas the Blueberry Festival is a weekend event, the Shrimp Festival lasts for three days. However, since the water taxis will be available, the mayor wants to make it a four-day event."

"What happens at the Blueberry Festival?"

He listened while she told him, loving how her mouth moved and how sexy he thought it was, even when she took a sip of tea. This was what he'd missed as well, sharing a meal with her. He couldn't say he missed hearing her talk because they honestly hadn't talked a lot. Again, it dawned on him just how much of their time had been spent in the bedroom doing other things than talking.

Jaye blinked when he realized she had stopped talking and asked him a question. "Excuse me? What did you ask?"

"I asked how things are going at the bank?"

"Great. More new accounts and less foot traffic into the bank now that everyone is getting the hang of on-line banking. We're planning to increase the number of drive-through lanes and add a couple of ATM lanes. I couldn't believe there're only two drive-through lanes, and an ATM that you can't access from your car."

"Larson Barrows didn't believe much in modern technology," Velvet said.

"Or making things convenient for his customers, either, apparently." When there was a lull in the conversation, he said, "These plates are nice, and the design is pretty. I haven't seen them before. Are they new?"

Instead of answering him, she stared at him with an odd expression on her face. "Is something wrong, Velvet?"

She shook her head. "No, nothing is wrong."

He knew that there was, and it was about the plates. What was it about them? She switched the conversation to something else—the forecaster's prediction that a cold front was headed to the cove next week.

He knew something was bothering her and it had to do with the dinnerware. When her conversation about the weather trailed off, he said, "The plates, Vel. What is it about the plates I should know or that I don't know?"

She hesitated before answering. "I was out shopping one day and saw this dinnerware set and fell in love with it. It was a couple of weeks before my twenty-eighth birthday and things between us were going so well. You had been so attentive, so loving and as usual so sexual."

Velvet stopped talking but Jaye knew there was more. "Go on."

She smiled, but he saw the pain in her eyes. "Silly me, I had convinced myself that I was getting an engagement ring for my birthday. When the saleslady told me that this particular pattern would be going out of stock, in my anticipation and excitement, I chose this dinnerware as the one I intended to put on my wedding registry. Of course, we didn't get engaged but I liked it so much that I bought it, anyway. If nothing else, I figured whenever I ate off of these plates, it would be a reminder."

A hard knot formed in Jaye's throat. "A reminder that I let you down?"

She shook her head. "No, a reminder that I let my own self down by believing something that wasn't true."

Jaye didn't say anything as he worked his brain to recall what he had given her for her twenty-eighth birthday. Then he remembered. He had given her a designer briefcase. It had definitely not been the engagement ring she'd been expecting.

"Velvet, I…"

"No, Jaye, it wasn't your fault. That's what I got for being overoptimistic, especially when you had told me countless times the nature of our relationship. I honestly had forgotten why I had them when I set the table. When you commented on them, I remembered."

He wished he could kick his own ass. She began talking about the weather again, pretty much letting him know any discussion about the plates was over.

"Do you have enough wood for your fireplace?" he decided to ask her.

"I've never used my fireplace since moving to the cove. From what I understand, the cold front headed this way is pretty unusual for this area."

"I'll make sure you have enough."

"You don't have to do that, Jaye."

He had to bite down to keep from saying that he took care of what was his. But after what she'd told him about the plates, his actions in the past had shown him that he didn't have the right to claim her, her time or her attention. To be honest, he didn't have a right to be sharing a meal with her served on plates intended to be a wedding gift. Their wedding gift. Knowing that made him more determined than ever to prove to her just how much he loved her.

They continued eating and eventually the tension between them eased away…only to be replaced by sexual vibes, which was evident by the heated looks they periodically exchanged with each other. The last thing he wanted on their minds was sex.

How many times in the past had they started a meal but then in the middle of it began tearing off each other's clothes when the vibes got too hot? It was a fix they didn't need to be in right now. So, he began telling her about all the plans they had for the new bank in Birmingham. That ploy helped them through the remainder of the meal.

When she stood to clear off the table, he stood as well. When their hands brushed, he heard her sharp intake of breath. Jaye knew it was time to leave or else he would be reverting to his old ways and take her on the table or the nearest wall. "Do you need me to help you?"

"No," she said rather quickly. "I got this."

He nodded. It was evident they both needed their space. "Then I think I better go and will see you in the morning."

Jaye made a move for the front door. He had wanted to kiss her goodbye but knew that wouldn't be a good idea. Once he pulled her into his arms and tasted her mouth, he would devour it. Then that would lead to other things.

He had nearly made it out of the dining room and headed to the door when she said, "I don't think going jogging with you is a good idea, Jaye."

He stopped and turned to her. "Why not?"

"I think you know why."

He didn't say anything as he held her gaze. "At any time have I gotten out of line with you, Vel?"

She drew in a deep breath and shook her head. "No, but it doesn't matter."

"And why doesn't it?"

"Because at some point I might get out of line with you. And if I do, will you stop me?"

His answer was quick and honest. "No."

"That's what I was afraid of."

He shoved his hands into the pockets of his slacks. "When it comes to me, Velvet, you shouldn't be afraid of anything. I've told you my position on sex-only relationships."

"Yet, you'd go back on that position if I wanted you to do so?"

"Yes, but only for you."

"Why only for me, Jaye?"

More than anything he wanted to tell her it was because he loved her, but he knew she wasn't ready to hear it. So, he told her what he'd told her weeks ago. "I will give you whatever you want. No matter what it is."

When she didn't say anything, he crossed the room and came to a stop in front of her. Drawing in a deep breath, he just stared at her, willing her to read in his gaze what she would not accept in his words. And then he drew her into his arms and kissed her.

Just in case she didn't get any reading from his eyes, he hoped this kiss would. He knew he should have kept walking and left, but when she'd asked her question and he'd given her his answer, it had undoubtedly left her confused. He had to try to unconfuse her somewhat.

He wasn't holding back anything, and neither was she. Devouring her, any part of her, had always been his favorite pastime, and when her tongue took charge of his with an intensity he felt in his groin, it made him groan. But he'd also heard her moan. They were both in a bad way and he knew she had an idea of just how bad at the feel of his throbbing erection pressing against her. He was getting that same idea with her scent. Whenever her womanly scent invaded his nostrils, he knew it was time to take her and thrust his body into hers, all the way to the hilt, and then ride her until they were both consumed in pleasure.

When his hands began to twitch with a desire to sweep her off her feet and carry her into her bedroom, he broke off the kiss. Although he wanted her with a passion that had seeped into his every pore, whenever they made love, she would have to be the one who initiated it. He refused to let her think that was still all he wanted from her.

He leaned in and whispered, "I won't knock on your door in the morning. You know what time I go jogging. You're always invited to join me, Velvet. I like having you with me and enjoy your company."

Without saying anything else, he turned and left.

CHAPTER NINETEEN

JAYE SWEPT HER up into his arms and carried her to the bed. It was a good thing he knew his way because their lips were still locked in what had to be the most intimate kiss they'd ever shared. When he placed her on the bed, he joined her there. They were both naked and she made a little protest when their mouths finally separated.

His gaze swept her body and her nipples hardened at the intensity of the desire she saw in his eyes. She knew that he intended to ride her hard, make her come several times and taste her all over. The thought of his plans for her made the area between her thighs throb.

Her gaze swept over him, and she saw how aroused he was and liked the thought that she'd done that. She was the cause of his huge erection and she intended to take care of him like she knew he would do for her.

And then he was back on the bed with her, pulling her into his arms and giving her a long intense kiss that left her panting. He whispered the words, "I want you, Velvet," as he moved into position over her. She was about to tell him she wanted him, too, but he kissed the words from her lips at the same time she felt him, his hard manhood meeting her womanly folds. She needed him, she wanted him, and this time, nothing was going to stop her from having him.

That one-and-done time hadn't been enough. How could she have thought it would be? Anticipation was clawing at her, and she felt he wasn't moving fast enough. She needed the feel of him sliding inside her and her inner muscles clenching him. She wanted him now.

Velvet's eyes flew open when her clock alarm went off, dousing her with the reality she was in bed alone and she'd only had yet another dream.

"I'M SO CONFUSED, RUTHIE," Velvet said as she turned over in bed and looked at the alarm clock that had gone off a short while ago. The only reason she'd called Ruthie so early in the morning was because Velvet knew Todd was still out of town and that Ruthie was an early riser.

After Jaye had left and she'd cleaned up the kitchen, she'd taken a shower and gone to bed with thoughts of the meal with Jaye dominating her mind and that parting kiss ruling her body parts. Specifically, those body parts had kept her awake most of the night. And when she'd finally dozed off to sleep, she'd had that dream…

"You're confused because he kissed you?"

"I'm confused by everything. I told you what he said before we kissed. That he would renege on his position on a sex-only relationship if I wanted him to do so. He would do it for me but not for any other woman. Only for me."

"What is there to be confused about? Sounds pretty clear to me. You're the only woman he wants to sleep with. He reneged on that position when the two of you made love a couple of weeks ago, so it wouldn't surprise me if he were to do it again."

"Yes, but that time was different."

"How so? Because you were in a bad way? Ready to jump his bones? Admit it, Velvet, you're in a bad way now, girlfriend."

"But that's just it, Ruthie. I shouldn't be. That one time with him should have been enough."

"Evidently it wasn't."

Ruthie had said the words Velvet did not want to fess up to. Yes, she wanted him again, but she should not want him. Considering the number of orgasms she'd had that night with Jaye, he should be well out of her system. But every time she saw him, she would remember how it felt to be held by him, to be in his arms in and out of bed, to be kissed all over by him, share orgasms with him. All those memories only intensified her desire for him.

"I told you what I think," Ruthie said, interrupting her thoughts.

Yes, but Ruthie didn't know Jaye like she did. "And I told you I don't agree with your assessment of the situation."

"Regardless, it's something you should consider as a possibility, Vel. It's not helping matters for you to do this, pushing yourself to the edge when you have a perfectly capable man as your neighbor who is willing to take that edge off. But since you're determined not to go anymore sexual rounds with him, I think you're doing the right thing by not going jogging with him this morning."

Velvet lifted her brow. "Why?"

"Because maybe you need to take a step back for a few days and think about everything that has been going on with you since Jaye came to town. I bet that after you do, you'll reach the same conclusion that I have."

"What? That for some reason Jaye is changing for me?"

"That, and the fact that you're falling back in love with him. If you ask me, you never stopped loving him."

Velvet quickly sat up in bed. "Ruthie, how could you even think that? You know how much I loved Jaye before. You know how much I wanted him to love me back. And you of all people know why I left Phoenix."

"Yes, I know. I also know how hard Jaye took your leaving. I told you he visited me a few times, trying to get me to tell him where you'd gone. He looked crushed and defeated."

Crushed and defeated… She did recall Ruthie telling her that. "And I will tell you the same thing now that I told you then. What was crushed and defeated wasn't his heart, but the fact he'd lost a bed partner. He would have been satisfied with us staying together for another three years with nothing but great sex keeping us satisfied. I deserved more."

"Yes, and maybe he's finally realized that you deserved more, Velvet. Think about it for a minute. Jaye coming to Catalina Cove and discovering you were there had to have been a real shocker for him. Maybe it shocked him into realizing what he'd lost, and he feels that he's been given a second chance. Then for the two of you to become neighbors was nothing short of a miracle for him to get it right this time."

"If what you say is true, then why is he putting limitations on us?"

"He's not, Velvet. You are. You're the one who set the rules. He's merely giving you what you want. Even you said how agreeable he's become. Maybe there's a reason for it."

Velvet heard what Ruthie was saying, but as far as she was concerned, the only thing Jaye had been shocked about was realizing he had lost a good thing when she'd left. However, that still didn't equate to love. All she'd ever wanted was Jaye's love. "None of that means anything, Ruthie, without his love."

"And you know why it isn't easy for him to love. It has to do with his mother."

A subject he'd brought up once, the morning after they'd made love. The same morning he'd told her his position on sex-only relationships. She'd hoped that he would bring up the topic of his mother again, but so far he hadn't. She then told Ruthie as much.

"You know what I've discovered from the time I've been with Todd is that men aren't as forthcoming with their inner thoughts and feelings as women are. Jaye's mother hurt him when she left. Her departure left him devastated. Maybe now he's healed and realizes that he wants your love."

Velvet released a deep sigh. "Jaye has always had my love, Ruthie," she said, knowing she was accepting what her best friend had said earlier about her falling back in love with Jaye. Deep down, she knew she had never stopped loving him.

"Yes, but what if he's trying to show you something, Vel?"

"Trying to show me what?"

"That now you have his love as well."

"That's the most ridiculous thing I've ever heard of."

"Is it? Take time away from Jaye, like I suggested, to think about it. Then the next time you spend time with him, pay close attention to what he says, how he acts with you and treats you. You've even said he's telling you more stuff now than before. For him, that might be a start."

"I still don't agree with your theory, but I do agree that Jaye and I need space between us if for no other reason than to keep me from jumping his bones whenever I see him. I've even dreamed of us making out in those blueberry fields."

Ruthie laughed. "I can see it happening."

Velvet could see it happening, too…but only in her dreams.

JAYE ABSENTLY TOSSED a paper clip on his desk while leaning back in his chair. Nearly a week had passed since he'd spent time with Velvet. She hadn't shown up to go jogging with him, but he had seen her leave for work every morning and saw her when she returned in the evenings. As much as he'd been tempted to do so, he hadn't sought her out but had given her space. Space she felt she needed because things were getting too hot between them and she couldn't handle the heat.

This past weekend had been the grand opening for the water taxis and he'd seen her there. They'd even been on the same taxi from the cove to New Orleans and back, but she'd hung out with several teachers from her school, intentionally ignoring his presence.

In a way, he wasn't surprised by her actions since he had a pretty good idea how her mind worked. She thought putting distance between them would solve the problem. It wouldn't. Just like putting distance between them two years ago hadn't solved anything, either. If she thought she needed time from him, then he would give it to her...up to a point. He refused to allow her to put distance between them too much longer. Hopefully, sooner rather than later, she would accept what he now knew. They were meant to be together.

Standing from his desk, he felt the need to get out of his office for a minute and breathe in a bit of fresh air. Although Velvet had never set foot in his office, he'd had many thoughts of her in here, and at the moment the intensity of those thoughts was consuming him.

He stopped at Ms. Carter's desk to let her know he was going to lunch. The moment he stepped outside, he thought the temperature had gone down since that morning. While jogging, he'd worn an extra layer, but forecasters promised it would be a nice weekend.

He headed for the Witherspoon Café. He had a taste for something filling and he'd heard their seafood pot-pie was pretty good.

The minute he walked into the café, he smiled when he recognized the person in line in front of him. Evans Toussaint. He'd met Evans at Vaughn's Super Bowl party. Since then, he'd run into Evans around town a few times and at the bank. He knew that, like many others, Evans had been born in Catalina Cove and since moved back to town.

Because of Evans's strong background in finance management and logistics, Vaughn, who would become

CEO of Lacroix when Reid retired later this year, had hired him on and put Evans in charge of handling Reid's low-interest loans, as well as Lacroix's new housing development. For that reason, Jaye often met with Evans and found him to be a likable person. He figured Evans was a year or two younger than he was.

"Evans, it's good seeing you," he said, shaking his hand.

"Same here. I see we had the same idea for lunch," Evans said, grinning.

"Yes, appears we did. According to Vaughn, this place has the best shrimp potpie."

"It does," Evans quickly agreed. "I'm getting their crab mac and cheese. That's my favorite and nobody makes it better than Chester Witherspoon."

At that moment, he and Evans were next in line to be seated. Since the place was crowded, they had no problem sharing a table. Once seated, a waitress quickly came to take their order. Jaye recognized her as one of the single women who'd shown up at his house with a platter of blueberry pastries after he'd moved in. He had thanked her for them and then sent her on her way without letting her cross over his threshold. He'd taken the pastries in to work the next day and they'd been a hit with his staff.

Today, the woman's huge smile was not for him but for Evans. After she took their orders, she looked at Evans with flirty eyes and said, "Anything for you, Saint."

After she walked off, Jaye couldn't help but grin at Evans. *"Anything for you, Saint?"* Jaye was aware that most people in the cove referred to Evans by his nickname, Saint.

Evans shrugged. "Cindy and I went to school together and nothing has changed over the years. She
likes to flirt."

For the next several minutes, they talked about
sports, namely football and what team should have
made it to the Super Bowl but hadn't. Jaye had felt the
Arizona Cardinals could have had a better season, and
Evans felt likewise about his favorite team, the New
Orleans Saints.

Cindy delivered their food, and when Jaye took a
bite of his potpie, he knew Vaughn and Evans had been
right. It was delicious.

"Are you going to the surprise party that Kaegan and
Bryce are giving Vaughn and Sierra Saturday night?"
Evans asked.

Jaye looked at him. "Yes, I intend to go. I understand
Kaegan lives in the Bayou. I've never been out that way
before, and I'm hoping I don't get lost."

"No problem. You can catch a ride with me. I know
my way. The Bayou is beautiful but it's like a swampy
wilderness at night."

Jaye had thought of using attending the party as a
way to catch a ride with Velvet but riding with Evans
was even better. Velvet would probably be there early
to help Bryce get things ready. Besides, since Velvet
hadn't mentioned anything about the party, chances
were she didn't know he'd been invited. He couldn't
wait until she discovered that he had.

"HEY, VELVET, WAIT UP."

Velvet, who was walking to her car after picking up
lunch, recognized the masculine voice and was tempted

to keep walking and pretend she hadn't heard Webb. However, she knew a few people had heard him call out to her and were glancing in their direction. It would have been rude to just keep walking.

She turned and moments later Webb came to a stop in front of her. "Yes, Webb?"

"How about going to the movies with me Saturday night?"

The man had to be kidding. Hadn't she made it clear— and most recently a few weeks ago—that she wouldn't go out with him? "I won't go out with you, Webb."

Instead of appearing disappointed or annoyed, he gave her a wide smile. It would have been a heart-stopper on the lips of any other man, but when you got Webb, you got the entire conceited package. "Come on, Velvet, you can't still be mad at me for letting those other guys know where I stand with you."

She crossed her arms, not caring if anyone seeing them could tell she was annoyed. "And like I told you, Webb, you don't stand anywhere with me. Why can't you accept that and move on? There are a lot of other single women living here, and I'm sure one of them will interest you." She didn't tack on that whether he interested them was another matter.

"You interest me. I figure sooner or later you'd realize that your teacher's salary won't give you all the things you want. I can. Take your car, for instance. It's nice but wouldn't you rather have a luxury vehicle? I'd get it for you."

"No, thank you. I don't need a man buying anything for me." If only he knew just how true that was. She looked at her watch. "Look, Webb, I need to be going."

"What's the rush? How about joining me for a drink."

The man just didn't know when to give up. "I won't go out on a date with you, Webb."

He smiled. "No date, just drinks."

"No, thanks. Like I said, I need to be going."

"Okay and I hope you know I don't intend to give up on you, Velvet."

Velvet tilted her head, gave him a real serious look and said, "I really wish you would." She turned and walked way, continuing to where her car was parked.

She pushed Webb from her mind, refusing to give him any space in her head. Now, pushing Jaye out of it was another matter. He seemed stuck, and no matter how she tried, he refused to go anywhere. Like those hot dreams she kept having where he always played a major role.

She'd had one every night since she'd intentionally put distance between them. However, she made sure that she was in her kitchen every morning to see him jog by the window, and she would inhale long deep breaths while recalling her dream of the night before. It would really be nice if in one of those dreams they finished what they'd started, but they never did. That only left her even more hot and bothered.

Jaye was usually home when she arrived, but he hadn't tried to seek her out. All she had to do was glance out her bedroom window to see him in what he'd turned into a workshop, busy on those rocking chairs he was building. Usually, he worked well into the night. She knew the exact moment he would call it a day when that part of the yard would darken. Then she would hold her breath, wondering if he would forego what she'd said and seek her out, anyway. He never did.

VELVET HAD JUST finished teaching the last class for the week. She was looking forward to the weekend, which included the surprise party for Vaughn and Sierra. Velvet smiled at the thought that her friend didn't have a clue. Vaughn's sister, Zara, had arrived in town that morning and Sierra's sister, Dani, had arrived last night. Both were staying on the outskirts of town at the lake house owned by Sierra and Dani's parents. Vaughn and Sierra wouldn't know their siblings were in town until they saw them at the party.

Velvet began packing up to leave. She wished there were somewhere else she could go instead of straight home. But then it would be just her luck to run into Webb Crawford again, and there was only so much of him she could take. She thought about going to the Green Fig to dine in, but if Sierra saw her, she might want to join her, and the last thing Velvet wanted was to let something slip out about the surprise party.

A few minutes later, she had called the Witherspoon Cafe for takeout. Tonight's special was their mouth-watering pork chops, Cajun rice and lima beans. She was about to put her phone back in her purse when she thought about calling Jaye to see if he wanted her to bring him dinner as well. That would be the neighborly thing to do. Besides, he had brought dinner to her last week. But would he expect them to share the meal together like they had then? If he did, that would only be asking for trouble.

She released a deep sigh. It had been well over a

week and a part of her wanted to connect with him in some way, even if it was with a text. She came up with a good reason to do so and began texting.

Jaye, the color I've chosen for the rocking chairs is blue.

Moments later he texted back. Blue? Not red?

She couldn't help smiling at his response. He knew red was her favorite color. Blue blends in better with the house's exterior.

Gotcha.

She waited to see if he would text anything else, and when he didn't, she tucked her phone into her purse. Did she expect him to engage in any kind of conversation with her, even via text, when she'd told him that things were getting too hot where they were concerned, and that she couldn't handle the heat and needed space?

Velvet finished gathering up her things when she noticed a writing pad on the floor by a desk. Evidently, one of her students had dropped it. Crossing the room, she saw it was an artist sketch pad with no identifying information on the front or back. She opened it up to see if there was possibly a name on the inside and was immediately amazed at the drawing she saw of what she knew was the statue of Jean LaFitté that was in LaFitte Square in the middle of town. She flipped through and saw other sketches that were just as impressive. She wasn't sure which one of her students had done the sketches, but they'd done a great job. This person definitely had an eye for detail and—

"That's mine!"

Velvet looked up and stared at Lenny Bordeaux. "Lenny. You must have dropped it. I was just trying to figure out which of my students it belonged to. The sketches in here are great."

She saw the surprised look in his eyes. "You think so?" he asked in an uncertain voice.

"Yes, I think so." She handed the sketch pad to him. "You are very gifted."

"Thank you," he said, stuffing the pad in his backpack.

Curiosity made her ask, "Are you taking any art or drafting classes?"

She heard the words *I wish* muttered under his breath before he said, "No."

She tilted her head to look at him. "May I ask why not?"

He shifted his feet and peered down at them a few times before looking back up at her. "My dad is depending on me playing professional baseball."

It was on the tip of her tongue to ask him if that's what he wanted to do. She had a feeling that although he might enjoy playing baseball, art was another one of his passions. It showed in his sketches.

"Maybe if you let your father know which you prefer, then—"

"It won't matter, Ms. Spencer. I am the last hope to restore honor to my family's name."

Honor to his family's name? Again, curiosity made her ask. "How will you playing baseball restore honor to your family's name?"

He hesitated a moment, and then said, "My dad was supposed to play for the Dodgers. He got hurt and now it's all up to me. He says it was meant for a Bordeaux to play professional baseball."

Velvet noticed the slumping of his shoulders. Shoulders that were carrying a lot of unjustified weight. Allen Bordeaux had missed out fulfilling his dream and now he was forcing that dream on his son instead of letting Lenny pursue his own passion.

"Ms. Spencer, promise you won't tell my dad anything? I don't want him disappointed in me."

Velvet heard the despair in Lenny's voice. It wasn't fair; his father was placing a lot on him. That was why she appreciated her parents so much. They never forced her to enter the family business and let her pursue her dream of teaching.

"Please promise me, Ms. Spencer."

She sighed. "Okay, Lenny, I won't say anything to him but maybe you need to consider telling him yourself."

"I can't." And then without saying anything else, Lenny quickly turned and rushed out of the classroom.

CHAPTER TWENTY

"Surprise!"

Velvet thought the looks on Vaughn's and Sierra's faces were priceless. It was evident neither had had a clue that the party given by Kaegan and Bryce was for them. And when Vaughn saw his sister, Zara, and Sierra saw her sister, Dani, they couldn't help but laugh.

"We got them good, didn't we?" Vashti said, coming to stand beside her with her camera in hand.

Velvet smiled. "Yes, we did. And I think the decorations are super." She had arrived three hours early to help Bryce, Ashley, Vashti and Donna with the decorations. The men had been outside, helping Kaegan with the food, and from the aroma that had seeped into the house, it smelled delicious.

A half hour later, it seemed the couple had gotten over their initial shock and were mingling with the guests. Velvet thought Bryce and Kaegan had a beautiful home. Connected to the first level was what was called the party house, a spacious building where they hosted their parties.

Sierra approached her a short while later with a scolding grin on her face. "I can't believe you didn't tell me anything."

"I wasn't supposed to," Velvet said, grinning.

"You just wait. I'm going to find a way to pay you back."

"You can try," Velvet countered.

"And I will."

Velvet looked at her watch. "Your bridal shower will begin in a half hour."

Sierra lifted a brow. "Bridal shower?"

"Yes. It's being hosted in another part of the house. And while we're having your shower, the men will help Kaegan set up for all the delicious food we will eat afterward."

Sierra rubbed her hands together. "Good. Kaegan's a great cook." Then she leaned in to ask, "How are things with you and your neighbor?"

Velvet knew why she was asking, given the last conversation they'd had. "I haven't talked to Jaye in over a week." As far as she was concerned, sending him that text yesterday didn't count.

Sierra raised a brow. "I thought the two of you were jogging together every morning."

She shrugged. "I felt the need to put space between us for a while." And knowing this was Sierra she was talking to, she added, "Whenever we're in close proximity, I can't think. All I want to do is seduce him. So, I'm giving myself a mental break since there's only so much torment my body can take."

A smile touched Sierra's lips. "Umm… I wonder how that's going to work out for you when the cause of your torment just walked in the door with Saint."

"What!"

Velvet turned and her gaze collided with Jaye's. She

hadn't expected to see him and desire suddenly rushed through her.

"Hmm…this is the first time I've been in the presence of the two of you since that town hall meeting and I can feel the heat you're both generating, Velvet."

Velvet broke eye contact with Jaye before others began feeling that same heat. "Why didn't you tell me he was coming?"

Sierra laughed. "Since I didn't know about this party, I wasn't privy to the guest list."

That was true, and neither Bryce nor Vashti would have had a reason to tell her, since they didn't know of her and Jaye's past relationship…or present one for that matter.

"Umm, now that's interesting."

Velvet tried to calm her racing heart after sneaking a peek at Jaye. "What is?"

"Zara just stepped in off the patio and seems to be having the same reaction seeing Saint as you had seeing Jaye. I didn't know they knew each other that well," Sierra said.

"Didn't they grow up here in the cove?"

"Yes, but Saint was in the class that graduated the year before Vaughn. That was five years before Zara and I did."

Velvet couldn't help Sierra in figuring anything out about Zara and Saint. All she could think about was how good Jaye looked in his jeans and button-up shirt. She didn't have to glance around the room to know other women were probably noticing as well.

Trying to get her heart rate under control, she asked, "Are Brody Dorsett and Freda McEnroe a couple now?

I noticed earlier they arrived together, and they were together during the water taxis open house."

She understood that both Brody and Freda had grown up in the cove but moved away after college. Brody had returned a few years ago to take over the job of fire marshal when Brody's father, who'd been Catalina Cove's longtime fire marshal, retired early due to an illness. Brody's father had subsequently passed away.

Like several others, Freda had returned to the cove last year. She'd opened a bakeshop, taking advantage of Reid's Lacroix low-interest loan program. Velvet thought she was a very attractive woman and Brody was a handsome man. Personally, she thought they looked good together.

"No, they're just good friends who enjoy each other's company. Both are recovering from broken hearts," Sierra said.

"I definitely know how that is."

Bryce let out a loud whistle to get everyone's attention. "The men are to follow Kaegan to the party house and, ladies, please follow me." She grinned and added, "The fun is about to begin."

"I GATHER YOU didn't get the memo, Jaye."

Jaye took a sip of his beer and looked at Sawyer. They had been talking about how the bank could support Catalina Cove's Police Department's athletic league when the women appeared, arriving from the bridal shower to join the men in what Kaegan called the party house.

"What memo?" He was trying to keep up with Sawyer's conversation while keeping his eyes on Velvet.

Sawyer chuckled. "The one I heard Webb Crawford sent all the single men in the cove, letting them know Velvet Spencer was off-limits."

Jaye wondered who else might have picked up on his interest in Velvet. Sawyer didn't count. He was the sheriff, and since moving to Catalina Cove, it hadn't taken Jaye long to discover that Sheriff Grisham made it his business to notice everything.

"Nope. I didn't get a memo. Webb Crawford paid me a personal visit instead."

Sawyer was about to take a sip of beer and the bottle stopped inches from his mouth. "You're kidding, right?"

"Nope."

Sawyer sipped his beer and then said, "For him to do that means he considers you fierce competition. I would love to have been privy to that conversation."

"I'm glad you weren't. Let's just say I all but told Crawford what he could do with his asinine directive."

Sawyer shook his head. "Good for you. It's a pity that he can intimidate others into following his orders. There's nothing I can do since no laws have been broken and, so far, none of the men have complained."

"All I got to say is that he doesn't know me," Jaye said.

"And I guess he also doesn't know of your past relationship with Velvet, either."

Jaye held Sawyer's gaze. "Do I have a past relationship with her?"

Sawyer's lips spread into a smile. "If there was any doubt in my mind before, there isn't any now. Whether you know it or not, the two of you generate a lot of heat. Sexual energy is nothing to mess with."

"Tell me about it. And what makes you think it's because of our past? Why can't it be because we met as neighbors and—"

"Cut the crap, Jaye. I don't know the particulars, but if anyone were to take the time to think about it long enough, they'll figure things out. Especially since both of you are from Phoenix. Most people never bothered to find out where Velvet lived before moving here, but if they did, they'd begin wondering. So why are the two of you pretending otherwise?"

Jaye released a deep sigh. "Velvet's choice, not mine. And you're right about our past. We were together three years and I fucked up big time. My being here in Catalina Cove is no coincidence. I came here to win back Velvet's heart and no one, especially someone like Webb Crawford, is going to stop me."

Sawyer gave him a leveled look. "So far Velvet hasn't filed any complaints of you being a nuisance, so I guess you're handling your business within the confines of the law."

Jaye couldn't help but smile. Leave it to Sawyer to look at everything as law and order. And as far as anyone in Catalina Cove noticing he was attracted to Velvet, he really didn't give a damn. Even now, he could barely keep his eyes off her. That's what she got for making herself scarce for over a week. Avoiding him only made the situation worse. Case in point, Velvet glanced over at him and when their gazes connected, he felt a deep stirring in his groin.

"Ahh…maybe this is where I need to make a suggestion," Sawyer said.

Without breaking eye contact with Velvet, Jaye asked, "What's that?"

"Unless you want every single person here to figure out that something is going on between you two, I suggest you and Velvet cool off the heat or leave and go take care of business."

VELVET TRIED NOT to look at Jaye but found it impossible. She had tried so hard to put distance between them and now here they were in Kaegan and Bryce's party house, across the room from each other, breathing in the same air and sharing stolen glances, and according to Sierra, emitting heat.

She felt his eyes on her again and, unable to ignore it, she turned and saw him looking at her. She knew that look and knew what it meant. If others paid close attention, they would know as well. She should care if they did, but…

"Are you enjoying yourself, Velvet?"

She switched her gaze from Jaye to Bryce when she walked up.

"Yes, I am, Bryce. And I think everything turned out great. Sierra and Vaughn received a lot of nice gifts, and the food is delicious as usual." The menu had consisted of a feast with all the shrimp, crabs, lobsters and oysters you could eat, and all harvested by Kaegan's shipping company.

"I'll let the cooks know that you thought so. You can never go wrong with both Kaegan and my dad in the kitchen. And I want to thank you for all your help, Velvet. I appreciate it."

"No problem. I enjoyed doing it. Sierra is a good

friend. Catalina Cove is a nice town and I'm glad I moved here and got to meet all of you."

Bryce smiled. "And we're glad you did, too. And just so you know, I was selective with my invitation list and you're here among friends you can trust."

Velvet wondered why Bryce was telling her that and was about to ask when a deep husky voice said, "Excuse me for interrupting."

Bryce and Velvet glanced up to see Jaye standing there. "Hello, Jaye," Bryce said, smiling brightly. "I'm glad you came."

"Thanks for inviting me." He shifted his attention to Velvet. "I was wondering if I could get a ride back to town with you when you left?"

Velvet swallowed. She and Jaye riding in the same car with all that sexual energy? Seriously? "How did you get here?" she asked.

"I rode here with Evans Toussaint. I didn't want to risk driving myself and getting lost."

Velvet was about to ask why he couldn't ride back with Saint and then thought better of it. She looked across the room and saw Saint standing in a group with Isaac, Brody and Ray, and they seemed to be sharing a joke. Zara was on the sidelines, talking to Freda and Donna. After Zara's earlier reaction at seeing Saint, she seemed to be ignoring him now.

There had to be a reason Jaye couldn't ride back with Saint. Maybe the man had made other plans when he left here. But still... "I'm not sure when I'll be leaving, Jaye. I helped plan the party and I might be needed to stay and—"

"Do nothing," Bryce broke in quickly. "Vashti,

Donna and I can handle everything, Velvet. Don't worry about it. But the two of you can't leave before the dancing begins to work off all that food we've eaten."

Suddenly, loud music began playing and Bryce grabbed Velvet's hand and pulled her toward the dance floor.

VELVET ENJOYED THE line dancing, where you didn't need a partner. She hadn't danced this much since Kaegan and Bryce's wedding reception. She liked dancing, always had, and Jaye would take her dancing all the time because he liked to dance, too. But he wasn't dancing tonight. Instead, he was sitting at a table with Sawyer, Ray and Kaegan. They were talking and Jaye was obviously pretending to listen because she felt his eyes clearly following her.

When the DJ announced he was toning things down with a couple of slow tunes, Velvet turned to Bryce to let her know she would be sitting the next ones out. But then she felt someone take her hand. She didn't have to wonder who it was.

Turning, she saw Jaye's face. The intensity of his gaze held her spellbound and he said in a low throaty voice, "Please dance with me, Velvet."

She knew without looking that several pairs of eyes were on them, and to avoid stirring up further attention, she nodded. He gently pulled her into his arms. The moment her chest pressed against his, she thought that maybe dancing with him wasn't such a good idea. They were two aroused bodies moving in sync to a slow tune.

She remembered the last time they had danced this way together—her body remembered as well. It recognized the solid muscular body that was holding her, and just like the last time, she was enveloped in his heat, his scent and all that was Jack Colfax, Jr. Automatically, she rested her head against his firm chest and closed her eyes, letting her mind and senses absorb everything about him. Even the sound of his breathing was soothing something within her.

She knew people were probably looking at them and wondering how a man and woman who barely knew each other could connect so perfectly. Velvet didn't want to think about the implications of that now. All she wanted was to feel Jaye's hand gently gliding across her back, stroking a need she couldn't deny.

The music came to an end and Jaye whispered into her ear, "Let's step outside for a moment."

She nodded and with his warm hand at the center of her back, he led her outside to the patio where a few couples were talking. He guided her to a darkened area that overlooked the Bayou. She inhaled the fresh air, loving the scent of the seasoned seafood that still lingered. But more than anything, she loved the masculine scent of the man standing beside her with his hand still at the center of her back.

Jaye hadn't said anything, but then no words were needed. They had come to a crossroad although nothing had changed between them. The relationship was still one-sided. She knew she still loved him, although for the past two years she'd tried fighting it. She had told herself she had eradicated him from her heart, but in essence she hadn't. Now, she was in the same predicament she'd been in two years ago that had driven her to leave him and not look back.

"Velvet, we need to talk. There's something I need to tell you."

She really didn't want to hear it. There was no need for him to reiterate that although he desired her, he could never love her.

"I don't want to talk, Jaye. I want to act. I don't love you and you don't love me. I think we've pretty much established that fact." She couldn't admit to him she still loved him and had never stopped loving him. She didn't want to think what that said about a woman who loved a man who would never love her.

"You said I was the only woman you would engage in a sex-only affair with, then that's all I want until you leave the cove. The one-and-done wasn't enough for me." There. She had said it, without shame. If physical pleasure was all she would ever get from him, then she would take it.

He'd leave in a few months, and when he left, she knew he would be taking a piece of her heart with him. But at least she would have this time with him. She intended to create new memories to sustain her.

He didn't say anything, just stared at her for a long while. Then when he spoke, he asked, "Are you ready to leave?"

She nodded and answered, "Yes, I'm ready."

CHAPTER TWENTY-ONE

WHEN VELVET BROUGHT the car to a complete stop in front of the house on Blueberry Lane, Jaye opened the door and got out. Hearing her again say that she didn't love him was a pain he would bear because deep down he believed if she loved him once, then she could do so again. Nothing had changed because he intended to do whatever he had to do to make that happen. Even if she thought for the time being that they were engaging in a sex-only affair. Each time they came together, it wouldn't be for sex but for love, and he hoped that eventually she would realize it.

He went around to her side, opened the door for her and then swept her into his arms. "Jaye! Somebody might see us."

"I doubt it."

Then, to make sure her mind wasn't on who might see them, he leaned in and kissed her. The drive from the Bayou had been tortuous as hell. He had let her concentrate on driving while he had concentrated on her.

He wasn't sure how he made it up the steps, holding her in his arms with their lips locked, but by time he pulled his mouth away, they were in front of his door. She had never been inside his home and he wanted her in his bed. Adjusting her in his arms, he fished the key from his pocket and opened the door, then maneuvered his way up the stairs.

When he reached the landing, she said, "You seem pretty good at climbing stairs with a woman in your arms."

"Only when you're that woman," he said, moving straight for his bedroom.

When they reached it, he placed her on her feet beside the bed and began devouring her mouth in ways he felt in every part of his body. And she was kissing him back and their tongues mingled greedily like this would be the only time they had. But he'd heard her say there were no longer any limitations until he left. Little did she know that he didn't intend to leave without her.

If she truly wanted to make Catalina Cove her home, then this was where they would both be. In fact, when she'd mentioned she wanted oceanfront property in Reid Lacroix's proposed housing development, he made arrangements with Reid to purchase it. If they didn't live in the cove permanently, it would certainly serve as their special vacation getaway.

He deepened their kiss and felt her immediate response. She tasted delicious, and her mouth was so hot it was practically burning his. It had always been this way when their mouths mated.

Jaye broke off the kiss when he felt her hand fumbling with the zipper of his jeans. He knew what she wanted and tonight and the days that followed he would give her whatever she wanted and whenever she wanted it.

He began undressing her, pulling her blouse over her head and tossing it onto a chair nearby. He removed her bra easily, and seeing the lush twin mounds, he knew he had to give them both quick licks before removing the rest of her clothing. Then, he made quick work of removing her jeans and sexy barely-there undies. When she stood before him completely naked, he removed his own clothes while she watched.

Jaye liked the intensity of her gaze, and as he removed each piece, she reached out and stroked him. First, his chest and shoulders. When she reached for his erection with warm hands, he sucked in a deep breath. "I wouldn't touch that too much if I were you, baby. It's too ready for you."

She smiled. "I doubt if it's more ready for me than I am for it."

"Want to bet?"

While holding his manhood firmly in her hand, she eased up to him and came inches to his lips and whispered. "Don't want to bet. I want to make love."

At least she hadn't used the word *sex*—and he doubted she realized it. For them, it would never be about just having sex. It would always be about making love, and it was up to him to prove that to her. Sweeping her off her feet, he placed her in the bed and then joined her there. When his mouth went for her breasts, she whispered, "Later. I need you inside of me, Jaye."

Intent on giving her any and everything she wanted, he moved in position over her and stared down and said, "Don't close your eyes, Vel."

If she found his request odd, she didn't say. More than anything he wanted her to read in his eyes the words she wasn't ready to hear. It didn't matter if she didn't love him. He loved her and for now there was enough love in his heart for the both of them.

Spreading her wide with his knees, he kept a tight grip on her hips as he slowly began easing inside her. Pressure was filling his belly as he pushed into her depths, and he could feel her inner muscles clenching him as he went. He'd always loved the feel of being skin to skin with her, something he'd never done with any other woman. He hoped she understood that was still true for him. She kept her eyes fixed on his, and he hoped she saw everything he wanted her to see.

He began thrusting into her with a precision he felt all the way in his belly. He wasn't holding back on anything. From the look in her eyes and the moans she was making, she was enjoying pleasure of the most intense kind. He knew just what she liked, how to angle his thrusts to ignite her body on fire. When sensation flooded his groin area, he increased his pace and nearly lost his grip on reality. But still, he didn't break eye contact with her.

"Jaye!"

When she whispered his name, Jaye was fully aware she was on the verge of an orgasm. So was he, and he wanted them to come together like they had so many times before. He wished he could go back in time to appreciate just how perfect mating had been between them.

"Come for me, baby, and I will come for you," he whispered in her ear.

As if his words pushed her over the edge, she screamed his name and he followed, hollering hers when everything within him ripped. And they were staring into each other's eyes the entire time.

He kissed her as they gave their bodies time to recover from their climax. When he released her mouth, he was moved by the glazed eyes looking back at him. He parted his lips to tell her he loved her, then stopped himself. Considering everything she'd said earlier, it would be up to her to realize he loved her, just like a part of him wanted to believe that no matter what she said, she still loved him.

"Thank you for doing this with me, Jaye," she said in a low voice.

Did she really believe she had to thank him? "For you, anytime, Vel."

"And I plan to hold you to that." She wrapped her arms around his neck and brought his mouth to hers.

VELVET SLOWLY OPENED her eyes. Glancing around the room, it took her a quick second to realize she was not in her bed. Sighing deeply, she closed her eyes again to remember everything, the hours and hours of what seemed like endless lovemaking. Once Jaye had brought her into his bedroom, the air surrounding them had become charged and intimate. But then the air had been that way between them at the party.

"Good morning. I see you're awake."

She shifted to look over at Jaye. He was standing in the doorway, fully dressed in a pair of jeans and a pullover sweatshirt that had *Colfax Construction* in bold letters across it. How had he left the bed without her knowing about it?

Sitting up in bed, she pulled the covers up when she realized she was completely naked. She wondered why the modesty now when several times she had been awakened with Jaye's head between her legs or him sucking on her nipples.

"Good morning," she said, not able to fight back a yawn. "What time is it?" She didn't see a clock anywhere in the room.

He glanced at his watch and said, "A little past noon."

"Noon? I've never slept this late before."

"Sure you have. All the time."

He was right, and it had always been after a night of endless lovemaking with him. There were times, especially whenever he returned from one of his business trips, that they couldn't get enough of each other.

"I picked up breakfast for us earlier, but didn't want to wake you."

"Where did you go?"

"The Witherspoon Café. I brought back a bag of their blueberry muffins and I got coffee going. Join me in the kitchen for breakfast…or maybe I should say lunch. Then after we eat, you can get dressed and help me outside."

"Help you outside?"

"Yes."

"With what?"

"The rocking chairs. With your help, I'll have them ready to paint this week."

"Oh, okay." She watched him cross the room to the bed and lean down to kiss her. But it wasn't a light kiss, it was one filled with all the desire she'd come to expect from Jaye. In no time at all, she was moaning and was about to suggest he take off his clothes and rejoin her in bed when he released her mouth and said, "Don't tempt me, Velvet, or we won't go outside to finish those rocking chairs."

"I won't tempt you if you don't tempt me," she countered.

He flashed her a dimpled smile. "I'll do my best."

"THANKS AGAIN FOR BREAKFAST."

Jaye turned at the sound of Velvet's voice. She was wearing a pair of jeans and one of his old T-shirts. Her hair was pulled back in a ponytail and he thought she looked cute and sexy.

"Glad you enjoyed it."

She smiled and gave him a dreamy-eyed look. "I appreciate the company *and* breakfast. You can't go wrong with blueberry muffins from the Witherspoon Café." And, as if it were the most natural thing for her to do, she leaned in and brushed a kiss across his lips. "And I happen to like the company just as much."

Deciding that wasn't enough, he pulled her into his arms and gave her his definition of an appreciation kiss. When he released her mouth, she said, "Remember, we aren't supposed to tempt each other."

He chuckled. "I'll remember—or I'll try to."

She shoved her hands into the pockets of her jeans and asked again, "So what do you need me to do?"

"I've finished that one chair," he said. "All it needs is sanding. I figured you can sand it for me while I finish up the second chair."

"I don't know how to sand anything."

Handing her a pair of safety glasses and work gloves, he said, "Don't worry, I'll show you."

He got some sandpaper for her. After demonstrating

how to start sanding in the direction of the woodgrain, he left her alone. While he worked on the other chair, on occasion he would glance over at her and see what a good job she was doing. He also couldn't help noticing just how good she looked doing it.

They didn't engage in conversation because of the noise from his saw. But more than once, he caught her watching him, like he was a puzzle she was trying to figure out. He wanted to tell her that he really wasn't that complicated, and that he was a man deeply in love with a woman whom he wanted a new start with.

They stopped to have dinner, feasting on the leftovers Kaegan and Bryce had sent them home with, including bottles of beer. Everything tasted just as good as it had last night.

"I think it's wonderful how Reid has lured so many people back to Catalina Cove with that low-interest loan program," Velvet said, after taking a sip of beer. "It was really an ingenuous idea."

Jaye agreed. "I think so, too. I guess it's his way of looking out for the cove's future."

After dinner, they went outside and continued working amiably together. He had finished the second chair and she'd begun sanding it. "When will you paint them?"

He shifted his eyes to her and smiled. "When do you want to paint them? I'd like to have this project finished this week."

She nodded. "That will work since I'll be leaving the cove next weekend to return to Phoenix."

He lifted a brow. "You will?"

"Yes. Another bridal shower. This time it's Ruthie's."

"Will this be your first time returning to Phoenix since leaving?"

"No. I was there for Ruthie and Todd's engagement party during New Year's."

So that's where she'd gone. Jaye had rushed back to Catalina Cove right after Christmas, hoping to see her at the cove's New Year's ball he'd attended as Reid Lacroix's guest, only to discover she wasn't there. At the time, he hadn't moved into the house on Blueberry Lane and was staying at Shelby by the Sea.

They continued working on the chairs and when the sun began to set, she removed her gloves and took off her safety glasses. "That's it for me today. I'm going home to relax before taking a shower."

Was she telling him that as a way of an invitation to join her in the shower? The thought made his lower extremities throb. He removed his safety glasses and gloves as well. "I think I'll call it a day myself. With your help, I accomplished a lot."

"Are you sure I wasn't in the way?"

"I'm positive. You did a good job sanding those chairs."

"Need my assistance in putting things away?"

"Thanks, that would be appreciated since I'm in need of a shower myself."

"Are you?"

"Yes." Then in what he thought was a soft ultra-sexy voice, she said, "Would you like to join me taking mine?"

He pulled her close to him to wrap his arms around her shoulders. "I was hoping you'd ask."

"And if I can be so bold to say, I'd like to try out

your shower, Jaye. I'm sure there's another old T-shirt of yours I can wear borrow."

"And if not, you can certainly wear nothing at all."

IT DIDN'T TAKE them long to put things away and head toward the house. Walking beside Jaye, Velvet struggled for control. More than once she had watched him work. His concentration had been focused on what he was doing while hers had been focused on him.

"We're going jogging together in the morning, right?" He moved aside for her to go up the porch steps ahead of him.

"I guess so, just as long as you know I'm still only doing one lap."

He leaned in and whispered, "I'll take any number of laps you'll give me."

He opened the door to his house and, after closing it behind them, he swept her into his arms. "I can walk up the stairs, you know."

"I know, but there's something about carrying you anywhere that makes it special."

She wished he would have thought that way when they'd been together before. She didn't want to think about that time, especially not now, and reached up and placed her arms around his neck to bring his mouth down to hers. The moment their tongues began tangling, all the desires and needs that he had taken care of last night had apparently replenished over the past few hours, as sensations rushed through her body.

When she felt them moving, she broke off the kiss. Halfway up the stairs, she suddenly said, "Stop, Jaye."

He stopped and looked down at her. "What's wrong?"

"I can't make it to the shower." She lowered her hands to unbutton his shirt. Understanding her need, he set her feet on the steps and began undressing her. Everything was happening so fast that she wasn't sure who was undressing whom until they were both naked.

Lifting her hips, he used their discarded clothing as a cushion for her against the wooden stairs. Before she could tell him that wasn't necessary, he kneeled between her thighs, slipped her legs over his shoulders, and buried his head there.

"Jaye!"

The moment she felt his tongue inside her, she fought hard not to come apart and grabbed hold of the railing as a multitude of sensations raced through her. Although no other man had ever done this to her before him, she was certain nobody could do this like Jaye. He knew just where his tongue needed to be to provide her with the ultimate satisfaction.

She screamed his name when intense pleasure took her over, thinking it was a good thing their neighbors were not in shouting, or screaming, range. He moved his mouth away, lowered her legs and then covered her with his body. Placing a tight grip on her thighs, he quickly thrust inside her and began riding her hard. Over and over again. They came together.

Intense pleasure consumed her, taking over her mind and body. Not holding anything back, he propelled her right into another orgasm. After she screamed his name for probably the fourth time, he lowered his mouth to hers, capturing it with one deep tongue-penetrating kiss.

Her body should have felt tired, worn out, but it felt

even more energized. She wrapped her legs around his waist so he could lift her up. "Now for our shower, Velvet." He carried her the rest of the way up the stairs.

CHAPTER TWENTY-TWO

"THE ROCKING CHAIRS are simply beautiful, Jaye," Velvet said, truly meaning it.

She knew Jaye had spent most of his evening hours working on them. On those days she hadn't taught gymnastics after school, she had joined him and even helped him paint them. She could honestly say it was a project they had done together, and she'd enjoyed it. He had told her he would spend the weekend looking for cushions that would complement the color. What he'd chosen were perfect.

She had resumed jogging with him every morning and it was like she hadn't stopped. She enjoyed hearing updates about the new bank in Birmingham, and sharing any news she had about her days at school. She told him about her conversation with Lenny and his passion for art. Like her, Jaye thought it was unfair for Allen Bordeaux to place so much pressure on his son.

She had spent the weekend in Phoenix, at Ruthie's bridal shower, and returned home before noon on Sunday. The moment she drove into the yard, she knew she'd find him in the backyard. When she saw her, he turned off his electric saw, set aside his safety glasses and gloves, and opened his arms to her. She walked right into them and they shared the kiss she had definitely needed. And from the way he devoured her mouth, he had needed it as well. Then he held her and whispered that he had missed her. He showed her everything, including his new project. He was building a couple of wooden planters that would hold blueberry bushes on the porch as well.

She had selected the color blue but he had chosen the perfect shade that blended in well with the house exterior. She also noted, while she'd been gone, he had painted the floor of the porch a dark gray. "Why are the rocking chairs on the back porch instead of the front?" she asked as they stood side by side with his arms around her shoulders.

He looked down and met her gaze. "I built these chairs for us, Velvet, and I doubted you'd want anyone to see us rocking together on the front porch. I put them back here so we'll have our privacy."

She held his gaze, slightly confused. He'd told her he was making the chairs to complement the style of the house. "You made them for us?"

"Yes. I recall you once telling me how your parents had rocking chairs on their porch at your childhood home in Seattle, and how they would sit together in the evenings to watch the sunset."

She blinked in surprise. "You remember me telling you that?"

"Yes, and I figured we could do that in the evenings when we get home from work. That way you can unload and tell me how your day went and I'll tell you about mine, as well as anything else we want to talk about."

What he'd said was a shocker. "Why? You never wanted that before, Jaye." She recalled she'd tried countless times to get him to sit on the patio with her at his place or hers and just talk. He'd said they could talk just as well in the bedroom. Only problem was, once there, they never really had.

"There are a lot of things I didn't do before that I want to do now. I've discovered it's not good to have no one to talk to, especially when you have a lot on your mind."

She nodded. "You've always had Mercury."

"Yes, he's always been my best friend and still is. I can talk to him about some things, but with a wife and a baby on the way, Mercury is busy these days."

And Mercury's outlook on life has changed, Velvet thought. Again, she couldn't help wondering if the reason Jaye was making all these changes in his life was not because he honestly wanted to, but because he felt compelled to do so because those he'd been close to for years had made changes. When she had suggested that to him, he had denied it was the reason for any changes he was making in his life.

"Well, I just wanted to let you know I'm back. I don't want to keep you from your work." She moved away from his side.

He reached out and pulled her back, bringing her even closer to his side. "Now that you're back, we can grab something to eat and then later, we can try out our chairs."

Our chairs. Three years ago, she would have given anything to hear him refer to anything as *theirs*. "Okay. I have a taste for ribs."

"Had I known I would have fired up the grill and had them ready when you got back."

"That's a sweet thought, Jaye, but you had enough on your plate with the chairs."

"How was the bridal shower?"

"It was great. Unlike the one we did for Vaughn and Sierra, it was the traditional girls-only. The Suns played and Todd and the guys went to the game. Everyone was happy they won. You still have season tickets?"

"Yes, I still have them. How about if I pick up ribs from The Shack."

She turned, wrapped her arms around his waist and tilted her head back to look into his eyes. "Barbeque ribs aren't the only thing I have a taste for." She wasn't sure why at that moment she decided to tell him what she wanted. A part of her was a little overwhelmed by his comment that he'd built those rocking chairs for them. She knew how much time he'd spent over the past weeks working on them.

He held her gaze for a long moment. "And what else do you have a taste for, Velvet?"

"For you, Jaye."

She saw the potent look of desire in his eyes when he said, "And I have a taste for you, too."

His words sent a sensuous tingling up and down her spine. Jaye was the only man whose deep husky tone, had the ability to do that. Then there was that look in his eyes that said how he would taste her and just where.

"Then I suggest we take care of these hot and sensual taste buds first. What do you think of that?" she asked, gently rubbing her hands down his arms.

"Whatever you want, Velvet, I will give it to you. No matter what it is."

She smiled. "I was hoping you'd say that."

"I'LL BE BACK in a few, baby."

Velvet opened sleepy eyes to the sound of the deep husky voice and saw Jaye standing by the bed. They had made love several times before slipping off to sleep for a nap. Now he was up and dressed and she was still in bed naked. "Be back? Where are you going?"

"To pick up the ribs." He grinned and added, "You know that other thing you had a taste for."

At any other time, she would have blushed, but not now. She was too exhausted to even bother. Jaye had practically worn her out. She was certain there were passion marks over every part of her body. And she had left passion marks of her own on parts of him.

"I remember," she said, shifting in bed and feeling the intensity of his lovemaking in several muscles.

She was about to close her eyes and doze off again, when she felt him nibbling at her lips. When she whispered his name, he slid his tongue inside her mouth and kissed her with enough passion to curl her toes. His kisses were always an all-out assault on her senses and in no time at all she was moaning. The pressure of his kiss eased up some, but that didn't stop the moans or all the sensations flowing through her.

After several deeper strokes of his tongue, he finally whispered against her moist lips, "Think of me until I get back."

She had no problem doing that and told him so. When she heard his door close behind him, she reached out and drew his pillow close to her to inhale Jaye's scent. She loved how he smelled. Instead of drifting back to sleep, she shifted on her back to stare up at the ceiling as a wondrous feeling swept over her.

Like she'd told Ruthie when her best friend had picked her up from the airport Friday night, she enjoyed being in a noncommitted relationship with Jaye because she didn't have to worry about a broken heart. Although she loved him, she had accepted that he didn't love her, and never would. With that acceptance, she felt satisfied. And speaking of satisfaction, since they'd agreed to their sex-only affair, Jaye was filling her nights with so much of it, she was smiling every day. She would miss him when he left Catalina Cove to return to Phoenix. She pushed the thought from her mind that she only had him for a few more months. He'd mentioned they had officially hired a new bank manager for the branch here in the cove. When the man arrived, there would be no reason for Jaye to hang around.

She sat up in bed and decided to get dressed. There was still a lot of daylight left and Jaye had said they would be trying the rocking chairs out today. She was excited about that. He had done a great job on them and what was even more special was that she had helped.

Just the thought he had remembered what she'd told him about her parents and their chairs gave her pause. She honestly thought he'd tuned her out when she told him but obviously he'd heard her. She also thought about what he'd said about realizing what he'd missed out on by not sharing himself with others. She would be the first to admit this Jaye was different, but the big question was how long he would stay that way.

BY THE TIME Jaye returned with dinner, Velvet had showered and changed into a pair of leggings and pullover top and, as usual, he thought she looked sexy as hell.

She'd opened the door to her home, letting him know they would be eating there.

"The ribs are delicious," she said when they began digging in. He felt a heady rush of desire when he saw her greedily lick her lips and recalled how she had licked him the same way earlier.

"Jaye?"

Suddenly, he realized she'd said his name while he'd been captivated by her mouth. "Yes?"

"Was the Shack crowded?"

He wondered if she was asking because it had taken him a little longer to return. Hopefully, she'd missed him. "No, but I did run into a few people."

"Oh? Who?"

"Ray and Ashley, Isaac and Donna and their little ones. They were dining in." He paused. "Just so you know, they noticed I was getting two take-out dinners instead of one."

He studied her expression as she kept eating. When she didn't comment, he asked, "Does that bother you?"

She shrugged. "After Kaegan and Bryce's party, I think some people might have their suspicions, anyway. We were giving off some pretty hot vibes." She stopped. "Something Bryce said that night pretty much confirmed others had noticed."

He lifted a brow. "And what did Bryce say?"

"She assured me we were among friends. Before I could ask her what she meant, you walked up. But I think I know what she meant."

"What's that?"

"That the people at the party, most of whom I've met

since moving to the cove and consider friends, can be trusted not to spread gossip."

Jaye nodded. "By gossip, you mean spreading news that we have a thing for each other?"

"Yes, a sexual thing."

He was beginning to not like any words that had the word *sex* connected to them. "Will you ever level with them—those you trust and feel close to—and let them know we once shared something more serious than a sexual thing?"

She tilted her head and looked at him, frowning. "But that's all we shared before Jaye—a sexual thing. My mistake was thinking it was more, remember?"

He could hear the hurt in her voice and reached out and took her hand, ready to tell her the truth. "Velvet, I—"

Velvet quickly pulled her hand back. "No, Jaye. Please don't spoil this moment for us. I don't want to talk about the past. I just want to focus on now." She wiped her mouth with a napkin, smiled and said excitedly, "I'm ready to try out our rocking chairs."

A SHORT WHILE LATER, with full wineglasses, Velvet and Jaye settled into the rocking chairs, admiring the view. Fields and fields of blueberry bushes stretched under the beautiful Louisiana sky. She was glad he'd decided to put the chairs out back instead of in the front. Not just for privacy, but because the view was a lot nicer and provided a sense of peace and tranquility. She hoped this would become one of their favorite places.

"This feels nice, Jaye. You did a great job."

"And you helped."

"Yes," she said proudly, grinning from ear to ear. "And I helped just a little."

"You helped a lot. I enjoyed working with you. We make a great team."

She refused to read anything into what he said and jokingly asked, "Is that your way of hinting that you want me to help you build those planters for the porch now?"

He chuckled. "That would be nice."

Velvet chuckled as well. "That can be arranged."

They rocked while sipping wine. Eventually, she said, "Sierra called after you left. The wedding is in less than two weeks, and I think she's getting nervous."

"Vaughn came into the bank Friday, and he doesn't seem nervous at all."

"That's a man for you."

He took another sip of wine and then asked, "Who's keeping their goddaughter while they're honeymooning in the Caribbean?"

"Things worked out great since they'll be gone the week of spring break. Just so happens, it's the same as spring break for schools in Atlanta, so Teryn will be spending the week with Dani, Emory and their kids."

He nodded. "I forgot all about spring break. What do you have planned for that week?"

She shrugged. "Nothing really. Last year Sierra and I took Teryn to Disney World in Orlando, and we had a great time."

Jaye stopped rocking and looked at her. She saw the serious look on his face. "Jaye, what's wrong?"

"I'd like to ask you something. You don't have to

give me your answer now, but promise me you'll at least think about it."

"What?"

"The week of spring break… Since you don't have any plans, will you go out of town with me, Velvet? Spending time with you here is nice but I'd like to take you out to dinner and do fun things with you outside of the bedroom."

She didn't say anything and took another sip of wine. That was a switch. Even when they went on trips together in the past, they would stay inside and in the bedroom most of time, being the two passionate beings that they were.

"Where would we go?" she asked, wondering what he would say. Usually, they'd gone to his family's cabin in the mountains of North Carolina, his place on Lake Tahoe, or skiing in Aspen.

"I want you to decide. Somewhere you'd want to go for a week to get away, wherever it is. I want to take you there. Where we can engage in unrestrained indulgences and won't be confined to this house."

Unrestrained indulgences…

Velvet thought about his offer. Honestly, she would love to go somewhere for a week. The only reason she hadn't planned something was because she hadn't wanted to sacrifice any time she could spend with him—inside the bedroom. Especially when she had no idea how much more time they had left.

She studied him. "Thanks for the invite, Jaye. I'll give it some thought and let you know my decision."

CHAPTER TWENTY-THREE

JAYE DREW IN a long labored breath as he and Velvet finished their warm-ups. The outfit she was wearing was so hot-looking, he was panting before they even started the chore of loosening up their muscles. Although, there was a certain part of his anatomy that couldn't loosen up. Instead, he could feel it getting hard every time he caught sight of her.

As they took off jogging toward the fields, keeping a steady pace together, he looked at her. "Is your outfit new?"

A smile stretched her lips, lips he enjoyed devouring every chance he got. "Yes. It was a thank-you gift from Ruthie for helping out with her shower."

"She did a great job selecting that outfit for you. You look great in it."

"Thanks."

They didn't say anything for a minute and then he said, "I went to see my mother a while back."

Velvet stumbled and he was convinced she would've fallen if he hadn't reached out to steady her. "You found her?"

"She wasn't lost, Vel. Not really. Since my college days, I've known where she was and how to get in touch with her if I wanted to. I never did. Neither did Dean or Franklin."

"I didn't know."

"The reason you didn't know was because I didn't tell you. That was another mistake on my part. I should have shared more with you instead of holding it in."

Velvet was quiet, and Jaye wondered if she was remembering all those times she'd tried getting him to talk about the mother who'd deserted him, his father and his brothers. One thing she did know about him was that he never displayed much emotion. For years, he'd thought that was a sign of weakness and made a point to keep his emotions in check. Whenever she'd broach the subject of his mother, he'd clam up.

"She's living in Texas with her fourth husband. Husband number two, the one she ran off and left us for, passed away after ten years of marriage. However, he left her pretty well off."

"Who was he?"

He remembered what his father had told him. "She met him at a department store of all places. He had a wife and she had a family. After they sneaked around, having an affair for six months, he decided to divorce his wife and she decided to ditch her husband and children. She divorced Dad, then the two of them moved to Texas."

After they rounded a bend in the trail, he said, "He died of a heart attack ten years later. Within a year, she married husband number three, a man twelve years younger. He nearly broke her financially. Husband number four was her divorce attorney."

Velvet eyed him. "She told you all that?"

"No. When I got older, Dad told me about husband number two. And before deciding to go see her, I hired a private investigator. He supplied information on the others. I wanted to be prepared, to know all there was about her."

"Were you prepared?"

He didn't say anything for a minute and then admitted, "Not as much as I'd have liked."

Jaye saw they had already covered the first lap and were back at their starting point. "It's time for you to split to get dressed for work. Let's finish this conversation this evening over wine and sitting in our rocking chairs."

She smiled. "I'd like that, but don't forget I have gymnastics class after work. Then I'm joining Sierra and Teryn for dinner at the Green Fig."

"Alright. Thanks for the reminder. I have a dinner meeting with Reid and Vaughn at the Lighthouse." Since moving here, he'd discovered the cove's lighthouse-turned-restaurant was one of the best places for fine dining, and you had to make reservations weeks, sometime months, in advance.

There was no need to tell her he was meeting with them to discuss his offer to buy the first piece of oceanfront property in Reid's new development, and his plan to give it to her, hopefully, as a wedding gift.

"I understand Reid and his wife are leaving on a cruise this weekend," Velvet said.

"Yes. They'll return for Vaughn and Sierra's wedding, and then they are leaving again to take their granddaughters to Hawaii for their college spring break."

"Sounds nice."

"Yes, it does."

When Velvet leaned toward him and tilted her mouth up, he knew what she wanted but teased her by planting a kiss on her cheek. She frowned. "Enough with those cheek or brush-of-the-lips kisses whenever we jog, Jaye. Why are you holding back when I know you can do better than that?"

He grinned. "Can I?"

"You know you can."

Yes, he could, but he'd been trying to show restraint and control, otherwise he would end up making love to her right in this blueberry field. Wrapping his arms around her, he said, "Let's see what I can do."

He loved stroking his tongue with hers and wished they had all the time in the world to stand here and do just that. Driven to get as much of her flavor as he could, he gripped her backside, wanting to feel his hands on her, not caring he'd ridden her ass before going to sleep last night. That didn't matter. There was never a time he didn't enjoy making love to her.

When he finally released her mouth, he continued to hold her bottom, pressed close to his front, wanting her to feel the extent of his desire for her. "Thanks, Jaye, I needed that," she whispered against their moist lips.

"You did?" he asked, smiling, tempted to kiss her again. Knowing he shouldn't, but still not willing to move his mouth away from hers.

"Yes. I have a parent–teacher meeting with Allen Bordeaux this morning. He's that father I told you about who refuses to accept his son is failing my class."

"Things haven't improved with that situation?"

"No."

"Then I'm sure you'll handle things just fine." He leaned in and kissed her again. By the time he broke off the kiss, they were panting for breath.

"I need to go," she said on a breathless sigh. "My parent–teacher conference is first thing this morning."

"Okay," he said, releasing her and taking a step back. "I'll see you later. If I arrive home before you do, I'll have the wine ready."

She smiled over her shoulder. "And if I get home first, I'll do the same."

THE MOMENT VELVET walked into the conference room and saw the deep scowl on Allen Bordeaux's face, she knew the meeting was not going to go well. "Good morning, Mr. Bordeaux."

He muttered something that sounded like he'd returned her greeting, but she wasn't sure. The minute she sat down, he lit into her. "What is the meaning of this letter you sent to me?" he said, throwing the document on the table."

"Just like the previous two letters, I think the meaning is pretty clear, Mr. Bordeaux. I will be submitting grades this week, since next week is spring break. As Lenny's parent, I just wanted you to know he still has not improved in my class and will be given a failing grade. There are only two more grading periods this school term for him to improve. If he doesn't, he won't advance to the next grade unless he goes to summer school."

The man's face hardened. "And like I told you, my son will not be going to summer school. You are teaching him stuff he won't need when he plays in the pros. Algebra didn't make sense to me back then and it doesn't make sense to my son now."

"Regardless, and like I told you, it is a required core subject to move on to the next grade. If you have a problem with it, then you need to take it up with the school board."

Without another word, the man snatched the letter off the table, stood and left.

It was dark when Velvet arrived home that evening and she smiled when she saw Jaye had made it home before her. Bringing the car to a stop, she grabbed her briefcase and got out. Moving quickly up the steps, she headed for her door.

Inside, she placed her briefcase on the table and removed her jacket. The weather was a little cool and that had her wondering if Jaye still wanted to sit out in the rocking chairs. She smiled when she heard the knock on her back door. Lifting the blinds, she saw it was Jaye and he was holding two glasses of wine.

Opening the door, she said, "Hi. How was dinner?" She took the glass of wine he offered her.

"Great and how was yours?"

"Delicious. Today's special at the Green Fig was my favorite. Black bean soup with crab meat and andouille sausage." She sipped her wine and said, "It's chilly outside. Are you sure you still want to sit in the rocking chairs?"

"Yes. Come see what I've done."

Closing the back door, she stepped onto the porch and stopped. Near the rocking chairs, he had placed one of those portable woodburning firepits. Even from where she was standing, she could feel the heat and it looked cozy and rather romantic. She also saw a blanket thrown across one of the chairs.

She glanced up at him and grinned. "You've certainly seen to our comfort tonight, Jaye."

"It's too beautiful a night for us not to sit out here. We might have missed the sunset but look up in the sky, Velvet."

She tipped her head back and saw how the dark sky was sprinkled with what looked like hundreds of stars. "It's beautiful, isn't it?"

"Yes, it is. Come, let's enjoy it."

When they settled into their chairs, he covered them in the blanket that was large enough to spread over both of them. "I love it," she said happily, taking another sip of wine.

"And what do you love?" he asked her.

"I love our rocking chairs, the blanket, the fire and the sky. I need this after today."

"I take it your meeting didn't go well with Allen Bordeaux."

She released a deep sigh. "Not the way I'd hope. In the end, I told him if he had a problem with the core subjects needed to advance to the next grade, then he could take it up with the school board. Hopefully, they will have the backbone that my principal obviously doesn't have."

She sipped her wine and said, "I guess Lenny didn't talk to his dad about his love for art like I had suggested. You should have seen the way his eyes lit up when I complimented him on those sketches. But he feels he needs to have the future his father wants him to have."

"That's sad," Jaye said. "I know my grandad always wanted Dad to go into construction, but Dad had a good head for numbers. At no time did he force a construction career on Dad." After taking another sip of wine, he said, "And Dad did the same for me, Dean and Franklin. All three of us were good with numbers, but Franklin was the one who loved working with his hands and building things a lot more than Dean and I. That's why Grandad took Franklin under his wing and taught him everything he knew. Now, Franklin has the best of both worlds and it has benefited him." He chuckled. "I'm fine juggling just one. I love banking."

"And you're good at what you do."

"Thanks."

She said, "Grades for this term go in on Friday and there's only two more grading periods left. If Lenny doesn't show any improvement, then he will not only fail my class but the grade."

"Maybe that's what he wants to do."

Velvet frowned. "Why do you say that?"

"He's a kid and probably figures if he fails, then that will keep him from having to play ball. He knows his father won't see it as his fault but yours, mainly because Allen Bordeaux expects you to do for his son what his teachers did for him."

Velvet thought about what Jaye had said. "I hope what you're saying isn't true."

"Not saying that it is, but it might be a possibility you shouldn't dismiss."

Not wanting to talk about the Bordeaux family any longer, she decided to change the subject. "Now, finish telling me about your visit with your mother."

"She was so different than I remembered," he said. "Older, of course. But still pretty. She's taken care of herself and has a classy look about her. Had I passed her in the street, I would not have known her. That's sad, isn't it?"

"No, not really. You were pretty young when she left, right?"

"Yes. I was twelve, Dean was ten and Franklin was seven. And none of us had seen her since. She never called or reached out to us on our birthdays. She walked out and never looked back."

"Was she surprised to see you?"

"Yes and no. I didn't just show up, if that's what you're asking. I called a week ahead and asked to see her. I invited Dean and Franklin to go with me, but they weren't interested."

It was hard for Velvet to wrap her head around a mother who would just leave her family like that. "Did she say why she did it?"

He took another sip of wine and looked at her. "Bottom line, she didn't offer any apologies for what she did and said we were better off without her. She wasn't cut out to be a mother and Dad was talking about having a fourth child because he wanted to try for a daughter. She felt that she needed to leave before she had a breakdown. Those were her words, not mine."

Velvet didn't say anything for a long moment. "Are you glad you went to see her?"

"Yes," he said, quickly, as if he didn't need to think about it. "For years I thought my parents' breakup was my fault."

She tiled her head. "Why?"

After taking a sip of his wine, he tilted his head back and stared up into the sky. When he finally looked at her, he said, "Although I was young, I knew what my mother was doing. At least I soon figured things out. Dad didn't know she was leaving us home alone while she met up with her lover, sometimes even at night, when Dad worked his second job at the university. I would wake up from a bad dream and she wouldn't be there. I was getting scared and when I got scared, Dean and Franklin did, too. Mom always got home before Dad got off from work and made it seem as if she'd been there all along.

"One night, Dean woke up with a bad tummy ache and Mom wasn't there. He was throwing up all over the place and I got scared. I didn't know how to reach Mom, but I knew how to get in touch with Dad at the university. I called him and he came directly home. He rushed Dean to the emergency room. It had been his appendix. Dad said if I had not called him to get Dean to the hospital, his appendix might have burst and killed him."

"Oh, my goodness."

"Dad was furious. I think that's when he found out what she'd been doing and about all the times we'd been left alone. Mom told me that it was my fault. I was the oldest and should have known what to do."

"What! You were only twelve."

"It didn't matter to her, but it mattered to me. She left after that and filed for a divorce to be with her lover. For years, I blamed myself just like she wanted me to do. I grew up believing all women were like her, or close to it. It would be just my luck to give my heart to one who would destroy it the way she destroyed Dad's."

"When you went to see your mother, did she have any remorse about what she'd told you all those years ago, when you were a child, and letting you think everything was your fault?"

"No. I knew then that she was right—the Colfax family had been better off without her. It took me coming face-to-face with her and talking to her to accept that. She thinks she has it all now, with her lavish lifestyle and a husband who dotes upon her. Little does she knows things aren't as peachy as she thinks."

"What do you mean?" she asked as he poured a little more wine into their glasses.

"That private investigator also had information that her present husband is having an affair with one of his employees, and soon he'll serve Jessica Colfax-Percy-Owens-Goodman divorce papers to marry a woman thirty years younger."

"Oh, well," Velvet said. "What goes around, comes around." No wonder he'd avoided talking about it. "What made you go see her, Jaye?"

"I needed closure. Since I was a kid, I'd allowed her to take up space in my head. I was messed up and she was somewhere enjoying three more marriages. Well, maybe husband number three wasn't such a joy since he screwed her over, but still."

"What did your dad think about you going to see her?"

"He felt it was time. Maybe it's a good thing that neither Dean nor Franklin wants to see her. They didn't have the issues about her leaving as I did."

Jaye grew quiet. It was as if talking about his mother had drained him mentally. He stood up and stoked the fire and when he sat back down, he said, "Did I mention the co-op program my bank has initiated with the schools here?"

She knew his question was his way of changing the subject, and she understood. He had shared more with her than he'd ever had before. "No, what program is that?"

She could tell from his smile that he was excited about it. "It's a co-op program where the bank will work closely with both the junior and senior high schools to give students the chance to learn hands-on how their financial decisions can affect their quality of life. I think it's best to introduce it to them before they leave for college or start their lives in the workplace."

"Oh, Jaye, I think that's a wonderful idea."

"Thanks. We will teach a banking class at both the junior high and senior high levels. We'll set up an actual bank within the schools where students can open accounts and learn how to save and invest. The principals and the school board have given their approval and are excited about it. We hope to have it implemented at the beginning of the next school year. Isaac Elloran has agreed to build most of the software. It will be the first of its kind here, and I hope to expand it to partner with my other banks and the schools in their areas." Isaac, who was married to Donna, was a technology expert, born and raised in the cove, who'd moved away after college. A few years ago, he'd retired and returned home.

She sipped her wine. "I can certainly see something like that being beneficial to Catalina Cove."

"I can, too, and honestly, you gave me the idea."

She was surprised. "When?"

"That day you told me how that kid in your class doesn't think he needs math because of all the millions he plans to make. Making millions is fine but knowing how to keep it and grow it is monumental."

"Well, I'm glad I was able to contribute even though I didn't know I was doing so." She set aside her empty wineglass.

He reached over and took hold of her hand. "Have you thought about what I asked a few days ago, Velvet? Is there someplace I can take you on spring break for unrestrained indulgences?"

She looked at him. "There is a place I'd like to go."

"Where?"

"The Keys. I've never been there before."

He leaned closer and placed a kiss on her lips. "Then consider it done. I'll make the arrangements."

LATER THAT NIGHT, they stripped and fell into each other's arms in bed. After sharing what he had with Velvet about his mother, Jaye wanted to make love to her with a new perspective and deeper meaning.

He kissed the top of her head. "I'm glad you're here with me, Vel."

She lifted to stare down at him and then shifted their positions when she eased her body over his. "And I'm glad you've agreed to take me to the Keys."

If only she knew. He would take her anywhere. "Whatever you want, Velvet, I'll give it to you. No matter what it is, and in this case, no matter where it is."

Pain flashed across her eyes. It had been so quick if

he hadn't been staring into them, he would have missed it. "Don't say things you don't really mean, Jaye."

He reached up and cupped her face in his hands and said in as tender a voice as he could, "Trust me, I won't."

She lowered her mouth to his and Jaye took it with a hunger he felt in every cell of his body. And then her tongue began mating with his. Soon it became obvious that she wanted to own this kiss and he let her, while loving every stroke and lap of her tongue. This was the kind of kiss that affected him in all kinds of ways, and she had to know it. He'd always had a weakness for her kisses. He'd taught her well.

When she finally released his mouth, Jaye exhaled a shuddering breath, but soon discovered she wasn't through with him. Leaning in, her tongue licked his bottom lip, then moved to the top one. By then, he was a mass of greedy need and he intended to make sure she felt the same way. He might not be able to tell her in words yet, but he intended to translate it with his actions every chance he got.

When she went for his mouth again, he used that moment to flip their bodies and now she was the one looking up at him. He leaned in and kissed her the same moment he slid into her body and began thrusting hard. Then harder and harder still. The deeper he went, the more his senses became overloaded in pleasure. It was as if something that had been holding him back had finally loosened him from its grip. Telling Velvet about his mother had broken chains and he was no longer bound. He was free.

Jaye loved seeing her thrash her head back and forth

against the pillow, and the way she was lifting and roll-ing her hips against him, as if enticing him to go deeper still. Somehow, he was able to oblige her. Her inner muscles clenched and it felt like he'd gone to heaven and back, and was getting ready to go there again.

"Jaye!"

The sound of her screaming his name compelled him to increase the pace of his thrusts. Passion had taken over and all he could do about it was growl his pleasure and hold tight to her hips, tilting her to hit the spot that he knew would push her over the edge again. They were skin to skin, flesh to flesh and, whether she knew it or not, heart to heart. One day she would know it and would never have reason to doubt that he loved her and just how much.

They climaxed together and sensations he only felt with her rolled through his body and curled his toes. He tightened his hold on her, feeling totally in sync with her. A short while later, he slowly shifted off Velvet and held her in his arms. He would have her for a week in the Keys, and their time wouldn't just be behind closed doors. He couldn't wait to take her out and engage in regular activities in the open like a normal couple.

"You're going jogging with me in the morning, right?"

She looked at him through glazed, satisfied eyes. He thought she looked amazing. "Hmm?"

"Tomorrow morning. Me and you. Jogging in the blueberry field. Okay?"

"One of these days we need to do something other than jog in that blueberry field, Jaye."

"You got any suggestions?"

She leaned in and whispered a few, which got him aroused all over again.

"And one day we will," he whispered before claiming her mouth.

CHAPTER TWENTY-FOUR

"ONLY A COUPLE of hours left to go," Donna Elloran said excitedly, smiling over at the three other women in the room. She, Velvet, Bryce and Vashti were bridesmaids in Vaughn and Sierra's wedding, and they had been housed in one of the twelve bedrooms at Zara Haven since noon. They had helped put on each other's makeup, worked on their hair, and in a little while, they would put on their bridesmaid dresses.

Sierra was in the master suite, which was located on a wing of its own, with her mother. While in another bedroom were the matron of honor, Sierra's sister, Dani, and her goddaughter, Teryn, who was junior maiden of honor and standing in for her deceased mother, Rhonda, who'd been Sierra's best friend. Vaughn's sister, Zara, another bridesmaid, was in a separate bedroom assisting Vaughn's twenty-year-old twin goddaughters, Jade and Kia—who were also bridesmaids—with their makeup and hair. Dani's daughter, Crane, was the flower girl and Vashti and Sawyer's son, Cutter, was the ring bearer.

Velvet was just as excited. Last night, Zara Haven had been theirs for the bridal party. Vaughn had held his bachelor party next door at Donna and Isaac's home. It, too, had been an all-night affair, and from what the women had heard, it had been a wild one. Velvet could believe it and had missed sharing a bed with Jaye.

The time spent with him over the past weeks had been more than she could have wished for. They jogged together every morning and then, after sharing dinner together, they would sit in their rocking chairs and enjoy a glass of wine or on those colder evenings, a cup of hot chocolate. At night, they made love until exhaustion drove them to sleep. It was as if they had carved out a world at the house on Blueberry Lane that was just theirs. And like she'd told Ruthie just that week, she was deliriously happy with the way things were going between them. After removing elements of love and forever, Velvet had settled into what *was* happening now. A short-term sexual affair.

Although he never said how much longer he planned to remain in Catalina Cove, she knew it couldn't be much longer with that new branch being built in Birmingham. That's why spending a week with him in the Keys meant so much to her. She was beginning to look forward to being in a place where no one knew them. That meant they would lift some of the restrictions she had placed on their affair while in Catalina Cove.

Not to call attention to both of them leaving town at the same time, she was all packed and ready to fly out tomorrow morning. Jaye wouldn't fly out until Monday. He hadn't liked the idea of her arriving in the Keys before him until she'd promised to make it worth his while when he got there.

She jumped when Vashti snapped a finger in her face. When she saw the other women grinning, she'd realized that she had been asked a question while her thoughts had been a million miles away.

Smiling sheepishly, she said, "Did I miss something that was said?"

"Umm, we were all wondering when you were going to fess up that something is going on between you and our sexy banker?" Vashti said.

Velvet's head fell back and she couldn't help but laugh. Yes, something was definitely going on between her and Catalina Cove's sexy banker. Jaye was rocking her world. She would even go so far as to say things were better than they'd been before. She figured it was because she'd removed the element of expectation. She wasn't expecting anything from him and knew the score. They were enjoying the moment and nothing more.

Not to make it too easy on her friends, she asked, "What makes you think something's going on between me and Jaye?"

"Excuse us, Velvet Spencer," Ashley said with a huge grin on her face. "We were at Sierra's bridal party when the atmosphere between you and Jaye Colfax was sizzling. Trust me, we all felt the intensity of your attraction to him and his to you."

"Heck, there were times when the two of you seemed to be out-staring each other, like you were the only ones at the party," Vashti added.

"The sexual chemistry was so thick you could slice it with a knife," Bryce tacked on.

"And then some," Donna brought up the rear by saying.

Velvet smiled as she glanced from one woman to

the other. Women, who like Sierra, she had gotten to know, women she trusted. It was time to level with them about a few things.

"There is more going on between me and Jaye than any of you know. We didn't first meet when he came to town."

"You didn't?" Ashley asked in surprise.

"No. Although I am from Seattle, I lived in Phoenix for four years. That's where I moved from when I came here. While I lived there, Jaye and I were involved in an exclusive relationship for three years."

"Wow!" Bryce said, totally surprised like the others.

"Yes, however, I broke things off when I saw it was a relationship that was not headed in the direction that I was hoping it would." There was no reason to come out and say she'd fallen in love with him, but he hadn't with her. She was sure they got the picture. "And as you can see, there has never been a lack of sexual chemistry between us. There still isn't."

"So, the two of you are working things out and getting back together?" Donna asked, and Velvet could hear a hopeful tone in her voice.

"No, that's not it. I fell in love with Jaye once and don't plan to do so again. He's not the marrying kind. A girl learns her lesson after a heartbreak. What we're sharing now is strictly physical and mutual. When he leaves Catalina Cove in a couple of months, for me, he'll be out of sight and out of mind."

The room was quiet and then Donna said softly, "There are times when things don't work out that way. Isaac and I were divorced for three years but there was never a day that went by that I didn't think of him, and my body didn't yearn for him. So, I wish you the best in that endeavor, Velvet."

Velvet knew exactly what Donna meant. She had gone through the same thing when she'd first arrived in Catalina Cove two years ago. It wouldn't be easy to erase Jaye from her mind but at least her body would be satisfied for a while. "There's something else I need to tell you. Something about me that only a few people in town know."

"What?" Ashley asked.

"My parents founded the Spencer's Corporation."

Nobody said anything for a minute as they just stared at her. Then when it clicked with them, Donna exclaimed, "Oh, my God! You're the Spencer heiress?"

Velvet smiled. "Yes."

"Wow," Vashti said in an astonished voice. "I met your parents years ago while working for the Nunes Hotel in New York. That was the first hotel to have a Spencer's. Your parents were wonderful and a joy to work with. I regretted hearing of their deaths."

"Thanks."

"Of all the times we've eaten together at Spencer's, why didn't you say anything?" Bryce asked.

"Because it's something I'd rather not share with a lot of people. I've discovered people often treat you differently when they know your financial worth. Besides, although I own the corporation, teaching is my first love, and a lot of people don't understand that. My parents understood and gave me their blessing. I have a capable executive team in Seattle that's managing things for me, and I'm satisfied with that."

Ashley grinned. "I just thought of something."

"What?" Velvet asked.

"I wonder how Webb Crawford is going to handle it when he finds out that you're not dependent on a teacher's salary, and that you're a lot wealthier than he is."

"By the powers vested in me in this great state of Louisiana, I now pronounce you husband and wife. Vaughn, you may kiss your bride."

Velvet watched the newlyweds seal their marriage vows with a huge kiss and was extremely happy for them. It had been a beautiful wedding. Sierra was a gorgeous bride and Vaughn, a handsome groom. The wedding planner had transformed the grounds of Zara Haven into a majestic wonderland. The wedding was held in late afternoon and numerous hanging lights had been strung all around.

The couple had said their vows beneath the gazebo that overlooked the gulf. The gazebo had been beautifully decorated with Sierra's favorite flower, white roses, mixed with peach-colored daisies. Her wedding dress of white lace and satin designed by her sister-in-law, Zara, had looked exquisite. The men wore white tuxes with peach-colored ties.

As the wedding party followed the bride and groom to the area on the estate where some photos were to be taken, Velvet forced her eyes not to find Jaye in the audience. She had seen him when she'd marched with the wedding party, and the way he'd been looking at her nearly took her breath away.

An elaborate sit-down dinner was followed by toasts, the cutting of the huge wedding cake, Vaughn and Sierra's first dance as husband and wife, and the father—daughter dance. Now, the bride and groom were mingling with their numerous guests. It seemed almost everyone in Catalina Cove had been invited and the large grounds of Zara Haven could accommodate all who'd attended.

The couple looked so good together, and at that moment, a part of Velvet couldn't help but wish such happiness for herself. But then hadn't she pretty much given up on love and forever after as part of her future? She glanced over at Jaye, knowing wherever he was her gaze would automatically find him. When she spotted him, he was staring at her with a pensive look. She couldn't help wondering what he was thinking. He'd told her he would be leaving before the tossing of the garter by Vaughn because as a single man he didn't want to get caught up in that. She understood. It wouldn't make sense for him when marriage was not in his future.

She didn't want to participate in the tossing of the bridal bouquet by Sierra, but knew her friend would expect her to. Unlike Jaye, she couldn't skip out without being noticed. Besides, as a bridesmaid, she would be expected to stay until the end, at least until after the bride and groom left for their honeymoon.

As luck would have it, an hour later she was the one who caught the bridal bouquet. She was glad Jaye had left already and hadn't been there to see it.

"You look beautiful, Velvet."

She was in such a happy mood today that even the irritating sound of Webb's voice didn't annoy her. She glanced up at him and smiled. "Hello, Webb."

He tilted his head and looked at her. "You look happy.

Is it because you caught the bridal bouquet, which traditionally means you're next?"

"Not at all. I'm happy because one of my dearest friends got married to the man she loves."

He chuckled. "Yes, Sierra Crane did well for herself by snagging a wealthy husband, who'll get even wealthier now that he's in line for Reid Lacroix's job. I can remember when her father worked for that gas station Vaughn's parents owned." He sipped his wine and then added, "I bet old man Miller is rolling over in his grave, knowing his son married beneath him."

Velvet studied him over the rim of her wineglass. Then lowering it, she said, "Is it always about wealth for you, Webb? Specifically, who has it and who doesn't?"

"Not always but usually," he said, grinning, like he was amused by her question. "Like Sierra, I have no problem with anyone wanting to better themselves by attaining a higher social class. If you recall, I've offered you the same opportunity, but you continue to play hard to get."

"All you want is me in your bed."

"Yes, for starters," he admitted. "And if I'm satisfied with you there, I have no qualms about proposing marriage. You are a beautiful woman who would make any man a trophy wife worth having."

The smile dropped from Velvet's lips. "Well, as far as I'm concerned—"

"Hi, Webb. Excuse me. Velvet could I borrow you for a second?" Bryce asked, looping her arm with Velvet's and not waiting for her response.

When they were out of hearing range of Webb, she looked at Bryce. "How did you know I needed rescuing?"

Bryce laughed. "Your expression. One minute you were smiling and then suddenly one of those I'm-about-to-read-his-ass looks appeared on your face, so I figured I needed to act quickly."

"And I thank you for doing so."

"No problem," she said. "And congratulations on nabbing the bridal bouquet. I thought Laura Crawford was going to plow everybody down to grab it. My gosh, she's been married before. I'm glad you were the one who caught it."

"Well, even with her back turned, I think Sierra deliberately tossed it to me." When Velvet saw the twinkle in Bryce's eyes. "My catching it doesn't mean a thing."

"Okay, if you say so."

When everyone began clapping and cheering, they looked to where Vaughn and Sierra appeared from inside the house, arm in arm and with so much love shining in their eyes that anyone looking at them could both see it and feel it. They were dressed for traveling and it was obvious to all that they were ready for their honeymoon to begin.

CHAPTER TWENTY-FIVE

VELVET FELL IN love with Key Largo instantly. Jaye had made all the arrangements and a private car had picked her up from the Miami airport when she'd arrived Sunday. The beautiful villa where they were staying was right on the ocean and had everything they needed.

She loved the ocean view from practically every room and especially liked the privacy fencing, affording seclusion on the beach. The Florida weather was perfect, beautiful and sunny, and she was looking forward to spending a lot of time outdoors. This was the first real spring break vacation she'd taken since moving to Catalina Cove.

Jaye arrived Monday around noon. The moment she heard the key in the lock and saw the door open, she crossed the room to be engulfed in strong arms. His kiss let her know he'd missed her, and she hoped the way she returned the kiss let him know that she'd missed him as well.

Instead of sweeping her off her feet and taking her to the nearest bed, like she thought he would, he suggested they walk on the beach. She'd figure that would come later, *after* they'd made love. She pushed aside the thought that all the times they'd made love had been her idea. Never his. Why? What if he wasn't feeling it with her like he used to? There was no doubt that he enjoyed their time in the bedroom and at no time had he held back on anything, but still…

Under the brightness of the day and the warmth of the Florida sun, Jaye kissed her again, and her thoughts vanished. She wasn't sure what affected her the most, the heat of the sun or the heat from his kiss. She decided it was from his kiss, which was causing fire to rush throughout her body.

By the time Jaye had released her mouth, she could barely stand on both legs. She had to clutch the front of his shirt in order not to sink to her knees. He lowered his head to murmur in her ear, "Tell me what you want, baby."

Why did she have to tell him when he knew? However, if hearing her say it was the only way she would get it, then she had no problem doing so. "I want you, Jaye."

That was when he swept her into his arms and headed back inside the villa.

JAYE HELD VELVET as she slept in his arms. The moment he had walked into the villa, he'd wanted to carry her to the nearest bedroom. But he'd held back, although he knew that wasn't what she was expecting. He didn't want her to assume sex was the only thing on his mind—even if it had been at the time.

He had suggested they go outside because he had needed to get his libido in check. But after they'd kissed and he'd seen the desire in her eyes, he'd known what she wanted. Still, he wanted her to speak her desires aloud and tell him what she wanted, and then he would give it to her.

She had yet to tell him that she wanted his love. Was she beginning to feel comfortable with not having it? Well, he didn't intend for that to happen and this week he intended to step up his A-game.

She stirred and her eyes opened. She looked at him and then at the clock on the wall. She frowned. "It's evening, Jaye. Why didn't you wake me?"

He smiled and tightened his arms around her. "You needed your rest."

She snuggled closer to him. "By all rights, Mr. Colfax, you needed yours. I was hoping to wear you out."

"You would have if I hadn't slept on the flight here."

"And my excuse is that I didn't get much sleep last night at all. I was missing you."

She had told him that when they'd talked on the phone. Velvet had called to let him know she'd arrived and how beautiful their villa was. She'd called again later to talk to him while he packed. When she'd called late at night, he'd been concerned until she told him how much she was missing him.

"And I missed you, too, Velvet. The reason I slept on the plane was because it was hard for me to sleep Sunday night without you snuggled close beside me."

She turned in his arms and when she offered her lips to him, he took them. He loved her and hoped he was displaying just how much with every kiss and touch.

He released her mouth and said, "I have dinner reservations at one of the restaurants just a short walk from here. It's on the beach."

"Okay. Are you still going jogging every morning?"

He chuckled. "Yes, *we're* still going jogging every morning. The sandy shores will replace the blueberry fields. Are you ready to get up for dinner?"

"Not yet." Then she pulled him close for another kiss.

THEY ARRIVED AT the restaurant on time for their reservation—just barely. Jaye thought it felt strange to walk into an establishment together, holding hands and not caring who saw them together. They were shown to a table that overlooked the Atlantic. The ocean was beautiful at night and the water reflected the light from the torches around the restaurant.

After they ordered drinks, Velvet looked at him. "So, what do you have planned for us this week?"

He smiled. "One thing is definite, I'm keeping you away from the bedroom as much as possible."

"Why?"

"I think you trying to kill me."

She broke eye contact with him to study her menu. "You're sure that's all there is to it?"

He heard the uncertainty in her voice. What was going on with her? Reaching out, he lifted her chin so their gazes could meet. "What other reason could there be?"

She shrugged. "Maybe you don't want me as much as I want you?"

Did she honestly think that because he was letting her decide when they made love? "I want you just as much, possibly even more, Velvet, but I'm letting you decide on when and how much."

"Why?"

He leaned closer so his words could not be overheard

and whispered, "Because if I don't, you'll never get off your back. My head would forever be between your legs, our reproductive parts would always be joined, and my tongue might as well become a permanent fixture inside your mouth."

She blinked and he smiled. Hopefully, that would put her doubts to rest.

THE NEXT MORNING, they got up before dawn and went jogging on the beach. After Velvet jogged her mile, she returned to the villa. Jaye was determined to do his five miles. By the time he returned, she had showered and was waiting for him.

After his shower, they walked to one of the cafés for breakfast. Just as Catalina Cove was known for their blueberry muffins, one of Key Largo's claims to fame was their key-lime muffins. She and Jaye thought they were incredible. Later, they walked on the beach, holding hands, and he told her all the things he'd arranged for them to do during the week.

"My goodness, Jaye. I'm not as young as I used to be."

He laughed. "So says the woman who tried wearing me out in the bedroom yesterday and last night. And as far as being young, if you recall, Velvet, I'm five years older than you."

Suddenly she released his hand and raced off and called over her shoulder, "Catch me if you can!"

Like she'd known he would, Jaye took off after her. She figured he could've caught her easily but decided to let her get ahead of him. She zigzagged around him and then raced back toward their villa. She appreciated that she got there before him.

By the time he reached their villa, she had the shower going and figured he'd know where to find her. He didn't waste any time removing his clothes and joining her.

When he opened the shower door, she teased, "About time you got here, Jaye. Those additional five years are showing. You're really getting slow in your old age."

"Slow?" He stood there and she knew from the look in his eyes he intended to show her just how wrong she was. They'd made out in showers plenty of times, but she had a feeling he intended this time to be one she long remembered.

Water poured down on them as he pulled her into his arms, and she loved the feel of his wet naked flesh against hers. He pleasured her first while on his knees with his head buried between her legs and then he took her hard and fast against the wall.

There was nothing slow about it. After soaping up and rinsing, he gathered her in his arms, dried them both off and headed for the bed. If she had anything to do with it, they would stay in bed until lunchtime. Her goal was to get her fill of him today since he'd mentioned they would be gone from the villa the next day.

She kept her arms wrapped around his neck when he eased down on the bed with her. Gazing into his eyes, she saw the same deep wanting and yearning she knew was reflected in hers. "I want you, Jaye. I need you."

"Are you sure, Velvet?" he asked, sliding his tongue along her collarbone and neck.

Why would he ask her that? Couldn't he tell? She'd

been ready to jump his bones the moment he arrived on Monday. Whereas he'd been trying to lessen their time in the bedroom, she'd been trying to do just the opposite. She needed to stock up on as much pleasure from Jaye as she could before he left the cove. But if for whatever reason he needed to hear it, then she had no problem stating it. "Yes, I'm sure. I want and need you," she whispered hotly against his lips.

"Then let me see just how badly you want and need me," he said, tilting her body in an angle for easy entry. He thrust hard inside her. Tightening her legs around him, they moved in sync and gazed into each other's eyes. She wanted him to see the depth of her need and want for him in her eyes.

He felt so good inside her, and when her inner muscles tried to hold him hostage, he responded by pumping even harder. Not to be outdone, she deliberately used her muscles to clench his erection even tighter.

That's when he angled her body farther and went straight for her G-spot. She screamed his name when her body seemed to explode and that's when he hollered her name as well. Then he lowered his mouth and ravished hers. She would never get enough of this or him, although deep down she knew she had to. They didn't have forever, just moments.

CHAPTER TWENTY-SIX

JAYE AND VELVET got dressed to attend another bon-
fire party.

She found it hard to believe their week in Key Largo
was almost over. Jaye had given her the time of her life,
memories to last a lifetime. For her, they had to. She
would need them in the late hours of the night when her
body wanted him and he wouldn't be there. Refusing
to dwell on her future, she thought about now. Here. In
Key Largo, Florida, with him.

They started each day by jogging together. After
their shower, they would enjoy breakfast at one of the
local diners. She had to admit it was nice being out
among people and not caring about being seen together.
After breakfast, they'd engage in whatever activities
Jaye had planned that day for them. One day, they'd
gone snorkeling, and usually every day they walked
to the pier to dolphin-watch. He'd given her a free day
to shop, and he'd tagged along. It felt good having him
with her as she visited several of the seaside shops, picking up souvenirs. They'd frequented a number of restaurants for lunch and dinner, and one day they'd taken
a tour of some of the other islands in the Florida Keys.

Then there were their daily walks on the beach and
their games of Frisbee in the evening to work off all the

food they'd eaten that day. They'd attended a few bon-
fire parties where they'd met several people—mostly
honeymooners. Every evening, in addition to walking
the beach, they enjoyed watching the sunset—although
they both admitted they missed their rocking chairs
back in Catalina Cove. Jaye had rented a boat and tomorrow they would go fishing after breakfast.

"I'm ready, Jaye."

He was standing at the window, looking out, and
turned at the sound of her voice. She recognized that
look of male appreciation in his eyes. "You look fantastic, but is that outfit legal?"

Velvet threw her head back and laughed, knowing
why he was asking. She was wearing a dress she had
purchased during her girls' weekend trip to New York
with Ruthie. It was short and the neckline daring. "As
long as I got a man with me, I'm good."

"Well, you better believe I intend to stick by your
side tonight, and I don't want you to dance with anyone but me."

"Getting territorial, are you, Mr. Colfax?"

"Call it whatever you like."

"I call it being territorial."

"Then that's what it is. Are you ready to go?"

An hour or so later, Velvet realized just how serious
Jaye was about sticking to her side and not letting her
dance with anyone but him. He'd behaved territorial
when they'd been together before, but not of this magnitude. When he'd held her close as they danced, she
could just imagine what anyone watching was thinking.
But she didn't care. They were people they didn't know
who didn't know them. A part of her regretted how

things would be when they returned to Catalina Cove and resumed their routine of not being seen together.

"Did you enjoy yourself tonight, sweetheart?" Jaye asked her as he opened the door to the villa hours later.

"Yes!" she said, excitedly. They had danced, talked, shared kisses that didn't have to be stolen, and fed each other the delicious food that had been served. She would miss this place, and especially miss being here with him.

"Whatever you're thinking about that put that look on your face, don't."

She looked up at him. "And what sort of look do I have on my face?"

He shoved his hands into the pockets of his slacks. "I'm not sure. It just didn't look like a happy one."

"Is this one better?" She gave him a huge smile, practically showing all her teeth.

He laughed. "Yes, that one is much better. Now come over here so I can give you something to make that smile even brighter."

"Brighter? Is that possible?" She moved toward him.

"Not sure, but I'd like to try."

There was no way she would stop him from trying, and figured she would appreciate his effort. When she stopped before him, for moment he just stared into her eyes. When she'd become mesmerized by his gaze, he swept her into his arms and headed for the bedroom.

SOMETIME BEFORE DAWN, Jaye climbed out of bed after detangling their bodies. He'd gotten a text earlier from his brother Dean saying there was a hiccup in Birmingham. Colfax Construction was ready to begin but there seemed to be a mix-up regarding a prior agreement with the city's restructuring of the roads around the bank. The restructuring was needed for smooth access to the bank.

That meant when he left Florida tomorrow, instead of returning to the cove, he would fly to Alabama. He sent a text back to Dean, letting him know of his plans. Moments later, he eased in bed beside Velvet, hoping he didn't wake her. She muttered his name in her sleep and snuggled against him. There was just something about the feel of her naked flesh touching his.

Jaye would miss this island and the time he had spent here with her. He hoped this week had shown Velvet he was capable of wanting more from her than just sex and eventually realize that he loved her.

"ARE YOU SURE about that, Angie?"

"I'm positive, Cassie. The papers came across my desk at the property appraiser's office. I'm telling you the truth. Our new banker, Jaye Colfax, purchased waterfront property costing over a million dollars in that new area being developed by Mr. Lacroix. Instead of putting it in his name, it's in the name of Velvet Spencer."

Allen Bourdeaux, who was in the waiting room of his dentist's office and flipping through a magazine, overheard the conversation between the two women, although they'd tried whispering. Angie Boston worked as a cashier at the pharmacy and Cassie Kirkwood worked in the property apprasier's office. He continued listening, interested in what they were saying.

"Velvet Spencer, the teacher?" Angie asked Cassie.

"Yes."

"Umm, I didn't know the two of them were an item."

"Neither did I," was Cassie's response. "Considering the cost of that property, it appears they're more than just *an item*. Of course, what they're doing behind closed doors is none of our business. I'd heard Webb Crawford was rather smitten with her. No wonder she didn't give Webb the time of day. She was holding out for someone even richer."

"There's nothing wrong with a woman wanting to better herself," Angie said.

"I agree and it looks like she struck gold, no pun intended."

Allen had heard enough. So the teacher who thought she could flunk out his son was sleeping with the banker and had managed to get property worth over a million dollars out of him?

Just like the two women had said, Webb Crawford fancied himself smitten with the woman. Obviously, she was playing Webb for a fool the same way Allen's ex-wife, Cheryl, had played him. Others, including his teammates, had known the type of woman she was, yet no one had seen fit to tell him. More than anything, he wished they had. It would have saved him a lot of heartache and misery. In the end, the only thing he had to show for their one year of marriage was Lenny. His son meant everything to him.

He tossed the magazine aside. He didn't consider him and Webb friends, but they had attended school together. Maybe he ought to enlighten him about what the teacher was doing behind his back to save him the pain that he'd gone through with Cheryl.

CHAPTER TWENTY-SEVEN

"How was your vacation?"

Velvet, who was sitting in a booth at the Witherspoon Café, glanced up and saw Sierra looking simply radiant. Marriage agreed with her.

"It was wonderful. And how was your honeymoon?"

Velvet really didn't have to ask. The huge smile on Sierra's face said it all. "It was amazing. There are times I think that I need to pinch myself to make sure I'm not dreaming."

"Well, I am happy for you. Are you here with Vaughn?"

"No, he had an early meeting at the office. I just finished walking Teryn to school and had a taste for Ms. Debbie's blueberry muffins. May I join you?"

"Of course." Debbie and her husband, Chester, owned the Witherspoon Café. Everyone loved her blueberry muffins, which made the café a popular breakfast place.

Sierra slid into the seat across from her and leaned over the table to whisper, "What about you and Jaye? How did your week in the Keys go?" Sierra was one of the few who knew where she'd gone and who she'd been with.

Velvet sighed. "Of course, we had a great time and I appreciated getting away but…"

"But what?"

Velvet shrugged. "But nothing." She sipped her coffee, deciding not to say anything else when the waitress came to take Sierra's order.

When the waitress left, Sierra looked at her and asked in a low tone, "How was it not to have to sneak around?"

She hesitated, and because this was Sierra, she said, "It was fantastic and it will be hard to go undercover with him again when he returns."

"He's out of town?"

"Yes. Instead of returning to the cove as planned, Jaye went to Birmingham. Some problem developed with the bank construction, and he'll be gone all this week. I'm not expecting him back until Sunday."

"Why do you think you have to go undercover when he gets back?"

"Because nothing has changed. He'll be leaving the cove soon and the last thing I want people talking about is my affair with him."

"It's really nobody's business, Velvet, what you do and with whom."

"I know, but there are some who would make it their business, and I'd rather not be the topic of anyone's conversation. Especially when Jaye deliberately didn't date any of the other single women in town."

"It was his right to do so. Just like a woman has the right to date who they want, so does a man."

Velvet knew what Sierra said was true, but for years she'd intentionally avoided drawing attention to herself. She loved Catalina Cove. It was her home now and it would be her home long after Jaye left. Although the past week had pretty much shown her how things could bc, she had to remember for her and Jaye, they would never be that way again.

The waitress returned with their food and they chatted for another half hour before Velvet had to leave for school.

"Ms. SPENCER, are you busy?"

Lenny was standing in the doorway to Velvet's class. It was nearing the end of the day and she was about ready to pack up to leave. "I'm never too busy for any of my students, Lenny. Come on in."

He closed the door behind him and came to her desk. His hands were shoved into his jeans pockets. Today, he looked a lot younger than the fifteen-year-old that he was. Maybe it was because there was a shyness about him that normally wasn't there. He was staring down at his shoes, and she figured he was trying to get his thoughts together. She had time to let him.

When he looked up, he said, "I don't want to fail the ninth grade, Ms. Spencer."

She nodded. Report cards went out this week and chances were that seeing his grade had been a wakeup call. "And I don't want you to fail, either, Lenny. You have two more grading periods to turn it around and I believe you can."

"Algebra isn't easy, but I know I can pass if I try," he said quickly.

"But you haven't been trying, have you?" she asked, speaking aloud Jaye's suspicions.

His gaze fell to his shoes again. "No. I figured if I didn't pass, Dad would see there was more to my life than baseball. I like to draw, too."

"And who says you can't do them both? I love gymnastics and took classes while growing up. I also wanted to become a teacher. I discovered I could do both. I teach here and I'm still involved with gymnastics by coaching after school twice a week."

His eyes widened. "I didn't know that."

"Well, I do. I know a basketball player who played for the NBA. In addition to his love of basketball, he always wanted to fly planes. He played basketball during that season and when he had the time, he learned to fly. He retired from pro sports last year, and now he's started a company that builds small planes."

"Wow!"

"He didn't limit his abilities, and neither should you."

A huge smile spread across his face and there was a gleam in his eyes when he said, "I can play baseball and when I'm not playing ball, I can do my art. One day, I can even use the money I made from baseball to open an art gallery."

Velvet laughed. "Yes, you can certainly do that. I suggest you talk to your father, Lenny, and tell him your plans and let him know you can do both and want to do both. But first you need to work on improving your grades. My offer to help you still stands."

He looked surprised. "It does?"

"Yes. I can give you extra assignments and even tutor you after class to get you caught up."

"Thanks, Ms. Spencer. I'll talk to my Dad about it when he gets home from work."

Velvet smiled. "I think that's a good idea."

WEBB GLANCED ACROSS his desk at the man who'd asked to see him. Al had graduated a few years earlier than he had, but he recalled that at one time Allen Bordeaux had been a hometown hero. He'd been picked by the Dodgers until a car accident shattered those dreams.

"So, what's the reason for your visit, Al?"

The man leaned forward in his chair. "I think most of the men in town know of your interest in Velvet Spencer."

"And?"

"And I think you forgot to tell the new banker."

Webb paused. "Why do you say that?"

"Because I heard he purchased a prime piece of real estate on the gulf, valued at over a million dollars, in Reid Lacroix's new development for Ms. Spencer."

Webb sat up in his chair, surprised. "Who told you that?"

"I'd rather not say. But I just wanted you to know what kind of woman you've fallen in love with." Allen Bordeaux checked his watch and stood. "I need to be going. The shifts change at the restaurant in an hour and one of my workers called in sick."

Webb sat at his desk for a long while after Al left. First of all, he wasn't in love with Velvet Spencer. Al was wrong about that. He would admit to being obsessed with having her in his bed, but only because she'd been the first woman he couldn't get there easily.

He stood and walked to the window. His jaw tightened at the thought that all the time she'd been brushing him off, she'd had no problem hooking up with the new banker. He bet the two were already involved when he'd gone to the bank to warn Colfax off. That meant she began sleeping with Colfax not long after he moved to town. And it must be some hot and heavy affair for the man to put out that much money on property for her.

It wasn't right that Colfax was getting a damn good roll between the sheets. A roll that Webb should be getting. Anyone in town knew not to get on a Crawford's bad side and it was time he taught Ms. Spencer that lesson. He wished he could teach Jaye Colfax that same lesson, but he'd heard Reid Lacroix had personally approved of Colfax's bank to take over Larsons Bank when Larson retired. Everyone in the cove knew that if Reid Lacroix—who was the wealthiest man in the cove—liked you, then the rest of Catalina Cove sure as hell better like you, too. Nobody in their right mind would want to cross Reid Lacroix. For that reason, he knew to leave Colfax alone, but Velvet Spencer was another matter.

Returning to his desk, he picked up the phone to call Dwight Beaks. Dwight was a member of the school board and Webb would bet there was something in a teacher's contract about her receiving expensive gifts. If there was a violation of any sort on Velvet Spencer's part, then Beaks would know about it. And if there wasn't, then Beaks, with a little push from him, could find one that would fit.

"I DON'T THINK I've ever seen you so happy, Dean," Jaye said to his brother. After attending yet another meeting about the Birmingham bank, they were on their way to grab dinner at one of the restaurants close by.

Dean, who was driving, chuckled as he slowed the car at a traffic light. "Lilly is everything I could ever want and we're ideal for each other." He continued driving and asked, "How are things going between you and Vel? You haven't said."

Jaye shrugged. "There's really nothing to tell. I'm still trying to show her how much I love her."

"Why don't you just come out and tell her, Jaye?"

"Not sure she's ready to hear it. In fact, there's a chance she won't believe me. When we were together, I did a very thorough job of convincing her I wasn't capable of loving a woman."

Dean raised an eyebrow. "Let me get this straight. Vel still doesn't know she's the reason you opened that bank in Catalina Cove in the first place?"

"No, she doesn't know that. She doesn't know I hired a PI to find her, either." Jaye rubbed his hands down his face. "There are a number of other things I've done that she isn't aware of as well." One was the engagement ring he intended to give her and the land he'd purchased for a wedding present. The latter wasn't contingent on her accepting the former. He would give her the land regardless.

"I don't understand. You took her to the Keys last week. Why didn't you tell her everything then? I'd think that was the perfect opportunity."

Dean's question reminded Jaye of what a wonderful time he'd shared with her, and his brother was right. It had been the perfect opportunity. In a way, it had been too perfect to ruin.

"Jaye?"

He glanced over at Dean. "Things were so perfect for us in Key Largo. I didn't want to risk ruining things. I'm not sure how I would have handled it if she refused my love, Dean."

"The way you refused hers."

Jaye drew in a deep breath. "Yes, the way I refused hers," he said softly.

Dean pulled into a parking spot and brought the car to a stop. He cut the engine and turned to Jaye. "Why are you letting what Mom did to us still stand in the way of your happiness? You went to see her and yet you're still letting her run roughshod over your emotions."

"You think that's what's happening?"

"Don't you? After you tell Velvet that you love her, and she still needs time to accept that you really do, then by all means give it to her. I'd think, considering everything—especially your relationship before and all that crap you told her about not ever planning to fall in love—that you'd understand. It doesn't mean you won't stop trying to get her to fall in love with you or make her believe you love her. At least she'll know how you feel and intend to do whatever it takes to make her part of your life again. This time not as your lover but your wife. Do you know what I'd do if I were you?"

Jayc couldn't believe he was getting advice from his younger brother. "And just what would you do?"

"I'd leave here tomorrow, go back to Catalina Cove and tell her how you feel, and if she needs time to digest it, give her that time. But at least let her know."

"What about tomorrow morning's meeting?"

"I suggest you take off right after that. I'm sure you can even get a straight flight to New Orleans and make it there before dark."

Jaye thought about Dean's suggestion and the more he thought about it, the more it seemed doable. "That means you'll be attending tomorrow night's dinner with the mayor alone."

"No problem."

"You're sure?"

"Positive. Now let's get something to eat."

CHAPTER TWENTY-EIGHT

VELVET WAS STANDING at her kitchen counter, pouring a glass of wine, when she heard a car pull up outside. She looked out the window, wondering who would be visiting. When she saw it was Jaye, a smile of surprise touched her lips at the same time shivers of excitement rushed through her body. She hadn't been expecting him back for a week. When they talked on the phone last night, he hadn't mentioned anything about returning home early.

She nearly jumped when she heard the firm knock on her door. What had he done? Taken her steps two at a time to have made it to her door so quickly? She set the wine bottle on the counter and didn't waste any time moving through her living room. After looking out the peephole to confirm it was him again, she opened the door.

"Jaye, I wasn't expecting you back until Sunday." She smiled and stepped aside to let him enter. This was her first time seeing him since leaving the Keys.

"That had been the plan until I found out I'd need to remain in Birmingham a little longer to take care of a few more issues." He closed the door behind him. "And I was missing you like crazy."

She'd been missing him, too. This house had seemed

so lonely without him. During the evenings, she'd sat in her rocking chair on the porch, but it hadn't been the same. Their nightly phone calls had been nice, but there was nothing like seeing each other in the flesh. And speaking of flesh...

She needed to feel his and moved toward him. The moment she'd opened the door, her body had responded to his. Sometimes she wished her body wasn't so needy and greedy where he was concerned, but it couldn't be helped. Her body recognized the one and only man who'd ever touched it. Pleasured it.

He pulled her into his arms and, as usual, his kiss made her weak in the knees and his unique scent enveloped her.

She was lifted off her feet and she knew exactly where he was taking her. Instead of placing her on the bed, he set her on her feet beside it. He began removing his clothes and, likewise, she began removing hers. By the time she stepped out of her panties, he had finished undressing.

Easing down to his knees, he rubbed his face against the juncture of her thighs. He lifted his head to look at her. "You are all woman, Velvet. Every inch of you and every part of you."

The eyes staring up at her were filled with heated lust and seeing that look, along with what he'd said, swamped her entire being with sensuous sensations. "And you, Jaye Colfax, are all man."

He smiled, then lowered his head between her legs and the instant she felt the invasion of his tongue, she moaned as tremors of pleasure began running all through her. "Jaye..."

Being a thorough man, it was a while—specifically two orgasms later for her—before he stood, picked her up and placed her on the bed. He joined her there and proceeded to take her the way she needed to be taken. It was utterly irrational to want a man this much, and the way he was pounding inside her let her know the intensity of his desire. He might not love her, but he wanted her.

Moments later, orgasms struck them simultaneously. When he threw his head back to holler her name just when she screamed his, she had a feeling it was only the beginning. By morning, they would have given her bed one heck of a workout and then some.

"I LOVE YOU, VELVET."

Velvet slowly opened her eyes and peered up at him. From her facial expression, Jaye could only assume that she thought she'd misunderstood his words. In that case, he had no problem saying them again. "I love you."

When he saw tears form in her eyes, he wrapped her in his arms and she buried her face in his chest. He hadn't expected his words to make her cry.

"Shh, Vel. I didn't mean to make you cry, but it was something I needed to tell you. I couldn't keep it to myself any longer."

She pulled back to swipe at her eyes and shook her head. "Please don't say words you don't mean, Jaye. That's worse than you never saying them at all."

He reached for her, but she moved back. She stood from the bed and slid into her robe. When she wouldn't look at him, he said, "I take it you don't believe me?"

She made eye contact then. "Of course I don't believe you. I was with you for three years and they were good years. Yet you didn't love me then, so why should I believe you'd be in love with me now?"

He drew in a deep breath and held her gaze. If she needed a timeline, he would give her one. "We need to talk, Velvet."

"No, we don't." She shook her head, frowning. "You've never lied to me about anything, Jaye, and I'm asking that you please don't lie to me now. Especially when you don't have to."

He sat up in bed. "Why do you think I'm lying?"

She crossed her arms. "Why wouldn't I think that? If you're not lying, then you're delusional and getting love mixed up with lust."

Now that made him mad. He stepped out of bed and pulled on his jeans. "We need to talk, Velvet. Outside. In our rockers."

"Outside?" She glanced at the clock. "Jaye, it's close to three in the morning."

"It doesn't matter. You get the wineglasses and I'll grab the wine."

She stared at him for a long moment and then said, "Fine."

"WHAT IS HE upset about?" Velvet muttered as she went into the kitchen and grabbed two wineglasses from the cabinet. She of all people knew Jaye was incapable of loving a woman, so why was he pretending otherwise? Like she'd told him, he was getting lust confused with love.

By the time she opened her back door and stepped out, he had placed a bottle of wine near the rocking chairs and was firing up the pit. It was a gorgeous night, and the sky overhead was beautiful as usual.

She knew his eyes were on her as she sat in the rocking chair next to his. She handed him both glasses and watched as he filled them. "Easy on mine," she said. "I have to go to work tomorrow."

Without a word, he handed her a wineglass. She took a sip and then asked, "So, what do we need to talk about, Jaye?"

"Why don't you believe I love you?"

"Maybe it would be easier to state why I *know* you don't love me."

"Well, then, tell me what you think you know."

She frowned. "First of all, I was gone for two years. If you loved me, you would not have let me go at all."

"I didn't let you go, Velvet. You left on your own, without my knowing."

She held up a finger. "Then let me restate that. Had you loved me, I would not have had a reason to go. And you certainly wouldn't have let two years pass without coming after me." She took a sip of her wine, then continued, "Second, you're a man who enjoys sex from women. No emotional entanglements. Stupid me, I thought I could be different, but you proved me wrong. And, number three is the fact that all you feel toward me is lust. I can tell the difference. Nothing has changed. You want me as much as you did before, and I'm nothing more than your lover until you leave Catalina Cove. Need I go on?"

He tilted his head. "There's more?"

"Of course."

OF COURSE? HONESTLY, JAYE had heard enough. Everything she'd said was all wrong and there were a few things she didn't fully understand. A dark scowl covered his face. "First of all, the reason I didn't come after you was because I had no idea where you'd gone. I admit, for a while I was mad that you left me, especially when you knew how I felt about love and marriage. But then, after my anger dissipated, I understood why you did it.

"Second, nobody, and I mean nobody, would tell me where you'd gone. Not Ruthie or the teachers you knew at school, and not your corporate executives. It was as if you'd vanished off the face of the earth."

"So, it wasn't easy to find me, and you gave up," she snapped. "I bet it was shocking when you discovered, after you'd gotten on with your life, that I was living here in Catalina Cove. The last place you thought I'd be."

He turned in his rocker to face her. "No, it wasn't. I knew you were here."

She glared at him. "There's no way you knew."

"There is a way because I hired a private investigator to find you."

It was a good thing she'd finished her wine because when she jumped from her chair, she nearly dropped the glass. After placing it on the table, she said, "You didn't do anything of the sort."

He stood as well. "An invoice from Douglas Investigations says otherwise. And once I discovered where you were, I devised a plan to get you back."

"Devised a plan? What are you talking about? What plan?"

"I bought Barrows Bank for starters. Then I made sure your neighbor leased me this house so I could be your neighbor."

"You did what? How dare you manipulate things

just to get me back in your bed, knowing I meant nothing to you," she snapped. "Did you do it for revenge?"

"Revenge? Of course not. I did it because I realized that I loved you."

"And just when did you realize this, Jaye? After you decided you were missing me as a bed partner? After your close friends began falling in love and you felt left out, and decided to give love a try yourself?"

His jaw tightened at her words. "I realized it when I came to terms with what you meant to me and the depth and intensity of my love for you."

She scoffed. "If everything you say is true, then you should have told me upfront, and not tried to manipulate me by coming up with some plan."

"If you recall that night when I came here to talk to you about my moving to the cove, you joked about me deliberately buying the bank upon discovering this was where you were living. Then you said that you knew I hadn't because it wasn't in my makeup to care that much for any woman. I decided to prove how wrong you were and that it is in my makeup to care that much. For you.

"And you're wrong in thinking I don't know the difference between love and lust. I wanted to court you properly, Velvet. To share more of myself, especially my emotions, than I did before. And I have. You know about my mother now and we spend more time out of the bedroom than in it. That's a deliberate move on my part. I didn't want you to think all I wanted from you was sex. As much as I wanted you, I held back and only made love to you when you wanted it and asked for it. I was determined not to sleep with you until I proved there was more between us than sex. You don't know how many times while we made love that I came close to telling you how I felt. How much I loved you."

A part of Velvet wished she could believe him, but something was holding her back. Namely, that part of her heart she'd vowed to protect. The pain had been so hard before that she'd pretty much convinced herself that Jaye was a man incapable of loving any woman, including her.

"We didn't make love, Jaye," she said. "For it to be making love, both parties need to be in love. We had sex."

"That's not true and you know it," Jaye countered. "We made love even those times I convinced myself it was just sex."

Then, Jaye picked up on something she'd said, whether intentional or not. Since she didn't believe he loved her, was she saying that she still loved him? He had to believe that she did.

For a long moment, Velvet just looked at him. Finally, she said softly, "I think it's best for you to sleep the rest of tonight at your place, Jaye."

He shoved his hands into his pockets. He remembered his brother's advice not to push, and to give Velvet time to think. That she would eventually come around. But what if she didn't? What if he'd told her so many times he wasn't capable of loving a woman, that she still believed it? The thought of losing her was a pain he just couldn't bear.

"If you want me to leave, then I'll do that, Velvet. But you're wrong about how I feel about you because I do love you."

She didn't say anything. Instead, she turned and walked into the house and closed the door behind her.

CHAPTER TWENTY-NINE

"WHAT DO YOU mean you don't believe Jaye loves you?"

"Just what I said, Ruthie. We were together for three years. Three solid years and he didn't fall in love with me then, but he wants me to believe he did it in three months? That's crazy and you know it." Velvet moved around her bedroom, getting ready for work. She felt tired because she hadn't gotten much sleep last night.

"But didn't he say he'd found out where you were and came after you? Think about it, Vel. The man bought a bank and then fixed it so he could be your neighbor. What do you call that?"

"Manipulation. I bet he did it to prove a point."

"What point?"

"That he could."

"You're not being rational and it's obvious that you're upset, and—"

"I am rational and, of course I'm upset."

"And you honestly think you have a right to be upset?"

Velvet rolled her eyes. "Yes, I do, and don't you dare try to convince me otherwise."

"I wouldn't dare since you're on a roll. But do me a favor."

"What?"

"Think about everything you've told me. Then put me in your place and Todd in Jaye's, and when you do, I believe you'll see things differently. Have a great day at school. Love you. Bye, Vel."

Velvet clicked off the call, not caring what her best friend had said. She didn't need to switch places with Ruthie and Todd. There was no way Jaye could love her, and she felt insulted that he thought she would believe that he did.

Her gut tightened when she heard a knock on her front door and figured it could only be one person. Glad she was fully dressed, she inhaled deeply before heading to the door. She opened it to find Jaye. A fully dressed Jaye in jeans and a shirt and not his jogging attire.

"Yes, Jaye?"

"Good morning, Velvet. I just wanted you to know I'm going back to Birmingham and will be there until the end of next week. I was wondering if you'd grab my newspapers and mail."

Of course she would. "No problem."

"Thanks." He turned to leave but stopped and looked over his shoulder at her. "I love you and have no reason to lie about it. Hopefully, one day you'll realize that."

She watched him sprint down her steps to his car. She closed her door, but couldn't stop herself from peeking out the window to watch as he backed out of the yard. How dare he leave her in one hell of an emotional mess? An emotional mess brought on by a man who didn't know the difference between love and lust.

The school day seemed to go by fast. She had gymnastic practice after school and before going home, she stopped by the Witherspoon Café and ate alone.

By the time she had pulled into her yard and gathered all her things to go into the house, she was in worse shape than she'd been that morning. Whether she wanted to admit it or not, she was missing Jaye.

"YOU'RE BACK ALREADY?" Dean sat in the chair across from Jaye.

Jaye eyed his brother. "Yes, I'm back." Avoiding further details, he asked, "How did last night's dinner with the mayor go?"

"Great. I think we've pretty much ironed out all the issues, but we'll need another week here to be certain when we meet with several more city officials."

Jaye attended back-to-back meetings that day and deliberately kept himself busy. It was late afternoon when he returned to his hotel suite and was tempted to call Velvet before getting into the shower—tempted to tell her again that he loved her. But he felt she needed time to think about the other times he'd said it, like just that morning before leaving for the airport. It was up to her to believe his words. Besides, he'd also use this time apart to consider everything she'd said and decide how to move forward. One thing was certain—he would not give up on her or their love.

At least he wouldn't be bored this weekend. Franklin would be arriving in the morning. There was never a dull moment around his youngest brother. He definitely knew how to keep things lively—and that's exactly what Jaye needed. There would be another meeting next Thursday with several city officials, so Jaye had no plans to return to Catalina Cove until after then.

Shoving his hands in his pockets, he went to the window. He thought his view of the downtown Birmingham skyline was spectacular. The Colfaxes had made the right decision to open their first Alabama branch here. Now they were eyeing a Florida location. He was also eyeing something else. Putting the ring on the finger of the woman he loved.

He hoped when he returned to Catalina Cove at the end of next week that he and Velvet could talk again, and that the conversation would go better than the last.

VELVET SAT DOWN in her rocker and looked wistfully at the empty one beside her. Over the past few days, she had replayed what Jaye had said over and over in her mind. The one thing she couldn't discount was that he *had* changed. She'd even mentioned that to Ruthie and Sierra. What he'd said was true. Each and every time they'd made love, she had initiated it. Not once had he suggested doing so, even those times when she'd known without a doubt that he'd wanted her.

I was determined not to sleep with you again until I proved to you there was more between us than sex.

She could no longer dismiss the fact that since she and Jaye had started sleeping together again, she'd been the one to limit their relationship to a sex-only affair. Another thing she couldn't discount was the amount of time they'd spent together out of the bedroom. Doing things like jogging, sharing meals and sitting in these chairs. Rocking chairs that he had built for them. To enjoy the sunset together like her parents had done.

And while sitting and rocking in these chairs, they had shared more than just the sunset. They had discussed a lot of things that they'd never talked about before. Including his mother.

And had he really bought Barrows Bank and arranged to move in next door, all to be near her? Was it manipulation, as she'd said, or was it the actions of a desperate man who'd realized too late that he'd made a mistake? Velvet continued rocking, knowing she still had her doubts about a lot of things, and because of those doubts, she was afraid of Jaye breaking her heart again. But what if he meant what he'd said? She took a sip of wine and knew she had a lot to think about. Though she missed him, she was glad Jaye wasn't around. He would only cloud her thoughts.

She reached for her phone when it rang and was surprised when she looked at the screen to see it was Mr. Dunning. Why would her principal be calling her on a Sunday evening?

"Hello?"

"Ms. Spencer?"

"Yes, Mr. Dunning?"

"The reason I'm calling is to let you know that you need to appear at tomorrow night's school board meeting at six."

Velvet raised a brow. "Why?"

"I understand that they have a few questions to ask you about a possible conflict of interest."

Velvet was even more confused. "What kind of conflict of interest?"

"Not sure, but I imagine it's a misunderstanding that you can clear up quickly."

There was *definitely* a misunderstanding if anyone thought anything involving her and her job was a conflict of interest. "Okay, Mr. Dunning. Where will the meeting be held?"

"In the auditorium at the senior high school."

"Thank you and I'll be there."

CHAPTER THIRTY

IT WAS PAST noon on Monday when Jaye walked out of a meeting that had started at eight o'clock and should have ended more than an hour ago. One of the other bankers in town, who was rumored to be entering politics, had wasted everyone's time grandstanding.

After talking to Dean and Franklin and making lunch plans, he pulled his phone out of his jacket and saw he'd missed a couple of calls, and all from Vaughn. He hadn't seen or talked to Vaughn since the wedding. Since the newlyweds had only planned to be gone a week, chances were Vaughn and Sierra had returned from their honeymoon by now.

He returned the call. "Vaughn, this is Jaye. I was in a meeting and see I missed your calls."

"Thanks for calling me back. There's something going on here in the cove that I think you should know about."

"What?"

"The school board is bringing Velvet before them this evening on a code-of-conduct violation."

"You're kidding, right?"

"I wish I were. It took a lot of digging to find out the reason, since some of the board members don't even know why. I understand Velvet doesn't even know, and they won't tell her until the board meeting tonight."

"And what's the reason?" Jaye asked angrily.

"Someone found out that you purchased land for her in Reid's new development and they are trying to say it is a conflict of interest."

Jaye gritted his teeth. "And just how is that supposed to be in violation of anything? Velvet and I are adults and it's nobody's business what we do. And it's my money to do with as I please."

"True, but no one knew you and Velvet were involved. I heard they first tried saying it was a morality violation but, just like you said, you're both adults and you can do as you please with your money. They knew that wouldn't stick so they went after a code-of-conduct violation since you're sponsoring that cooperative bank at the junior high school."

"What does that have to do with anything? Velvet isn't involved with that and, even if she was, how would anything that would benefit the school cause a problem?"

"It doesn't and shouldn't. Once the school board agreed to allow you in to partner with the schools, they're saying since your purchase of that land was a gift to her, she should have disclosed it."

"What the hell? Velvet doesn't even know I purchased that land for her. It was going to be a surprise wedding gift."

"The two of you are getting married?"

"I'm working on it. Damn. I've been working on it since coming here, but dumb crap like this will not put things in my favor with her, Vaughn."

All Jaye had to do was remember what Velvet had said the last time they'd talked. She'd seen his coming to town and taking over the bank and deliberately becoming her neighbor as manipulations. He could just imagine what she'd think when she discovered he'd bought that land for her, too.

"If you ask me," Vaughn said, "it sounds like someone has it in for Velvet and is trying to shame her into admitting the two of you are involved in an affair that no one knew about. There are some in Catalina Cove, even members of the school board, who feel it's their God-given right to know everything."

"Well, I got news for them, it isn't. And if they were so concerned about it, then why didn't they contact me or bring me before the school board? This is nothing but bullshit and I'm not having it." Jaye rubbed his hand down his face, not wanting to believe any of this. "What time is that school board meeting?" he asked.

"At six."

Jaye glanced at his watch. In order to make that meeting, he would need to leave now. "I'll be there."

VELVET PULLED INTO the school's parking lot and when she saw all the cars, she figured a basketball game was probably going on as well. She checked her watch as she swiftly walked up the steps and entered the school.

"Velvet?"

She turned upon hearing her name and saw Sierra, Vashti and Bryce. Smiling, she headed toward them. "Hey, guys. Are all of you here for the game?"

Vashti looked confused. "What game?"

She gestured at the parking lot. "I saw all the cars and figured there was a basketball game going on."

Sierra shook her head. "Those cars are here for you."

Velvet's eyes widened. "For me? What on earth for?"

"Word got around the cove that a teacher was being brought before the board for some conflict-of-interest issue, and everyone is curious as to what it is. Nobody seems to know."

Velvet shrugged. "Neither do I. And aren't school board meetings private when it's a one-on-one with a teacher or school employee?"

"No," Sierra said. "All Catalina Cove school board meetings are public and we're all here to give you support."

"Why would I need support?" Velvet asked, confused. "Mr. Dunning felt it was nothing more than a misunderstanding that could be cleared up at this meeting."

"Well, let's hope that's all there is to it, but I heard that Dwight Beaks called the meeting, and that made me uncomfortable," Vashti said.

Velvet's brows drew together. "Who is Dwight Beaks?"

"Dwight Beaks used to be an attorney in town," Bryce said. "And if you ask me, I think he's been on the school board way too long. Heck, he's been a member since my brothers were in high school."

"To show you how conservatively he thinks," Vashti explained, "he's the one who called for a vote to kick me out of high school when I got pregnant."

"And it passed?" Velvet asked, shocked.

"Before they could take the vote, my parents sent me to a home for unwed mothers," Vashti said. "However, there is no doubt in my mind had he pushed for a vote, he would have gotten one in his favor. He pretty much rules the school board. Always has."

"That's what's bothering me," Sierra said. "Nobody seems to know what this meeting is about and those who do are keeping it hush-hush. I don't like it."

"I don't, either," Bryce said. She smiled when she looked beyond Velvet's shoulder. "There's Ashley and Donna."

When Ashley and Donna approached, Ashley said, "The guys are outside talking and will be inside in a minute."

"What guys?" Velvet asked.

"Our husbands," Donna said. "When I heard Mr. Beaks called the meeting, I figured there would be trouble. We're here to support you."

Velvet sighed. That's the same thing Vashti had said, and both Donna and Vashti had grown up in Catalina Cove. This Dwight Beaks sounded like someone who was known to stir up mischief. She hoped that wasn't true because she really wasn't in the mood.

VAUGHN CHECKED HIS watch and said to the men standing around him, "The meeting is about to start. We're all here and the place is packed. I contacted Jaye and he's flying back tonight. Evidently, Dwight Beaks intends to try to shame Velvet in front of the entire town like he tried doing to Vashti."

Sawyer, who was leaning against a lamppost, straightened upon hearing his wife's name. "When did Dwight Beaks try shaming Vashti?"

Every man heard the sting in Sawyer's voice. Before Vaughn could respond, Kaegan said, "Calm down. It was years ago, Sawyer. When Vashti was pregnant at sixteen and refused to reveal the identity of her baby's father, Beaks called a board meeting to get her kicked out of school."

"What the hell!" Sawyer exclaimed angrily.

"Did they kick her out?" Ray Sullivan asked, who, like Sawyer, hadn't grown up in the cove.

"No," Isaac said. "If I recall, her parents sent her away to have her baby before that happened."

"Babies. She had twins, remember," Kaegan said, grinning, trying to lighten the conversation.

It didn't work with Sawyer. His jaw was still tight when he said, "I knew I never liked Beaks for a reason."

Isaac chuckled. "Very few people do. They tolerate him but I'd figured he's too old for this kind of non-sense."

Vaughn's phone rang. He pulled it out of his jacket and after glancing at the screen said, "It's Jaye." He answered the call. "Hey, Jaye, where are you?"

"Bad weather caused delays, but we've just landed in New Orleans. I should be there in an hour or less."

Vaughn was glad Sawyer hadn't heard that because, as the town's sheriff, he would have taken issue with the *or less*. "The meeting is about to start, so hopefully you'll get here in time." And then he added, "Drive carefully."

VELVET GLANCED AROUND the crowded room. Whatever the school board thought they had on her, they intended for this to be a spectator show. And why was Webb sitting on the other side of the room and staring at her with a smirk on his face? Did he have anything to do with this? And if he did, why and how?

Drawing in a deep frustrated breath, she broke eye contact with Webb and glanced down another row and saw Allen Bordeaux. When their gazes connected, he quickly looked away. Was she mistaken or had she seen a flash of guilt in his eyes? If so, why? She decided not to waste her time trying to figure out who might be behind tonight's meeting. Hopefully, it was just a misunderstanding like Mr. Dunning had said.

She looked toward the front of the room where six men and one woman sat at a long table. The man she figured was Dwight Beaks occasionally glared over at her with what looked like disgust on his face. The other board members avoided eye contact with her. Now she was beginning to get concerned. Mr. Dunning had once said Allen Bordeaux was a popular person in town. She had suggested to him that if he didn't like the required school's curriculum that he should take it up with the school board. Had he done so in a way that made them question her integrity? Surely, failing Lenny Bordeaux wouldn't constitute any type of conflict of interest when he didn't deserve a passing grade, so she remained baffled about the purpose of the meeting.

She let out a deep breath. Even with her friends and their husbands sitting around her for support, she wished the man she loved were here, too. But it was her fault that he wasn't. She accepted that now. Over the past few days, she'd had time to think about everything Jaye had said. Then there had been the look in his eyes when he'd said it.

Velvet wished that she hadn't overreacted, but it

might be too late now. A part of her refused to believe
that it was. Love didn't work that way.

If no further complications occurred in Birmingham,
he would be coming home Thursday. She would have a
lot to say to him. She had thought of calling him today
just to hear his voice, but knew what she had to say was
best done face-to-face.

"Are you okay?"

Velvet looked over at Sierra. Before she could answer, the lone woman on the board stood.

"Good afternoon, everyone, and welcome to this special meeting of the Catalina Cove school board. Since
I only got word of this meeting today—" the woman
didn't hide her annoyed tone "—I'll let Mr. Beaks in-
form everyone of the reason for this meeting."

Velvet found that odd. A meeting was called by the
school board, yet some of the members didn't know
why? She had never heard of such a thing. As if Sierra
knew her thoughts, she leaned close to her and whispered, "Only in Catalina Cove."

The microphone was passed to Mr. Beaks. Instead
of standing, he remained seated and said, "Ms. Velvet
Spencer, could you come forward, please?"

Sierra gave Velvet's hand a squeeze as she stood. At
that moment, she felt like more than a hundred pairs of
eyes were on her, but since she knew she hadn't done
anything wrong, she walked to the front with her head
held high.

When she came to a stop, she said, "I'm Velvet Spencer. Could someone tell me what this is all about?"

"We will in a minute, but we need you to confirm a
couple of things," Mr. Beaks said.

She lifted a brow. "Confirm what?"

"That you teach ninth grade at Catalina Cove Junior High School. Is that correct?"

"Yes, that's correct."

"And you've been teaching there for close to two years. Is that correct?"

Velvet wondered where all this was leading. "Yes, that's correct."

It seemed Dwight Beaks was taking his time to ask the next question, clicking his ink pen with his fat little fingers like he, and everyone present, had all the time in the word. She suddenly understood his ploy. If he thought for one minute that he would make her squirm, he was mistaken.

"Your next question, please," she said, not hiding her annoyed tone.

Dwight Beaks frowned when he heard several chuckles from the audience. "Do you think this is an amusing matter, Ms. Spencer?"

She lifted her chin. "No. In fact, I have no idea what the matter is. Amusing or otherwise." If she sounded flippant, that was too bad. She refused to let this man intimidate her.

He leaned back in his chair and eyed her speculatively and said, "You were once overheard saying you intended to purchase some of the property in Reid Lacroix's new development. In fact, you spoke specifically about a tract of land on the ocean."

Velvet wondered what that had to do with anything and what business was it of his or anyone else's. "Yes, I said that."

She could recall just when she said it and who was

around her when she had. It was at the town hall meeting when Reid Lacroix announced the news about the development. She had been talking to Sierra, but her words had been overheard by Webb and his sister, Laura.

"Of course, you knew at the time you said it that such a thing was impossible on a teacher's salary."

At that moment, Velvet was tempted to tell the man that she could buy anything she wanted, but decided not to. She wanted to see how this all intended to play out. In the end, she would put Mr. Beaks and anyone else who thought her business was their business in their place.

"What concern is it of the school board how I spend my money?" she asked.

"It deeply concerns us if it's money you don't have."

She heard a few chuckles and snickers from the audience and refused to look back, certain one of them was from Webb. "I honestly don't see why."

"Obviously, you didn't read your teacher contract thoroughly. If you had, you would have noted that any gifts over a thousand dollars that is exchanged between teachers, administrators, or school partners must be disclosed."

She wondered why he was telling her that. "I am aware of that."

"Then would you like to explain to this board why our new banker, Jaye Colfax, who is also your neighbor…in fact the two of you live in the same house on Blueberry Lane, although you maintain separate residences…purchased land for you, in Reid Lacroix's new development that cost over a million dollars?"

Gasps sounded around the room and Velvet's mouth nearly dropped open. Jaye had done that? He had purchased land for her in that new development. But why? She recalled mentioning to him once that she planned to buy property there. Had he bought it for her instead? Then she remembered what he had told her more than once... *I will give you whatever you want. No matter what it is...*

"The board is waiting for your response, Ms. Spencer."

She drew in a deep shaky breath and finally said, "I wasn't aware he had done that."

Mr. Beaks laughed as he threw his pen on the table. "Surely, you can do better than that, Ms. Spencer. A man you barely know buys you property worth over a million dollars, property you let it be known you wanted, and you don't know he bought it for you?"

Velvet frowned. Now she understood the reason behind Mr. Beaks's earlier questions. He had deliberately painted a picture of her as some sort of gold digger who was sleeping with the banker to get perks. Namely, a piece of property that cost millions.

"I didn't say that I don't know the reason he did it, Mr. Beaks. I said I didn't know that he had done it. And since I didn't know he had bought that property for me, there's no way I could have filed a disclosure."

There were several chuckles from the audience, which didn't sit well with Mr. Beaks. He leaned over the table and said in a loud irritated voice, "That's for this board to decide, Ms. Spencer, as to whether a conflict of interest has occurred. And since you didn't know he was buying you such an expensive piece of property, but know why he did, will you please advise us of the reason he did it?"

"Did you ask him?" she replied smartly.

Mr. Beaks frowned. "You're the one claiming the conflict doesn't exist."

"It doesn't, and the reason Jaye bought me that land," she said, not caring that using his first name indicated a personal closeness between them, and making sure she spoke loud enough for everyone to hear, "is because he loves me."

There, she'd said it and had done so with the confidence she now felt. Jaye did love her, and buying her that land was just another way he'd wanted to prove that he did.

"If she believes that, then she needs her head examined," a feminine voice in the audience said out loud.

Velvet knew without turning around that Laura Crawford had made the comment. Velvet's gaze remained on Dwight Beaks. He was grinning like he agreed with Laura.

"Honestly, Ms. Spencer. Do you actually think a man of Jaye Colfax's caliber would fall in love with a—"

"Teacher?" she finished for him. "I don't see why not because he certainly fell in love with me," she said with self-assurance and poise.

"And, I most certainly did."

Velvet jerked around at the sound of that masculine voice. And she, like everyone else in the auditorium, watched Jaye walk forward. His expression might be unreadable to some, but Velvet knew that look. He was fighting mad.

CHAPTER THIRTY-ONE

JAYE HAD TAKEN note of the number of people at the meeting and that had angered him even more. He switched his gaze to Velvet and kept his focus on her as he approached. For her to state in front of a room full of people that he loved her and with so much conviction in her voice, it meant she truly believed it. He was glad because he did love her with every bone in his body.

He came to a stop beside her and gave her an assuring smile before turning his attention to the seven individuals sitting at the table. "I want to know what right any of you have to question Ms. Spencer about anything I purchased for her? Especially when it was to be my surprise wedding gift to her."

Loud gasps sounded around the room behind him, but Jaye didn't care. Granted, he hadn't asked Velvet to marry him yet, but now that she knew he loved her, the proposal would come when they were alone.

"Wedding gift?" Mr. Beaks exclaimed. "When did the two of you become engaged?"

When the eyes of everyone at the table went to Velvet's left hand, Jaye said, "Not that it's anyone's business, but my proposal was something I'd planned to do in private when I felt the time was right. That's all you need to know."

Dwight Beaks looked flustered. "But the two of you were never seen around town together. And you've only known her for a few months. If you came here looking for a wife, you could have done better. We have several well-bred women living here from good families that are more on your social scale."

Hearing the man's absurd spiel, Jaye and Velvet looked at each other, and unable to help themselves, they laughed. That angered Dwight Beaks. "The two of you find something funny about what I said?"

"They aren't the only ones," a loud voice said. "Although I'm not laughing."

Every head in that room swiveled around to find who had spoken. Reid Lacroix stood in the back. Silence descended as he made his way to the front. Unlike Jaye's earlier expression that had been unreadable, there was no mistaking the anger on Reid's face.

"Mr. Lacroix, we didn't know you had returned from your trip to Hawaii," one of the board members, who had remained quiet all this time, quickly said. "We hope you had a nice time with your lovely wife and beautiful granddaughters."

Without answering the man, Reid came to stand beside Jaye and Velvet. He demanded, "What's going on here?"

When all the men at the table appeared too ill at ease to answer him, the lone woman on the board said, "From what I gather, Mr. Lacroix, there are some members on this school board who are trying to fire Ms. Spencer because Mr. Colfax purchased land as a gift for her. They feel that constitutes a conflict of interest."

Reid frowned. "Why?"

Dwight Beaks found his voice and said, "Because since Mr. Colfax will start a co-op bank in both the junior and senior high schools, that makes him a partner of the Catalina Cove school system. Velvet Spencer is one of the teachers. It's our understanding that he purchased land for her worth over a million dollars. No disclosure of the purchase of that land was made by either of them."

Reid waved off his words. "I'm the one who sold Mr. Colfax the property knowing full well who it was intended for. Since I consider myself a partner of the Catalina Cove school system, due to the numerous programs I've put in place, such as the internship program for high school seniors, I didn't complete a disclosure, either. Am I in violation of a conflict of interest as well?"

Nobody on the board said anything, but a few shook their heads.

Reid Lacroix asked, "Then why are they?"

When no response was provided, Mr. Lacroix said, "Frankly, I am offended by what this school board tried doing to Ms. Spencer here tonight, mainly because I'm the one who personally invited her to come to Catalina Cove."

From the loud murmurs around the room, Jaye figured what Reid had just revealed was news to everyone.

"You?" several board members said in surprise.

"Yes, me. Velvet's parents were good friends of mine for years. And as far as anyone questioning her social class, just so you know, Velvet Spencer owns every Spencer's restaurant in the country. Even the one located here."

More gasps were heard, even from the front table.

"Just think," Reid added, ignoring the shocked faces of the individuals sitting before him, "Catalina Cove has had an heiress—one who is probably twice as wealthy as I am—living among us for two years, and tonight all of you treated her like crap."

"But—but we didn't know. We thought she was a mere schoolteacher," one of the board members said.

"It should not have mattered if she was a garbage collector. Everyone, regardless of their occupation, deserves respect. And maybe it's time for some of you to stop looking down on teachers. If you feel they aren't getting paid enough, then you ought to vote to give them raises." From the cheers heard around the room, it was obvious several teachers were in attendance.

"And another thing," Reid said when the room got quiet again. "Some of you have been on this board a long time. Too long. Maybe you need to do what I'm about to do in a few months. Retire. In fact, I strongly suggest it."

Instead of commenting on Reid's suggestion, Dwight Beaks switched his gaze from Reid to Velvet. "Ms. Spencer, this school board apologizes for any inconvenience or embarrassment your appearance here tonight might have caused you. That was not our intent."

"Wasn't it?" Velvet said, frowning deeply as her gaze moved from one board member to another. "Teaching is my choice and a profession I love. The one thing I've noticed since working in the Catalina Cove school system is the inferiority reference that's always made to teachers. That needs to stop. I agree with Reid that all the teachers should get a raise."

"At least thirty percent or more," Jaye tacked on and grinned at the shocked look on several members' faces.

However, by the applause around the room, a lot of people evidently agreed.

"That's a good idea," Reid said, nodding. "It's not like this school district can't afford it. I suggest you make it happen even if you have to reduce your own salaries to do so. Just think of all the young people who left here after college to teach elsewhere. It's time they were given an incentive to come back home."

Dwight Beaks loosened his tie and said, "That suggestion will definitely be taken up at the next board meeting."

"Make sure that it does," Reid replied.

Beaks nodded and said, "Tonight's meeting is adjourned."

Jaye turned to Velvet and, not caring they had an audience, pulled her into his arms, tenderly kissed her forehead, and held her close. He would kiss her the way he wanted to later when they had privacy. When he released her, she was surrounded by her friends, who gave her hugs.

Vashti had a huge grin on her face when she gave Velvet a high five. "After the way Mr. Beaks treated me when I was a teen and pregnant, it felt good seeing you put him in his place. And then for Reid to suggest he retire was icing on the cake. I'm going to be smiling for days."

Ashley, smiling broadly, said, "I wished you could have seen the look on Webb's face when Reid Lacroix announced how rich you are. It was priceless. And just to think, all this time he assumed he was the prize you should have been grateful to get."

"And I don't think Laura Crawford has picked her jaw off the floor yet," Bryce added.

Reid approached Velvet and said, "I know you preferred to keep your identity a secret, Velvet, but I was standing out there in the hall and had heard enough. I hope you know that not everyone in Catalina Cove are pompous asses."

Velvet smiled. "Yes, I know that, Reid." She looked around at the group surrounding her who'd given her their support tonight. "I've made good friends while living here. Friends who accepted me for who I am and not for what I have."

Jaye and Velvet thanked everyone for being there to give her their support. "We're headed over to the Witherspoon Café," Vashti said. "You and Jaye want to join us?"

Jaye chuckled. "Since I haven't eaten since breakfast, that sounds good."

Velvet looked at him. "You haven't eaten since breakfast?"

"No, I got that call from Vaughn right before noon, and I immediately made arrangements to return here."

She glanced over at Vaughn, who shrugged and said, "A man has to handle business when it comes to his woman. Even if she's capable of handling it herself. That's what love is all about."

Velvet nodded, knowing Vaughn was right. That's what love was about. Jaye placed his arm around her shoulders and they walked out of the auditorium with their friends.

JAYE AND VELVET left her car parked at school and rode together to the Witherspoon Café. He would drop her off to retrieve her car in the morning on his way to the airport. The only reason he was returning to Birmingham was because there was an important meeting that he didn't want to miss tomorrow. Knowing he had rushed back to Catalina Cove after Vaughn had called him meant everything to Velvet.

Once inside the car, he pulled her into his arms and gave her the kiss he hadn't given her earlier.

Hours later, after a delicious meal at the Witherspoon Café, they pulled into the yard of the house on Blueberry Lane and saw a car parked in their driveway, a car neither of them recognized. "Stay put until I find out who it is," Jaye said.

When the other driver got out, Velvet saw it was Allen Bordeaux. She wondered what he wanted. Jaye and the man conversed for a few minutes. Then Jaye returned to the car and said, "Bordeaux wants to talk to you, Velvet. I'm okay with it if you are. I'll see you safely inside and then I need to go up to my place for a minute, anyway."

She nodded. "Okay."

Jaye walked her to the door and even went inside with her to start coffee. Then he left, leaving her alone with Mr. Bordeaux. She turned to the man. "You wanted to talk to me about something, Mr. Bordeaux?"

He nodded. "I came here tonight to give you this." He took a folded sheet of paper out of his pocket and handed it to her.

Velvet read it and glanced up at him. "You're resigning as manager of Spencer's?"

"Yes. I figured you would be firing me, anyway."

She tilted her head. "And why would I do that?"

"Because of what happened tonight at that school board meeting."

She studied him. "Are you saying that you're the person who was behind what happened tonight? The one who provided that information to the school board with the intent of making me look bad?"

"No. I never talked to anyone on the board. I did, however, tell Webb Crawford what I'd overheard about Mr. Colfax buying you that land. But I did so only because I knew he was in love with you himself. For that reason, I felt he had a right to know based on what happened with me and Lenny's mother. I was in love with her, but I didn't know she was only in love with money. She left me for another one of the players on another team. I was trying to spare Webb heartbreak."

There was no need to tell Mr. Bordeaux that Webb didn't love her; he just wanted her in his bed. "I'm sorry Lenny's mother did that to you, and since you weren't the one trying to get me fired tonight, then—"

"No, I would not have tried getting you fired. Lenny talked to me this weekend, and he told me how you offered to help him get his grades up. I knew he liked to draw but I didn't know he was intentionally failing math because of me. I told him that you were right, he could do both. I hadn't realized how much pressure he was under because of what I wanted my dream for him to be."

Velvet nodded. "Now that you know, I'm glad you will support Lenny in fulfilling his own dreams. And as for your resignation, I'm not accepting it." She handed the letter back to him. "You're doing a great job as manager of Spencer's. You always get outstanding reviews and the people you manage enjoy working for you. I couldn't ask for more than that. Besides, our connections as parent and teacher have nothing to do with your employment."

He released a deep sigh. "Thank you."

"You're welcome and I look forward to helping Lenny bring his grades up so he can move on to senior high school in the fall."

"And I appreciate you for that as well. I don't know if you and Mr. Colfax plan to make Catalina Cove your permanent home after you marry, but I hope so. We can certainly use more teachers like you."

Velvet gave him a broad smile. "Thank you. That means a lot coming from you."

CHAPTER THIRTY-TWO

VELVET WAS IN the kitchen about to pour coffee into cups when Jaye returned. The moment she saw him, she crossed the room to be engulfed in his arms. The kiss he gave her was toe-curling yummy, just like she knew it would be. When he finally released her mouth, she tilted her head up and looked at him. "You knew what Mr. Bordeaux wanted, didn't you?"

Jaye nodded. "Yes, he told me. I guess he felt as your fiancé, I had a right to know. Trust me, I would not have left you here with him if I didn't think he was sincere."

She nodded. "I know." She then gave him a curious look. "And are you my fiancé?" she asked him, grinning.

"I hope to be." Then he said, "I miss sitting in the rocking chairs with you."

"Same here. It's a beautiful night."

"Come sit out there with me a while."

"Okay."

Suddenly, Jaye swept her into his arms. "Jaye!" She laughed.

"It's okay. I got you."

Yes, you do, Velvet thought as he opened the back door and carried her out to the porch. Instead of placing her in her rocking chair, he eased down to his and cuddled her in his lap. With his warm arms, he held her as close to him as he could manage, and she wrapped her arms around his neck. That's when he lowered his head to hers for another kiss.

The moment their lips connected, shivers raced through her body, and when his tongue eased into her mouth, she knew heaven. When he deepened the kiss, she groaned as blood rushed through her veins.

He abruptly broke off the kiss and she immediately felt the loss. "I love you, Velvet."

She doubted she would ever tire of hearing those words from him. "I truly believe that you do, Jaye."

"When did you accept it?" he asked.

"All that time I had alone to think while you were in Birmingham. I knew that I loved you and had never stopped loving you, even though I tried and at times convinced myself that I had. I thought about everything you said and everything you did and have done since moving to the cove. And I realized that you had done them just for me and to show me how much you loved me. I no longer saw it as manipulation but as a revelation. You were revealing to me in your own special way what I had come to mean to you."

"It might have taken me a while, Velvet, but I came to realize just how much I loved you, and then I was determined to do whatever I needed to do to win back your heart and to prove how much I loved you. There was no way I could live without you."

He paused a moment and then said, "I'm glad you realized the depth of my love for you. You don't know how it made me feel when I arrived at that high school and saw you facing down that school board and declaring you knew that I loved you. At that moment, I could have hung the moon. It meant everything to me, knowing you believed me."

He stood with her in his arms. He turned and placed her in the chair, and then got on bended knee. "I came to Catalina Cove to win back your heart, Velvet. I knew it wouldn't be easy, but I also knew I wouldn't give up. Whatever it took, I intended to do it."

She chuckled. "Such arrogance."

"I saw it as desperation and determination. I promised myself that if I ever got you back, I would never give you a reason to leave me again."

He took her hand into the warmth of his and gazed directly into her eyes. What she saw in the dark depths made her draw in a trembling breath when he said, "Will you marry me, Velvet? I promise to love you always and make you happy."

Filled with an abundance of emotions, she couldn't stop the tears that rolled down her cheek. This was what she'd always wanted. His love and to be his wife. "Yes, Jaye. I will marry you."

She felt him slide a ring on her finger and she looked down at her hand. Her eyes widened at the huge diamond. "Oh, my goodness. Jaye, it's beautiful. When did you get this?"

"I've had it since the day I arrived in Catalina Cove. Like I said, I was determined to win your love. I had told myself that I wouldn't leave the cove until you left here with me as my wife, and I meant it."

Smiling broadly, he stood and pulled her into his

arms. After a long drugging kiss, he released her mouth and she wrapped her arms around his neck and asked, "When do you want to get married?"

"This weekend."

She laughed. "Sorry, we can't marry before Ruthie and her wedding is in June. Besides, I want to finish the school year." She then thought of something. "When is Dean getting married?"

"Not until December. And since I vowed not to return to Phoenix without you as my wife, that means I'll remain here as well. The manager we hired for the bank starts here next month. That means I'll be traveling back and forth to Birmingham to check on the progress there, so I will stay here with you until we get married. With Delisa coming back in a few months, I guess I'll be moving in with you."

She grinned. "And you are welcome to do so."

"Thanks, and how about an August wedding?"

Velvet smiled up at him. "August will work fine. That way I'll be ready to return to the classroom in September."

"Good. Plan on a month-long honeymoon." He paused, then asked, "So where do you want to live after we get married? I bought that land for you. We can live here or we can live in Phoenix. I'll let you decide."

She knew how much he loved Phoenix. It was his home and for years it had been hers as well. "I want to move back to Phoenix. The house we build here on the gulf will be our vacation home."

"That sounds like a plan."

"And thanks for buying that property for me."

"You are welcome, baby." He swept her into his arms again and carried her into the house and straight to the bedroom.

AFTER PLACING VELVET on the bed, Jaye stepped back and watched her. He loved seeing her undress for him. He had a feeling that tonight she would be naughty, and nothing could stimulate him more than a naughty Velvet.

He watched her slowly remove her blouse, taking her time to unbutton it. Then came her bra. Then she reached up and ran her fingers through her hair that fell around her shoulders. The gesture made her breasts lift. Just seeing her like this filled him with even more desire and almost pushed him over the edge.

He moaned. When she heard it, she chuckled, and the sound carried through the room and played havoc on his senses.

Jaye watched as she removed her shoes before proceeding to take off her skirt and panties. Seeing her completely naked sent heat rushing through his entire body. Her scent was strong and extremely alluring, causing the ache below his belt to intensify.

"Your turn, Jaye."

Yes, it was his turn, and he didn't waste time getting out of his clothes. He gazed at her for a long time before moving toward the bed to join her. The physical chemistry they'd always shared was even more powerful tonight.

Easing on the bed, he drew her into his arms. "I love you, Velvet."

"And I love you."

Her words caused a deep pounding in his heart, and brushing back a lock of hair that had fallen in her face, he said it again, "I love you." Jaye loved saying it and knew he would keep saying it for the rest of his life.

Leaning in, he captured her lips and took her mouth with a greed he'd never felt before. Tonight, he felt like the luckiest man in the world because this beautiful woman, who he loved more than life itself, had agreed to be his wife.

Releasing her mouth he eased into position over her; he needed to be connected to her, inside her. Deep. With their gazes locked, he whispered her name as he slowly entered her, loving the feel of her inner muscles clenching him. And then he felt her legs wrap around him, tight.

"Say my name," she whispered, her gaze still locked with his.

"Velvet. Now say mine."

"Jaye."

He began moving with hard but slow thrusts. He increased the pace of his strokes, and then when he knew neither of them could handle holding back any longer, he whispered, "Come with me, baby. Now."

An explosion ripped through them, and he knew their lives together would be filled with all the love and happiness any couple could possibly endure—and then some. They had the rest of their lives to prove him right.

THE ALARM WOKE Velvet early the next morning. Sitting up in bed, she found she was alone. Where was Jaye?

"Looking for me?"

She glanced to the doorway. He was standing there dressed in his jogging attire. She rubbed sleep from her eyes and yawned. "You're going jogging?"

He smiled. "*We're* going jogging. Now get up, sleepy-head."

She dropped back down in bed and buried her head in the pillow. "How can you expect me to have energy left for anything after a night like last night?"

"You'll manage. Meet me outside in thirty minutes or you'll be late getting to school. Remember, I'm taking you to get your car on my way to the airport."

Unfortunately, she remembered.

Thirty-five minutes later, she joined him outside. When she noticed the huge blanket he carried, she asked, "What's the blanket for?"

He smiled at her. "You'll see."

She should have suspected something when he told her there was no need to do warm-ups today. But she got an idea of his intent as he led her deep into the fields without bothering to start jogging. Then he ventured off the path to a small patch of grass surrounded by a thicket of tall blueberry bushes and trees. Still, she decided to play dumb. "And just where are you taking me?"

He chuckled. "Just where you are. The blueberry fields." He obviously felt they'd gone deep enough and he spread the blanket on the ground. Easing down on it he said, "Blueberry fields forever," and extended his hand to her.

She laughed as she took it and joined him on the blanket. "I think it was *strawberry* fields."

Jaye pulled her into his arms and kissed her neck. "Whatever. For us, it will always be blueberries." And then he proceeded to show her why.

* * * * *

*After a passionate three-year romance, rancher
Maverick Outlaw and Sapphire Bardello aren't just
lovers but close friends too. But, when Phire
announces she must marry at her father's urging,
it looks like their relationship is coming to an end...
until they learn she's carrying Maverick's baby.
And he'll stop at nothing to claim the woman he loves
and their child, even if that means breaking free
of their controlling families...*

Read on for a sneak peek of
The Outlaw's Claim
by New York Times *bestselling author*
Brenda Jackson

Maverick's cell phone vibrated. He had turned off the ringer during the wedding ceremony and now wondered who would be calling him. Most of his female acquaintances only had the number to his burner phone. Anyone he considered important was here, attending his brother's wedding.

Except for Phire.

He felt a slow roll in his stomach after pulling out his phone and seeing it was her, Sapphire Bordella, the woman who'd once been his friend with benefits.

He and Phire had met in Paris three years ago, when he'd been on a business trip. They had been attracted to each other immediately. He had quickly discovered she was someone he could talk to and enjoyed spending time with—both in and out of the bedroom. They were friends who understood each other, and at the time neither had been looking for anything permanent. One thing they had in common—they both had domineering fathers. Maverick knew how to handle his, but Phire had yet to learn how to handle hers. He was convinced the man was as much of a manipulator as Bart. Possibly even more so.

A year ago, Phire had decided it was time for her to pursue a serious romantic relationship. By mutual agreement they had ended their FWB relationship. However, they had maintained their close friendship and would often call each other to see how things were going. Lately, he'd noticed her calls had become infrequent. He had assumed she'd met someone and things had gotten serious, and he'd been delegated as a part of her past.

"Phire?"

"Yes, it's me."

Maverick heard the strain in her voice. "Is everything alright?"

"No."

That single word stoked his ire at whatever was bothering her. The one thing Phire would never admit to was not being okay. He walked to an area in Westmoreland House where he could hold a private conversation. When he entered an empty room, he realized it was the huge playroom Dillon had added to the design of the building so the youngsters in the family could have a place to enjoy themselves. This room looked like an indoor playground.

"What's wrong, Phire?" he asked, closing the door behind him.

There was hesitation before she said, "I know we're not together anymore, but I need to see you, Maverick."

He heard the urgency in her voice and glanced at his watch. "I'm at my brother's wedding in Denver, but I can be in Paris in—"

"I'm not in Paris—I'm in Texas."

"You're home?"

"I told you this ranch hasn't been my home in years, Maverick."

Yes, she had told him that a number of times. "Alright. I have my plane. Just give me time to refuel and I'm coming to Texas."

"I hate for you to leave the wedding."

"The reception is about to end, and Jess and Paige will be leaving for their honeymoon in a little bit, anyway."

"If you're sure it won't inconvenience you."

A part of him knew Phire could never inconvenience him. "It's no problem. I can fly into Austin's airport and—"

"No, I prefer meeting you someplace else."

"Where, then?"

"Dallas. I can leave here for Dallas in a few hours."

"And I'll meet you there. I'll make all the arrangements and text them to you."

"Okay, and thanks, Maverick."

"Don't mention it. I'll see you soon."

After he clicked off the phone, he checked his watch as he left the room. He hoped to have all his questions answered as to what was bothering Phire in a few hours.

* * *

"And just where do you think you're going, young lady?"

Phire didn't bother to glance up from tossing items into her overnight bag. The last thing her father needed to know was that she had plans to meet Maverick. The best thing she'd done over the last three years was to keep Maverick's identity shielded from her father.

When he had ordered her home from Paris a couple of days ago, all he'd said was that she should come home immediately. Once she had arrived at the ranch, it didn't take long to find out why she'd been summoned. He had selected the man he wanted her to marry.

Phire's mother had passed away when she was twelve. Less than a year later, her father, Simon Bordella—an attorney turned rancher—sent her to live with his older sister in Paris. He hadn't even sent for her to come home during the holidays or summers. If it hadn't been for her aunt, Phire honestly don't know what she would have done. Lois Priestly had been a godsend for her.

As Phire got older, two things became crystal clear. Although her aunt Lois never had anything bad to say about Phire's father, she'd never said anything good about him, either. There had definitely been a disconnect in the brother-sister relationship. Granted, there was a fourteen-year difference in their ages, but Phire would have thought they'd have a closer sibling bond.

More than once she'd tried getting her aunt to talk about it, but she never would. The only thing Aunt Lois would say was that whatever was done in the dark would eventually come to light. Phire often wondered what she meant. Another thing her aunt had warned her about was never to cross him.

When Phire finished high school at seventeen, her father had finally sent for her, saying he wanted her to attend an American university. After college, Phire decided to make her home in Paris, and at the age of twenty-one, nothing her father did or said could make her change her mind. She reminded him that she was now an adult and old enough to make her own decisions. Besides, why would he want her around when he hadn't before?

After she'd been living back in Paris for a year, her aunt had a massive stroke, which left her without speech and paralyzed in the legs. That meant Aunt Lois was in need of constant attention in a long-term care facility. When the funds for Aunt Lois's care ran out, a frantic Phire had no other choice but to reach out to her father, convinced he would come to his sister's aid.

Simon Bordella had agreed to provide the funds for his sister's care, but not out of the goodness of his heart. He'd told Phire that he would only agree to help on one condition—Phire would agree to marry whatever man he chose for her without any questions asked.

At first, Phire thought he was joking. When she saw he was not, she was appalled. It was only when the doctors stressed what could happen to her aunt without proper long-term care that, out of desperation, Phire agreed to her father's terms.

"I asked, where do you think you're going, Sapphire?"

She turned around. "I need to think, and I can't do it here."

"What is there to think about? I kept my end of the

agreement and provided the best care possible for Lois. Now it's time you kept your end of the deal."

Phire narrowed her gaze at him. "I had hoped you wouldn't hold that agreement over my head. I'd begun thinking that you were providing the best of care to Aunt Lois because she is your sister."

"Well, you thought wrong. Lois and I never got along. The only reason I've been paying those exorbitant fees for three years is because of the deal you and I made."

"Why, Dad? Why is it important for you to select the man for me to marry?"

"The reason doesn't matter. All you need to know is that now that you're twenty-five, it's time for you to settle down and Jaxon Ravnell will make the perfect son-in-law."

Phire frowned as she thought of the man she'd been introduced to last night at dinner. "Why? Because he's wealthy and you think he can be easily manipulated?"

Her father smiled as if he found what she'd said amusing. "Jaxon does have more money than he knows what to do with, so what's wrong with me helping him decide the best way to use it?"

Phire didn't say anything. She would admit that thirty-two-year-old Jaxon was definitely a handsome man. He was the CEO of several technology firms in Virginia and was in Texas looking for land to expand. Her father had met him a few weeks ago at one of those Texas business meetings, where the red carpet had practically been rolled out for Jaxon.

Over dinner last night her father had tried his hardest to sell Jaxon on the idea that he needed to invest some of his millions by buying up a lot of the land in the area. Mainly land her father owned that was adjacent to the ranch.

She'd always been good at reading people, and it had been obvious to her—even if hadn't been to her father—that Jaxon *wasn't* a man who could be easily manipulated. For some reason, she had a feeling Jaxon was actually playing her father by pretending the opposite. That was something she found rather interesting.

What her father had said earlier was true. He had made sure her aunt had the best of care in one of the finest facilities in Paris. He had kept his end of their deal, and whether she wanted to or not, she would keep hers.

"I need you back here in two days, Sapphire. I could tell over dinner that Jaxon was taken with you. He said he'd be in the area for at least six months and you two should spend time together. I want a wedding to take place no later than the spring. Understood?"

When she didn't say anything, he continued, "Just in case you don't understand, maybe now is the time to tell you that I had Lois moved."

"You did what?" she asked furiously, crossing the room to her father.

"You heard me. Just in case you try to wiggle out of our agreement. Don't worry, my sister is still getting the best of care, just in a nondisclosed location. I won't tell you where until *after* you and Jaxon get married."

"You can't do that!"

"As her legal guardian, I can do whatever I want. Don't worry about your aunt. What you need to concern yourself with is getting Jaxon to make you his wife by spring. As far as I'm concerned, there's nothing you need to think about. However, if you feel the need to get away to accept your fate, then by all means, do so. But I expect you back in two days with a smile on your face, ready to convince Jaxon that you are the best thing that could ever happen to him."

When her father walked out the room, Phire sank down on the bed.

Maverick checked his watch as he paced the confines of the hotel room. He hadn't expected to arrive in Dallas before Phire and had texted her all the information she needed, including the fact that a hotel key in her name was at the check-in desk.

He knew everyone was wondering why he'd left Denver unexpectedly, when he and his brothers had planned to remain in Westmoreland Country for another two days. His brother Sloan had made a wisecrack that it must have something to do with a woman. His brother was right on that account. What Sloan was wrong about was in thinking this was a hookup.

Maverick considered Phire more than that.

From their first meeting it had been easy to see she was unlike any woman he'd ever known. In addition to her striking beauty, she had wit and a personality that drew him even when he hadn't wanted to be drawn. And the more he had gotten to know her, the more he'd appreciated their friendship. Entering into a FWB relationship had been the first of its kind for him. Before Phire, he would never have considered such a thing.

As he waited for her arrival, he couldn't help but recall when they'd first met. It had been his and Garth's second night in Paris, and Maverick had decided to check out the nightlife at a pub someone had recommended. Since the place was a few blocks away and it had been a beautiful night in April, he'd walked.

As Maverick gazed out the hotel window at downtown Dallas, he let himself remember when he'd met Sapphire Bordella. It was a night he would never forget…

Don't miss what happens next in…

The Outlaw's Claim
by Brenda Jackson,
the next book in her
Westmoreland Legacy: The Outlaws series!

Available November 2022 wherever
Harlequin® Desire books and ebooks are sold.
www.Harlequin.com